W9-BZV-368

BIRDLAND

By the same author

Plot Twist

BIRDLAND

Eric Adams

Kendra,
To stories for
the young at heart
All the Best,
Eric J. Adams

Hodder & Stoughton

First published in Great Britain in 1997
by Hodder and Stoughton
A division of Hodder Headline PLC

10 9 8 7 6 5 4 3 2 1

British Library Cataloguing in Publication Data

Adams, Eric
Birdland
1. Thrillers
I. Title
813.5′4 [F]

ISBN 0 340 64017 0

Typeset by Palimpsest Book Production Limited,
Polmont, Stirlingshire
Printed and bound in Great Britain by
Mackays of Chatham PLC, Chatham, Kent

Hodder and Stoughton
A division of Hodder Headline PLC
338 Euston Road
London NW1 3BH

To Kathy,
wings and all

ACKNOWLEDGMENTS

For insights into the life and art of Alfred Hitchcock, and for assistance of every conceivable kind, my sincere thanks go to George Lucas, Robert Graves, Muriel Anderson, Craig Von Weiderhold, Gary Sherwood, Christine Whyte, Ronnie Benjamin, Naomi Richman, Steve Trenam, Wendy Wasik, and the folks of Bodega Bay. And to the inspiration from A.H. himself, always the master.

They sicken of the calm,
who knew the storm.

Dorothy Parker

CHAPTER ONE

When the doctors summoned Katie from the waiting room she thought it was mercifully over. But her mother, sucking her final breaths, had saved one last emotional sword to jab into Katie's heart.

The intensive-care room was cluttered with the apparatus designed to forestall death one day, one hour, one minute. Tubes and wires crisscrossed in a jangled mess. Gangly metal arms held up monitors that cycled rapidly along fixed paths of light. An oxygen tank breathed monotonously with a life of its own.

'She called for you,' whispered a young nurse flashing a saccharine smile, a dismal attempt at camouflaging her true opinion of the patient. Or maybe Katie was projecting her feelings again.

Katie searched the faces of the doctors and nurses for clues. They averted their eyes or struck up conversations in mid-sentence, willing to share a space with Katie but not her burden.

Her burden. Katie moved toward her mother, Gloria Jacobs, shrunken by the ravages of lung cancer and emphysema, a distant ghost of the beauty she had once been.

Only her vanity remained intact. 'No tubes up my nostrils,' Gloria had demanded when wheeled into the hospital three weeks earlier. Nothing to obstruct her *visage* as she referred to it, no mouthpiece smothering her flame-red lips. She insisted instead on an oxygen tent, a device so out of favor that San Francisco General had to scramble to rent one.

At certain angles behind the tent's wrinkled plastic jacket, Gloria looked mysterious and aloof, like the celluloid queen she had forever aspired to be. But at angles where the jacket was bent from storage folds, Gloria's image appeared distorted, like an absurd caricature in a Fellini film or a crumpled snippet of film laying on the cutting-room floor.

Katie parted the tent wall and gazed upon the perishing icon. Jaws slack, milky eyes barely visible behind a narcotic haze, skinny legs the color of boiled chicken, only Gloria's hollow cheeks billowing in quick huffs suggested the possibility of life.

With two nicotine-stained fingers Gloria motioned Katie closer. Katie had once so admired those delicate hands, now knots of knuckle under splotched skin, capped with fingernails as curved as the Wicked Witch of the West's.

Katie lifted the tent jacket higher and entered the strange atmosphere of hissing oxygen. She had always needed an arm's length from her mother for sanity, a room's length to carry on a conversation, and a city block to carry on her existence as best she could. This artificial cocoon that breathed life into Gloria suffocated Katie. But these might be her mother's last words and there was no denying them now.

Gloria struggled to lift her head, a wobbly mass of sagging wrinkles and jowls, despite endless primping and three facelifts.

'Katie,' she groaned.

The pain drove her back to her pillow. She pumped her fist twice to speed the morphine on its way. Katie tried to speak, to console her mother, but her cracked lips forbade it.

Instead Katie leaned closer and rested her ear on the bristly whiskers of her mother's upper lip.

'Yes, Mother?' Katie whispered, her ring clattering on the cold metal bed rail.

'A secret.'

'What, Mama?'

'A . . . a . . .' Gloria pushed with a labor as unbearable as childbirth.

'*A bradda*,' Gloria muttered finally with more breath than word. She fell against her pillow to gather strength for another push.

'A *what*?' Katie asked gently.

Gloria mouthed the words with the exaggerated enunciation of a first-year drama student. 'A *brother*.'

Then she launched into a coughing spell so fitful Katie thought the end had surely come.

'Nurse!' Katie called.

A nurse ducked in and fluffed the pillow behind Gloria's hacking head, which did nothing to alleviate the attack.

'Isn't there something more you can do?' Katie begged.

The nurse shrugged, suggesting all complaints should be directed to Gloria, the de facto manager of her care.

Katie stroked her mother's hair, cradled her head, breathed for her. Nothing helped. Not until a bloody strand of lung tissue slithered from her mouth. The nurse poked her head in and wiped the discharge with a coarse napkin.

So often Katie had wished for her mother to die, mercifully, for her own sake. Now Katie squeezed her mother's hand, hoping to pump a few brief moments of life into the fading body, enough to solve this cruel riddle composed of a single word.

The murmuring doctors, the blipping machines faded into oblivion as she pressed closer, listening by osmosis more than sound.

'Brother what?' Katie asked.

'You have a brother,' Gloria muttered effortlessly.

Katie sat upright and bumped her head on the oxygen-tent frame. A hundred questions reached her lips but only one emerged. 'A brother?'

'I'm sorry,' Gloria whispered.

It was the first time Katie could remember her mother uttering an apology.

'Sorry for not telling me or sorry I have a brother?' asked Katie.

Gloria glanced up with her languid eyes.

'Just . . . sorry.'

A brother. Katie had never conceived of such a possibility. An only child was all she ever had been, her defining trait. How many times as a child had she stared out the window praying for her mother to come home, her father, nothing but a faint memory, to come back, and more than anything, a sibling to share her joy and misery.

'Does he have a name?' Katie inquired.

Gloria's eyes opened. Wide. She emitted a high-pitched half-chuckle followed by a squeal of delight, the utterance of a circus monkey or a homeless woman. Her face filled with anxious panic, then transformed into the childish surprise of a Christmas morning.

'Mother!'

Gloria's lip ceased trembling. Her billowing cheeks stalled in mid-breath. The heart monitor slipped into a soap-opera shrill of alarm.

'Move away!' a doctor ordered. He ripped away the tent and clawed open Gloria's nightgown, pumping furiously on her sunken breasts. The staff, so utterly indifferent before, now surrounded the body with grave infatuation.

'Stop it!' Katie shouted. 'D – N – R. It's on her chart.'

The team looked puzzled by the request.

'Do not resuscitate,' Katie felt the compunction to explain. 'It's what she wanted.'

The chief doctor checked the clipboard and nodded to the staff. They pulled away, reluctantly, creatures of habit denied their routine.

'A brother,' Katie whispered.

'What?' the doctor asked.

'Nothing.'

Katie searched her mother's face, her visage, for signs of life. If she followed form, a revival was imminent – back to life to spite her daughter or to prove once again her mastery over dramatic exits.

The doctor checked for pulse, then let Gloria's wrist slip from his grasp.

'She's gone.' He nodded solemnly.

'I'm sorry,' Katie said, hoping to assure him it wasn't his fault, once again apologizing for events out of her control.

A nurse flicked the monitor off. Another nurse rolled up the tent walls. The doctors left the room with nervous excuses. The resurrection was not to be.

'Would you like a minute?' asked a nurse.

A tinge of sorrow surprised Katie. This was it, the end of twenty-nine years of woeful motherhood. The end of a faceless parade of men, all willing to take a moment to endear themselves to the little daughter, yet unable to hide their eagerness to steer Gloria into the bedroom. The last of countless jaunts to Hollywood and New York, some for weeks at a time, that left Katie under the care of her invalid grandmother and with only a bay-window view of San Francisco Bay to console her.

'No,' said Katie wistfully. 'We said our good-byes long ago.'

Dead in six months, the doctors had predicted when Gloria was first diagnosed with inoperable lung cancer, way back when she returned home for good and demanded from her daughter the devotion she had never thought to provide as a mother. Six months dragged into four years. Four years of sponging bedsores and scrubbing bedpans. Four years of obeying cranky orders and ignoring snippy remarks. Four years of listening to the incessant drone of late-night television forever tuned to obscure channels broadcasting old movies.

In truth, Gloria had played only bit parts in movies here and there – one line, maybe two – opposite Gene Kelly or Vic Morrow. But she swore she had hobnobbed with them all – the actors, producers, directors, and cinematographers. From her red vinyl lounge chair, cigarette in hand, she held court on each one of them as if she were the marquis star.

Preminger was an alcoholic. Ingrid Bergman a prima donna. Montgomery Clift couldn't get it up. Crawford was thoroughly misunderstood. Hepburn's breath stank.

But in all her ravings, Gloria had never thought to mention a brother. And it was just like her to spit it out the moment she no longer had time to explain.

Katie stole one last look at frozen Gloria, her raspy hair spread across the pillow like a fraying death shroud, two fingers spread eternally apart, smoking in heaven, or hell, or wherever she was.

Katie found her grandmother in the waiting room engrossed in *People* magazine, looking almost younger than Gloria had of late. She wheeled her chair around to face Katie. Grandma's expression said it all.

'So, she lived a good life, most of it,' said Grandma. 'What more can you ask?'

'Cigarettes.'

'Cigarettes, shmigarettes. Look, honey, *it is written*. When it's your time, you go. Did she ask for me?'

'No,' Katie said.

'Figures. Well, may she rest in peace.'

'A brother,' Katie said softly.

'A what?'

'She told me I had a brother.'

Grandma wheeled a little closer. 'Did she, now? Well, they say drugs can make you delirious.'

'Grandma, *don't*. You always cover for her.'

'Maybe.' Grandma nodded. 'Maybe I do. But she was my number two and I owed her. You're just not as careful with the second one, you know. You'll find that out if you ever get married. You're so careful with the first child, making sure their shoes are tied and the dirt is scrubbed from behind their ears. But when the second one comes, it's not the same. They run barefoot, slip and fall on hand-me-down roller skates, their scraped knees go untended. They go out with older boys, come home after you're asleep. That was your mother.'

'You're doing it again.'

'All right, all right,' Grandma sighed. 'I guess you may as well know, you're old enough. You surprised the heck out of me by finishing college. Anyway, I'm not interested in keeping her dirty little secrets anymore.'

'I do have a brother, then.'

'Yes, you do. An older brother.'

'What's his name?'

'Vincent.'

'Vincent.' Katie closed her eyes to conjure an image but couldn't. 'Where is he now?'

Grandma waved away the annoying question. 'You don't want to know, believe me.'

'If I have family, I'd like to know about it.'

'What am I, yesterday's breakfast?' said Grandma.

'You know what I mean; a brother is different.'

'Well, there isn't much I can tell you.'

'Tell me everything.'

Grandma set down the magazine and bit her bottom lip like she always did when she was ready to recount a story.

'He was born six years before you. October, I believe, rainy, cold, a button-up, inside day. No, not October, December. It was December, I remember now because Christmas decorations were up all over. Yes, now I remember, a bitter, gloomy day. When I reached the hospital I saw the doctors whispering in hushed tones like they do when something's amiss. I wasn't let into the room but I knew something was wrong. That child wasn't right from the start, something with the birth, forceps, breech birth, I don't know, I wasn't there and your mother never tells me anything. It took him days to learn to suckle, I know that. He had this odd gaze, one eye shooting this way, the other eye another. You never knew when he was looking at you. Stayed in the hospital for about a week, if I remember. It was sunny and cold when she brought him home. A real bright day.

'Oh, but that child was colicky. Screamed morning, noon, and night. Couldn't stand to be touched, and your mother couldn't stand to touch him. I didn't get a moment's rest and neither did she. Screaming and crying, screaming and crying. I'm not one to call a child difficult, but he was a nightmare. She kept him for about two weeks, longer than I figured she would, but I don't have to tell you about your mother. Not exactly the nurturing kind. Anyway, it was for the best. She was always running around making movies, or trying to. And believe me, your generation wasn't the first to experiment with drugs. I couldn't care for that child myself, no way. She had no choice. I think it was the only selfless decision she made in her life.'

'What did she do?'

'She let him go. It was best for the child, really.'

'What do you mean, *let him go*?'

'Adoption. Except I'm not sure it was legal – at least, I don't think papers were signed.'

'Who took him?'

'Now *that* your mother never told me, and I wasn't there the day they made the switch. I was at my orthopedic surgeon, getting the pin replaced in my right hip. Painful procedure. But when I came home Vincent was gone, the crib was gone, diapers gone. Only a rattle remained, and your mother chewed on it like a baby herself, between puffs of her cigarette, naturally.'

'So you don't know who adopted him?'

'That's not what I said.'

'Then who did?'

Grandma paused, weighing the wisdom of her revelation. 'Katie, take my advice; forget your mother ever said a thing. Forget your brother.'

'There's no way.'

'You don't want to get mixed up in this, I'm telling you.'

'*Grandma.*'

Grandma sighed. 'All right, but don't blame me. I don't know why I'm doing this, but what the hell, I'll die easier. Secrets take up so damn much room. Young people don't realize that. The little sins you hide grow like a tumor, and before you know it, your body, your soul, has to shrink to make room. You may forget the pleasures that make you sin, but, oh, you never forget the sins themselves.'

'Please continue.' Katie wanted it all.

Grandma hunched closer.

'Before your mother moved to San Francisco, she was working up the coast on a film, in Bodega Bay, I believe. A bunch of them Hollywood types all crammed into trailers. Excess, lasciviousness, your mother's type of fun, if you know what I mean. Your mother had a friend or an acquaintance, a lady friend.'

'An actress?'

'I don't think so. But she was tied to the movies somehow.'

'What's her name?'

'I told you, I never found that out. But each time a letter came postmarked Bodega Bay, well, your mother got hell bent out of shape and didn't come out of her room until her cigarettes ran out. I guess she had a motherly streak in her after all.'

'I know that town,' said Katie. 'And you think he's up there?'

'Let me finish.' Grandma slipped into her serious tone. 'Many years later, a few years after you were born . . . I remember the day clearly, a stifling heat in the city, earthquake weather. Your mother was nervous all morning, peeking out the window waiting for someone, something. Finally a car pulled up, a long top-down Packard or Hudson or some such beauty they don't make anymore. It was cream yellow, polished to the nines, and driven by a black chauffeur in a creased uniform and driver's cap. A real sight. Your mother raced downstairs. I had my left hip break then so I couldn't follow, but I watched from the window above. In the back seat there was a lady, a curious sort, divine and affluent. She wore dark sunglasses and a brimmed hat, so I couldn't see her face very well. Beside her sat a carrot-topped lad, a bright little thing. As soon as your mother saw him she fell into his lap and wept. The boy looked up at me only once. He waved and gave the cheeriest of smiles.'

'Vincent.'

'Your mother stroked the boy's hair, exchanged a few words, some angrily with the woman, and then the Packard zoomed down Lombard Street. When your mother returned she looked at me with the most awful gaze. *He's all right*, she said, as if it were a big surprise or a curse. She locked herself in and bawled for three days. To this day I don't know why she cried. Was it because he wasn't the peculiar creature the doctors had predicted, or because she couldn't stand the idea of someone else enjoying something that was rightly hers? You know how jealous she could get. Anyway, we never saw the boy or the woman again. Your mother said she wasn't *allowed* to see him, whatever that meant. The letters stopped coming and your mother hardly mentioned Vincent at all. Until, that is, she found it necessary to break the news to you.'

Katie studied her grandmother, fidgeting, hiding something still. 'What do you mean, *hardly* mentioned him?'

Grandma folded her arms across her waist. 'No, that's it. I'm finished.'

'Grandma, please, don't leave me hanging.'

'Trust me, Katie. You don't want to know.'

Katie squirmed with anticipation. 'I have to know. He's my brother.'

'*Half* brother,' Grandma corrected.

'Whatever he is, he's all I have.'

Grandma took a deep breath and unfolded her hands. 'I guess I've gone this far, I might as well go on, against my better judgment, mind you. Now, this is sheer speculation, so you'll understand why I hesitate to even share it with you. Understand?'

'Understood.'

'About twenty years ago, one of your mother's boyfriends

came through town, stayed a night or two. But he was a loud talker, hard of hearing, I gather. I didn't try to overhear the conversation, mind you, but the walls are thin in that apartment, I don't have to tell you that. Bert was his name, or Bart. Anyway, he was a producer or location director, I don't know what. People change titles in that business like lovers. Anyway, he was on his way up the coast on business or something, and your mother pleaded with him to find news of Vincent. She was insane, your mother.'

'And?'

'And he came back a few days later and said he'd found out some news through some strange coincidence which I couldn't quite make out – he knew somebody who knew something. I don't know. Anyway, he told your mother that something had happened to Vincent, something terrible, a head injury or something, and that he was missing or had disappeared. Bert or Bart, whatever his name was, said there was talk Vincent might even be—'

Grandma's voice trailed off.

'—dead?'

'No, not that. Like I said, I wasn't even listening to the conversation. I just happened to catch this bigmouth talking. He used the word *deranged.* That's how he described Vincent.'

'What do you mean, deranged?'

'Maybe he said *demented.*'

'Demented?'

'Come to think of it, he may have said *disturbed.* My memory's not serving me right just now.'

'Didn't Mom try to find out?'

'Your mother? After her stint up there on the movie, she avoided that town like the plague. There were times we drove up the coast after we got the van with the wheelchair lift. She grew silent when we passed that town, and you know how hard it was for her to keep silent.'

Grandma picked up *People* and calmly began reading again.

'Tell me more.'

'That's all I know. God be my witness, and God rest your mother's soul.'

Katie thought for a moment. 'So he might need our help.'

Grandma dropped the magazine to her lap. 'There you go again. Another lost puppy to bring home.'

'I have to find out.'

'Now, you see why I didn't want to tell you?'

Something told Katie to leave it alone, not to disturb it, him, whatever it was that her mother had created. But she couldn't control her desire to touch, feel, see a brother. 'I'm going up there.'

'Oh, no, you don't.'

'I have to.' Katie's mind raced with possibilities, plans, hopes.

'You're crazy, like your mother,' said Grandma.

'Bodega Bay. What movie did Mom work on up there?'

'Huh?'

'What movie was she working on . . . in Bodega Bay?'

'Oh, I don't know,' said Grandma. 'Some Hitchcock film or something. I'll take a good book any day.'

'*The Birds*,' said Katie.

'The what?'

'*The Birds*. He filmed it up there.'

'Oh, yeah, that's it,' nodded Grandma. '*The Birds*.'

CHAPTER TWO

The funeral was a simple affair, certainly less grand than Gloria would have liked, but with the modest amount she had set aside, and even with Katie's generous contribution, there was little choice. The funeral director had quickly understood the futility of his upsell attempts and left his son to handle the details.

Since Gloria hadn't stepped into a church in her entire adult life, Katie had difficulty finding a priest. One had stopped by once on his hospital rounds and asked Gloria if she had any regrets in life. 'I wish I'd taken better care of my teeth,' she told him. The priest muttered a quick Our Father and slipped out to find a more devout patient. When he was summoned days later to administer the Last Rites, Gloria shooed him away. 'Too depressing,' she said. Katie implored her with a recitation of all the actresses who had won Oscars by dying dramatically on screen, a handsome priest by their side. But Gloria wouldn't hear of it.

For the funeral Katie did manage to find a priest at the last minute, an intense young man not two weeks out of the seminary. He led the Mass with a simple dignity, no false testimony concerning the character of the deceased, just a modest meditation on loss and love.

It was lucky Gloria wasn't around to tally, as she surely would have, the small number of mourners. Fifteen, maybe sixteen, all rousted by Katie or Grandma the evening before and reluctant to come. Aging Hollywood character actors mostly, spun away from the Hollywood orbit, not a lick of work in decades, but always a glimmer of hope with each ring of the telephone. In her many years around them, Katie had learned that actors possess a rare gene for foolish optimism. Directors carried the inverse gene for pessimism, both equally preposterous.

The funeral turned out to be a reunion of sorts, especially for the older entertainers who had long ago ceased driving the San Francisco hills and arrived by cab, Katie's treat. They hugged, held hands, and shared stories of glory days gone by. In their graying golden years they were beautiful, all of them.

It was a sunny, cloudless October day with a hint of a breeze – weather that would have disappointed Gloria. Not atmospheric enough, she would have complained. Lighting is *everything*, she had reminded Katie time and time again.

Katie wore dark sunglasses, thankful for the excuse of a bright sun. She felt no compunction to share her feelings with the few distant relatives and former friends in attendance. As it was, Katie experienced sadness and confusion and a million other emotions that blended together to create a neutral nothing, like mixing all the colors in a child's paint kit and winding up with a dull brown.

Grandma spent the funeral weeping as if she were to blame for Gloria's three-pack-a-day habit. Gloria's sister, Millie, had flown in from Seattle and wore glasses darker than Katie's. After the service, Millie politely inquired after Katie's well-being, feigned mild interest, then kissed Katie on the cheek and dashed off to catch a plane back home, without an invitation to continue the relationship.

Sunday evening was spent fretting over the details of dismantling her mother's estate, quite a euphemism for a room full of third-hand furniture and a bank book that reached hundreds of dollars on good days and spare change on most.

Katie asked Grandma why she had cried so hard at the funeral. Grandma said it felt wonderful to have her two daughters together again.

Katie took the coastal highway, a notoriously treacherous

stretch of road as it passes through the Marin headlands and into Sonoma County. Still, she wasn't quite prepared for the surprise of screeching motorists flying around each hairpin turn. Or the spit of gravel pounding the underside of her convertible when she veered too close to the road's edge. At the same time she marveled at the colorful dashes of tiny mountain flowers hidden among the parched grass. She could hardly contain her excitement with every roller-coaster grade that sent her car dropping beneath her. And she caught herself laughing when the uneven pavement rolled and pitched her like a personal earthquake. Several times she thought of rejoining the inland route, the safe route to Bodega Bay, but she fought the inclination to surrender. Besides, the ocean was too compelling as it stretched out as endless and blue as life itself.

Normally at this hour on a Monday morning she would be making her way to work on a crowded Muni bus. Thankfully, there were only a few final layouts to arrange for the travel magazine, simple department pieces: a Jamaica inn, a secluded beach on the Mediterranean, restaurants in Oslo. The rest of the art department would handle the details well enough, though Katie secretly hoped they'd miss her *special touch*, as they called it.

She had packed an overnight bag with mostly jeans and T-shirts, a slicker for the threatened rain, and a mauve mohair sweater she invariably received compliments in, just in case she met someone by pure chance, which never happened.

No, Katie counted the passing time by lost earrings and lost relationships, always wondering how she could break up so many pairs of both. She understood the earrings but never the lovers, an odd assortment of could-have-beens, would-have-beens, and losers. There was Joe, the musician who loved so freely, but only when he wanted. David the dentist who wouldn't floss because his father had forced him into dental school and it was his way of rebelling. Michael, the puppy-eyed junior executive who was devastatingly affectionate, a trait

Katie relished with schoolgirl ardor until she learned he was equally affectionate with everyone in town, boy and girl. There was Jimmy, the demon bartender who insisted on making love only at dawn, to preserve his 'chi', he said, which was all right with Katie except she was always so tired at dawn. Then there was blue-collar Richard, with his thick arms and wavy hair the color of copper. Katie fancied him a sailor, especially when he wrapped those thick arms around her from behind. She never felt safer. These were the men, give or take one or two in college and one or two more on distressfully lonely nights, for which Katie had pardoned herself, sort of. Fewer than her girlfriends, more than she would have liked, but Katie promised herself not to live with regret, a promise she broke often, which led to more regret.

Her mother was no help with men or relationships. *Don't get pregnant, and herpes will stain your face*. Gloria repeated her mantra until Katie was fifteen, then the admonitions ceased. From then on each time Katie broke up with a boyfriend, Gloria scolded her for losing another. Losing another, as if Katie were a careless child dropping lunch money on the way to school. But her mother was right. It was Katie who pushed them away. Katie who panicked at growing intimacy. Katie who retreated into the comfort of her loneliness, art, work. She was powerless to stop it, as powerless as her mother was with her smoking, or chasing stardom, or falling into bed with every man who resembled Mario Lanza. Anyway, relationships meant marriage, and marriage meant children, and children meant the chance to fail, again.

Maybe things would change if Vincent were still alive. Did he share Katie's inadequacies? Her desires? Could she feel comfortable at last with a man who wasn't a father figure or a potential lover?

These questions consumed Katie as she wound through fields of grass scorched brown. Upon the first drizzle, the grass would turn a luscious green and smell sweeter than flowers. But now, after months of summer drought and unusual heat, even the leaves of the eucalyptus trees looked a dreary shade of green, as if they had been bleached by some unseen hand and returned to their branches to hang lifelessly.

On the edge of Bodega Bay, Katie caught sight of a colony of new condos. They stuck out glaringly, an anomaly on these craggy rocks and cliffs that defied alteration or permanence. Once in town, Katie saw that not much had changed since Hitchcock's day; brightly painted storefronts and swinging signs hawked saltwater taffy, bait, and kites, but the facade did little to mask the unsettled, ominous feel of the town, still a perfect location for a story about inexplicable attacks by birds. Not hawks or vultures, but ordinary birds like sparrows, sea gulls, crows. Swarms of them, amassing at the most unlikely moments, terrifying little children, pecking out the eyes of lonely farmers, scratching schoolteachers to death. And for what reason? Katie never understood even after countless late-night viewings with her mother beside her puffing nervously.

Katie slowed to a crawl as she passed The Tides Wharf & Café, looking much as she remembered it from the movie. She flashed on that frightening scene when the patrons at the windows watch in horror as a stream of gasoline snakes toward a traveling salesman lighting a cigarette outside. They call to him, pound on the glass, wave their arms frantically, but he doesn't see them or realize the danger. He lights the match, drops it, and half the town blows sky-high.

Katie searched for the gas station, but it was gone, or had never been there in the first place, another trick of the camera. She knew that the small universes created on film were constructed of fiberglass and cardboard, false fronts and matte paintings. Shots here, shots there, shots a thousand miles away, a disjointed bundle of celluloid made to appear real in sweaty editing booths, worlds as fictional as the stories that drove them. Still, Katie felt a tinge of disappointment. The movie fan in her wanted it to be real.

At least the bay looked as she remembered, a symmetrical slice of coastline surrounded by a clutter of sullen shacks and stores hugging the hillside. The air reeked of brackish water and fish guts. Crusty wooden fishing boats knocked gently against splintering docks. Crab traps and fishing nets lay in tangles everywhere. The town folk moved in slow motion, heavy with a strange provincial gravity as they meandered down sidewalks or engaged in unhurried conversations.

Instinctively, Katie glanced across the bay to where 'the Brenner place' had been in the film. The house was gone, too, replaced by a parking lot and a boat launch of some sort, as best Katie could tell. Still, she imagined renting a skiff, as Tippi Hedren had done to bring those two gentle lovebirds to Rod Taylor's younger sister, all on a playful lark. The sequence came rushing back to Katie now. Tippi so elegantly stepping into the boat, kindly assisted by a salty dockhand. Tippi pushing the boat around. Tippi throttling briskly until the breeze brushed back her hair. Tippi, what a gorgeous sight.

As a little girl Katie had thought it absolutely wondrous that a woman could pilot a boat at all, let alone with a confident smile. How graceful Tippi appeared in her smart green outfit, her lustrous hair tastefully wrapped, her chin held queen high. What bedazzling confidence. What a revelation to see a woman with no need to look behind her, a woman who predicted the future by brashly creating it. Ah, the movies.

Katie recalled the very sensation she had experienced the first time she watched that scene. She straightened her eight-year-old shoulders, breathed deeply, and shared, just for a moment, Tippi's confidence as she rode the bay breeze. For days Katie savored the sensation despite the grisly outcome of the movie itself. Inevitably, the image faded and the depressing reality of Katie's life settled around her again. Even at that tender age Katie knew she could never be like Tippi Hedren, or any of the other leading ladies who represented infinite possibilities for her and an equal measure of jealousy for her mother.

Art did not imitate life, nor did life imitate art. Art was life's escape, the cruel reminder of what life could be but wasn't, a wish in Panavision. Anyway, what seemed so brave for a woman in 1963 seemed so simple today. Katie was sure she could handle a skiff, no problem, or at least she told herself she could.

She struggled to remember what judgments her mother had conferred on the cast: Rod Taylor, Tippi Hedren, Suzanne Pleshette, and Jessica Tandy. Strangely, Katie couldn't recall a thing.

Several shops along the way advertised *The Birds* memorabilia. Katie stopped at one but found precious little aside from a few posters and bird key chains. No, Bodega Bay itself was the best memento of all, frozen in time, unwilling or unable to change, an aging, pitiful mistress waiting for the glorious master's return.

Katie's eyes were drawn to the gables of a tall Victorian mansion a few blocks off the main drag. She jumped into the car and followed several turns until a stately bed-and-breakfast came into view. It was 'The Nest,' said the elaborately carved sign, named no doubt to attract Hitchcock aficionados. At four stories high and with its many upper-floor nooks and crannies, it dwarfed everything around it in both size and style. The front garden burst with primroses, gardenias, poppies, and forget-me-nots. A copper weather vane of a proud rooster caught a faint breeze in its tail and faced north.

Inside, the B&B was meticulously appointed, with Persian carpets, richly embroidered mahogany furniture, and a custom-made front counter of carved wood, which was unoccupied at the moment. Katie waited sometime for assistance, feeling guilty for her unsupervised presence, as if her intent was to thieve or rob, and someone would surely incriminate her for her devious plans. She thought of tapping the shiny brass bell on the counter but hesitated to break the museum silence.

Instead, she studied the Audubon bird portraits and bird-related reproductions that crowded the walls in their gilded frames. She stopped at a painting she remembered from art school and to which she had always been curiously drawn. It was a Victorian piece, a lush romantic rendition of a garlanded angel holding a spear as he gently invited a dark-robed pilgrim into a thicket of thorns and brambles.

'Good morning.'

The voice was masculine and soothing. But it startled Katie as she whipped around to face its source. 'I'm sorry. I didn't hear you.'

'Don't be sorry. Life's too short.' He smiled confidently and brushed back a shock of dark wavy hair.

Katie waited for more, but it didn't come. 'You must be the owner,' she said.

'No, not quite,' he said. His blue eyes pierced Katie.

Katie checked his left hand but didn't find a wedding band. 'A guest, then?'

'No. I don't even live here. My name is Rob.'

He smiled graciously and left it at that, as if it explained everything, and as if nothing were on his schedule or hers this morning but to calibrate their magnetic fields. As much as Katie enjoyed the attention, she felt terribly self-conscious.

'Beautiful painting,' she remarked to break the silence.

'*Love and the Pilgrim*,' he said.

'Yes, by Edward Burne-Jones,' Katie added. 'You know him?'

'One of my favorite paintings,' said Rob. He moved from behind the counter, looking sophisticated and earthy all at the same time in a gray sports jacket and blue cotton shirt, unbuttoned.

'I love his work,' said Katie.

'Me too. The technique is not exceptional, but there's just something about him, this painting in particular.'

A man who could talk art. 'I never figured it out either,' Katie replied.

'Ah, but look closer.'

With a wave of his hand Rob invited Katie in until their shoulders nearly touched. She felt his nearness, the texture of his jacket, his masculine scent. She restrained an impulse to lean up to inhale the smell of his neck.

He pointed to the angel. 'See that?' he said, speaking as if he alone possessed the secret to the work and was now prepared to share it.

'An angel leading a poor traveler into wild bushes,' Katie said, feeling immediately foolish for stating something so obvious.

'Those are not just wild bushes. It's a representation of love.'

'Love?' Katie turned to him. His eyes were bright, intelligent, yet strangely sad. She felt almost naked in the intensity of his gaze.

'Yes,' he said with passion. 'Love is chaotic, dangerous, unpredictable. We rush in and find it as unmanageable as a tangle of thorns.'

That certainly had been Katie's experience. But why was he telling her this? Had it been his experience, too, or was he toying with her after a quick study of a single woman traveling alone?

'Fairly bleak assessment, don't you think?' she said, covering her bases.

'Bleak? No. Look at the birds circling above, and the angel hovering,' he said with a twinkle in his eye. 'See their concern? They won't leave the traveler stranded. They're going with him on his journey, to lead him along the way, because love brings chaos—'

'—but protection as well,' Katie finished the sentence.

Suddenly it all made sense to her.

'Exactly.'

Katie clasped her hands in delight. 'That's wonderful!'

'Isn't it?' he said.

'*Isn't it?*' mimicked a female voice.

Katie swung around to face a petite strawberry blonde standing behind the counter, possessing all the features you're supposed to have – sharply cut cheekbones, small chin, full lips.

'I'm sorry, I—' said Katie.

'Sorry for what?' the woman interrupted, cocking her head ever so slightly, like a schoolteacher waiting for an answer she knew wasn't coming. She wore a blue two-piece suit with dramatic lines sailing down from her bust to her thin waist. A ruffled silk shirt was gathered at her neck by a large cameo. Katie's eyes watered from the woman's perfume.

'Sorry for—' But Katie wasn't sure for what. And she wasn't sure why she felt so uncomfortable. 'Katie,' she said. 'My name is Katie Jacobs.'

'I'm Lois, and this is my small enterprise. I see you've met the good doctor.'

Katie turned to Rob. No more good vibes from this guy.

'Informally,' Katie muttered. Her body shrank an inch. 'I didn't know he was a doctor.'

'*Dr* Robert Du Maurier, and my fiancé; proposed just last week.' Lois flashed a perfect set of white teeth.

'I'm a psychologist, really,' Rob explained. 'I have a therapy practice in town.'

'The *only* one,' Lois added. 'How many nights?'

'Well, I'm not sure I'm staying. I'm just checking rates, really.'

'Let me save you time,' said Lois. 'I have the best rates in town, the nicest accommodations. I'm just a little too far off the main road for most people, that's all.'

'Any bags?' asked Rob.

Katie felt cornered. Saying no was never one of her strong points. 'All right, then.'

'Good. If you'll sign the book.'

Katie turned to Rob. 'Just one bag, in the car, the red one with the dented fender – the car, not the bag.'

Now she felt like a complete idiot.

'I'll be right back.' Rob stepped out, all too willingly, it seemed.

Lois opened the register book and dipped a quill pen in a well of ink. How quaint, Katie thought. She signed her name without splotching ink, an accomplishment that made her feel immensely proud.

'Welcome to The Nest. And how long will you be staying?'

'One, two days, tops.'

'Wonderful. Single or double?'

'Single,' answered Katie.

'I ask only because we don't get many single women traveling alone up here. Business?'

'No, well, yes. I'm art director for *Adventure & Travel Magazine*, scouting locations,' she lied.

'I'm a faithful subscriber. Though I don't get to travel much, regretfully, with the demands of the hotel.'

Katie swung around for a quick journalistic judgment. 'I'm surprised we haven't written about you. It's so . . . quaint.'

'It would be nice if you did,' said Lois with genuine enthusiasm.

Katie turned back and eyed the full rack of keys dangling on the pegboard behind Lois. *Maybe you'd actually have some guests if we did*, Katie thought of saying, but bit her lip.

Rob returned with the bag and plopped it near Katie's side. No door-to-door service here.

'Fourth floor, room sixteen,' said Lois. 'The bridal suite. We're not expecting any wedding parties in the next few days. Who gets married on a Monday?'

'How nice of you,' said Katie.

Katie picked up the bag and gave Rob a polite smile, but no more. She didn't have time to play petty games of jealousy with these two; let them work it out themselves. Besides, she was eager to get started on her mission. Her brother was near; she could feel it. She grabbed the bag and headed for her room.

'And Katie,' said Lois.

'Yes?'

'Breakfast is served at 7:00.'

'Please, start without me.'

* * *

Lois stretched her neck to watch Katie climb the stairs. She held the position until she and Rob heard the last echo of Katie's footsteps winding up the four flights.

'She's very pretty,' Lois said.

'Yes, she is.'

Rob felt it coming.

'In a provincial sort of way. Don't you think?'

Rob thought about answering back, but didn't. He had learned long ago to dodge Lois's petty snares.

Lois examined Katie's signature. 'Look at all these loops and flourishes. Immature, don't you think?'

Rob leaned over. 'I kind of like it.'

'Like it? How could you?'

Rob looked at it again. 'I just do.'

Lois closed the book. She hooked Rob's arm and strolled him to the painting. 'If you want her, you can have her, you know.'

'Lois, stop.'

'I wouldn't mind, really, though I'd worry about catching a disease.'

'I was just being nice. She's a guest. Remember those?'

'Don't get smart with me, Robert. All I'm saying is that it's best not to flirt if you can't follow through.'

'I wasn't flirting.'

'Be careful what you wish for, Rob.'

He slipped his arm out of hers. 'I'll take it under advisement.'

'If only she knew,' Lois snickered.

'I don't need this, Lois. Really, I don't.'

'Wouldn't she be disappointed.'

CHAPTER THREE

The post office doubled as a general store, one of those mom-and-pop operations with hand-scribbled signs everywhere and dog-eared postcards tacked on the wall behind the cash register. It was also spookily silent, and every slight shift in Katie's weight caused the wooden floor to creak and moan beneath her. Katie browsed the sparsely stocked shelves, reading labels on cans of meat and potato-chip bags, searching for the gumption to speak. The elderly clerk beat her to it.

'Help ya?' he asked from beneath his green visor. A rubber thimble on his thumb helped him flick letters effortlessly into tiny boxes.

Katie stepped out from behind a dusty kiosk of cheap sunglasses. 'Yes, can you, please?'

'Depends what you're looking for.' He spoke without glancing up.

'I'm looking for a friend, a relative really, but I don't know his last name.'

'Makes it tougher. Lots of people moving in from the city.'

'I know, but I think he's been in town awhile. His name is Vincent.'

'You mean Vincent Jacobs.' The clerk sent another letter flying to its destination.

'Jacobs? That's my—'

Of course. Why hadn't Katie thought of it? That was his last name, wasn't it? But how unusual for an adopted child to retain his original surname. 'Yes, that's him. Do you know where I can find him?'

'I can't tell you where to find him, but I can tell you where he gets his disability checks.'

'You can?' Katie flipped up her sunglasses and rested them on her hair.

The clerk saw the eagerness in Katie's wide eyes. 'You from the IRS or something?'

'No, not at all. Really.'

He gave her another once-over. 'Jilted lover? Because we've had some domestic shootings 'round here lately. Seems no one talks it out anymore.'

'Honestly, he'll be glad to see me. Please believe me.'

'Well, I shouldn't. But you got a nice face. You an actress?'

'No.'

'Maybe you just remind me of somebody famous, an old-time actress.'

'I can't think of who.'

'Me neither, but you're a lovely little thing, if you don't mind my saying.'

Katie did mind, but she wasn't going to object now. 'Thank you.' She smiled, big and pretty, school picture-like.

The clerk set down his mail, all but one letter which he used to flag his directions.

'There's an old junkyard about two miles east of town, a quarter-mile off the main road. In the back there's a trailer. Behind the trailer there's another trailer. Green, I think. That's where the mail goes.'

'And you're sure it's Vincent Jacobs?'

'That's what the envelopes say. I can't guarantee anything after that.'

'Thank you.' Katie slapped down her sunglasses and turned to leave.

'And lady.'

'Yes, sir?'

'Be careful.'

'Why?'

'Because it's a man's world.'

'What do you mean by that?'

'Just what I said.'

Katie hurried into the heat, unsure of what to make of the cryptic warning but with no inclination to decipher it now.

She ducked into the very next store to select a gift for Vincent; even in a rush she couldn't go empty-handed. However, she was confronted with an instant dilemma. The store was two shops in one, flowers and liquor. An odd combination, she thought, until she realized the genius of it all. Sell liquor for the evening's wild reverie and flowers for the inevitable pleas of forgiveness that follow.

Would Vincent prefer a mixed bouquet or a bottle of scotch? Before she could venture a guess, the jingle of the door bell announced the arrival of a customer, an elderly woman, uncharacteristically solid. Katie glanced up instinctively, then found it hard to take her eyes off the commanding presence. Everything about the woman looked old-money rich and exquisite, but somehow out of place, or rather out of time in this harbor town. The woman's hair was cropped short and covered by a beige French beret dipped jauntily over her brow. She wore a rusty single-breasted wool herringbone jacket and brown leather riding gloves, which she took off upon entering. These were old clothes, two generations old or older, yet remarkably preserved as if tailored this morning.

The proprietor, a busty woman busy at the front counter with a bundle of receipts and a chirping calculator, swept away her work and jumped from her stool.

'Good day, Madame Charay.'

'Marvelous afternoon, isn't it? And rain is on the way, I hear. Have my orchids arrived?'

'Yes, ma'am.'

The proprietor unconsciously bent in a slight curtsy as she stepped from behind the counter and slipped by Madame Charay on her way to the back room. Katie hid behind a lemon tree to observe Madame Charay, obviously very familiar with the shop, take a quick tour. The woman hardly noticed Katie as she examined with great care the tips of the flowers and the underside of their leaves. Katie picked up a sad bunch of chrysanthemums. The proprietor returned cradling a bouquet of exotic orchids, six flowers, each with voluptuous white petals encircling a small, rich purple sack in the center, so erotic Katie felt herself blush.

Madame Charay lit up. 'Truly divine. You find the best.'

The proprietor smiled, pleased at the compliment. 'Two hundred and fifty dollars, as usual. No tax.'

Without pause Madame Charay pulled out a man's money clip and from a crisp flash of green snapped out three one-hundred dollar bills.

The shop owner made quick change and Madame Charay vanished out the door. 'Ta-ta.'

Katie checked the price on her own bouquet then placed it on the counter. So much for a bottle of scotch.

'Find something you like?' asked the proprietor.

'Yes, these will do, I think. Expensive flowers she just bought. What were they?'

The proprietor swelled with pride. '*Paphiopedilum lawrenceanum.* But not just *any Paphiopedilum lawrenceanum.*'

'Obviously, but why?'

'They're *immortal.*'

'Immortal?'

The shopkeeper plucked off a few dying leaves from Katie's bunch. 'You're not an orchid lover, I take it.'

'I appreciate them, I guess.'

'If you were, you'd know about *Paphiopedilum lawrenceanum*; they've caused quite a stir in the orchid community. This particular variety was first discovered in Borneo late last century, a rare find to begin with, until they vanished.'

'Vanished?'

'Stopped growing, really, but a mystery nonetheless. Collectors searched the jungles for years. It became sort of the holy grail for orchid lovers. Then about ten years ago the orchids started appearing again, in the very same fields they had first been discovered a century earlier. Orchid lovers flew in from the world over. You can imagine the excitement it generated.'

'Naturally.'

'In orchid circles they started calling the flowers the *immortals* because of their extraordinary reemergence – you just don't find flowers reappearing after a hundred years as if a single winter had passed.'

'I've never heard of such a thing,' said Katie.

'Except there's one peculiar trait about the *new* Borneo immortals.'

'What's that?'

'It's terrible, but quite romantic.'

'Tell me.'

'They die dramatic deaths.'

'They do?'

'Yes. As soon as they're exposed to even a hint of cold, they die. You can watch it before your eyes. Their petals turn from white to a flaming purple, then shrivel and die. Kaput. All in a matter of minutes, even seconds.'

'Just like that?'

'Just like that,' said the proprietor with a snap of her fingers. 'I keep them in the bread warmer of my Chambers stove until she picks them up.'

'She does so regularly?'

'Every other day, like clockwork.'

'Rich?' Katie did the quick math and glanced out the window for signs of the extravagant woman, but she was gone. Only waves from the unusually stifling heat traveled the streets.

'And eccentric,' said the proprietor. 'A real Hitchcock nut, I understand.'

'Isn't everyone around here?'

'Not like her.'

The owner wrapped Katie's flowers in paper and handed them over. 'Anything else?'

'No, nothing.'

'That'll be four dollars, eighty-six cents.'

Katie uncreased a five-dollar bill and pushed it across the counter. She put the change in a donation jar for the Sonoma County Society for the Prevention of Cruelty to Animals.

'Grave?' asked the shop owner inquisitively.

'No. Relative.'

'One leads to the other, doesn't it?'

Katie stopped and turned. 'What do you mean by that?'

'Oh, nothing. Just a little black humor. Nothing else to do in this town.'

'Pretty quiet around here?'

'A regular Monday matinee.'

In her excitement Katie nearly missed the peeling hand-painted sign for 'J&J's Wrecking' and the dim arrow directing traffic down a bumpy dirt road. The ruts rippled through her body as she approached the junkyard encircled by a corrugated metal fence topped with a tangle of barbed wire.

An angry dog began barking even before Katie stepped from her car.

'Hello?' she called.

The unlocked gate was ajar only a sliver. Katie tried but couldn't budge it and was forced to squeeze sideways through the narrow opening. A pit bull, the dog's front paws waving helplessly in the air as he fought the short chain. Katie searched for human life but saw only piles of transmissions, engines, leaking batteries, and the carcasses of cars piled high.

'Hello,' she called again, provoking no response except to silence the pit bull, which seemed perplexed by a female voice. She ventured deeper inside, past the rusted shells of pickup trucks and a long wall of hubcaps. The trail beneath her was slippery from engine oil, and she felt the slime on the bottom of her sneakers.

She reached the first trailer after having traveled farther than she had promised she would.

'Anybody here?'

She walked around back to find the second trailer, presumably belonging to her brother. She wasn't sure now she wanted to meet him.

Katie flung back her hair, stretched her T-shirt so her breasts wouldn't be so prominent, and practiced a pleasant smile.

She knocked politely. The thin door swung open. Katie hated when that happened, and she hated it more in this ungodly place.

'Anyone home?' The trailer gave Katie the creeps. This whole town gave her the creeps.

Katie heard a voice inside. A radio, she thought. But it repeated itself with an intonation that was mechanical and frightening. Katie cupped her ear and stepped one foot beyond the threshold.

'Help, Mama . . . Mama, help!'

A wave of goose bumps ran over her.

'Vincent?'

'Help, Mama . . . Mama, help!' The voice grew louder, filled with fear and impending harm.

'Help, Mama . . . Mama, help!'

The ranting of a lunatic. Katie delved inside in search of the being so in need of help.

'Help, Mama . . . Mama, help!'

The incantation bounced off the walls, bombarded Katie from every angle. She spun to face the kitchen cluttered with filthy dishes, only to hear it behind her, bouncing off the living-room walls covered with pinups from porno magazines. Its location was masqueraded, but the voice remained unwavering. That fear, that urgency.

'Help, Mama . . . Mama, help!'

Katie closed her eyes and let the words swirl in her mind.

She spun once more to face a dark corner, a blanket thrown over a box or a cage or some contraption.

She approached with one hand in front of her, one behind. Crouched, ready to strike, ready to flee.

'Help, Mama . . . Mama, help!'

Katie placed her hand on the blanket.

'Help, Mama . . . Mama, help!'

She closed her eyes, waited for a fleeting impulse of courage.

'Help, Mama . . . Mama, help!'

She ripped the blanket from its mooring and stared into the eyes of the creature.

It was a bird.

A big, old, restless, multicolored macaw with a thick beak and leathery claws.

'Help, Mama . . . Mama, help!' crowed the bird from its perch. It plucked a sunflower seed from the filthy cage bottom and expertly cracked the shell.

'Help, Mama . . . Mama, help!' It swallowed the seed and eyeballed Katie.

A bird. Katie laughed at herself, at the liberty of her wild imagination, at being duped by a near-brainless animal. Bodega Bay, a bird, what else?

'Who the fuck are you?' a voice growled behind her.

Katie spun around bad-breath close to a seething, greasy brute gnawing at his jaw and squinting as if viewing Katie from a million miles away.

'I said who the fuck are you?'

'Katie,' she gulped.

He moved closer, sniffed like a dog.

Katie stiffened. He smelled like sweat and sperm and oil. She squeezed her knees together.

'Vincent?' she asked, trembling.

'What the fuck is it to you?' He circled her, leering at her butt, her breasts.

'I'm a relative. Distant cousin. My grandmother was cousin to your grandmother. That's what they tell me.'

He licked his lips. 'That's what *who* told you?'

Katie stepped back. He stepped forward.

'You are Vincent Jacobs, aren't you?'

'You tell me. *You* broke into my house.'

'I didn't mean to . . . the man at the post office . . . the bird over there. If you're not, I can leave right now. Honest.'

'Honest, huh? You being honest with me?'

Katie avoided his murky eyes. 'Look, obviously this is a big mistake.'

She glanced at the door. With a head start she could make it all the way to her car. She could run fast, always could.

'I should be going.'

'What for? I *am* Vincent,' he said.

Katie stopped and turned. 'You what?'

'But you ain't no distant relative.' A smile lifted only one corner of his mouth.

Katie stole a look at this greasy cruelty covered with stubble.

'How do I know you're really Vincent?'

'Ask me something.'

'What color was your hair as a child?'

'Red. Flaming red.'

'Who is your mother?'

'Adopted or biological?'

'Biological,' said Katie.

'Beats me. I was adopted.'

Katie glanced out upon the rusty junkyard. 'I don't believe you.'

'Wanna see my driver's license?'

'That would help.'

He reached into the back pocket of his sagging jeans.

'No funny tricks,' said Katie.

He flipped open the wallet and stretched it at arm's length for Katie's inspection.

The license had expired by two years, but the name was Vincent Jacobs, accompanied by a photo of him looking only slightly less menacing. He shared her eye color, but little else.

'I got other identification, if you want to look.'

'No, that will be fine, thank you.'

'Now, what can I help you with?'

The dog started yelping. The sun sank behind a cloud, the first one in days.

'Nothing,' Katie said.

He slithered closer. 'Because I'm an expert at helping ladies like you.'

Suddenly he grabbed her by the wrist and pushed her against the wall.

Oh, Lord, Katie prayed. Then she kicked him in the groin with her knee, ripped away in an instant, and dashed out of the trailer.

'Come back here!' he groaned.

Katie bolted down the trailer's rickety stairs.

'Get back here or I'll call the cops!'

She kept running, running.

'You're not my brother,' she whispered to herself.

'What'd you say? Get back here, you whore.'

Katie ran, knees chopping high, hands slicing the air. She ran past the hubcaps, past the transmissions, past the chained dog. She slithered through the gate and kept running, running, running until she reached her car, not glancing in her rear window or turning her shoulder, not even when she fishtailed onto the coastal highway or swerved into town. She ran from her car into The Nest, past Lois and Rob twirling in the lobby to watch her rush by. She ran up the four stories, three steps at a time, ran until she reached the safety of her room, where she locked the door, drew the shades, and hid her face in a pillow. Hid because she had found her brother, and he was everything she feared he would be.

CHAPTER FOUR

The morning-sharp rays of sun wrested Katie from a deep sleep. She was safe, she thought at first, in her cluttered apartment overlooking the narrow park where old men dressed in white played boccie until dusk. But a few glances around the room and the brisk scent of ocean air returned her to sobering reality. Any doubts were dispelled with one look under the sheets at yesterday's clothing, soiled with junkyard soot.

She didn't want to touch her dirty jeans after a shower, let alone wrap them around her clean thighs. She berated herself for not packing another pair, for rushing up here, convinced a brother she could adore would be waiting with open arms. She tidied the room, made the bed, and trudged downstairs. And if she didn't feel lousy enough, there was Lois waiting at the counter, all prissied up and wide awake.

'Leaving so soon?' Lois said. 'I hope it wasn't the accommodations.'

'No, they were fine.' And they had been; the room was glorious.

'Then I gather you didn't find what you were looking for.'

'I guess not. Things changed. Everything changed,' said Katie.

'I'm so sorry.' Lois wore a lavender velvet dress with a flared skirt and a low bust line, much more risqué than her outfit yesterday. The modern and the Victorian, the sexual and the repressed, Lois could do it all, and Katie felt herself no match in her dusty jeans and T-shirt that revealed her navel. Katie had encountered women like Lois before, women who feel threatened by other women, territorial when nothing was at stake, never saying what they meant or meaning what they say, always scheming for the upper hand, then graciously returning it under the proviso that it's a bequest to be revoked at any time. Facing this Revlon poster-child served only to remind Katie that the world competed against her even when she wasn't competing herself.

Katie paid up with cash, wanting no record of her stay here. She was both saddened and relieved not to catch a final glimpse of Rob. She did allow herself a last glance at the painting that had drawn them together, the gentle angel with his mischievous smile. 'Love brings chaos but protection as well,' he had said. Yeah, right. The chaos part Katie believed, but protection, well, the painting was nothing but a fairy tale.

'I hope you'll still consider writing about us,' Lois said.

'Of course,' said Katie.

She picked up her receipt and stepped out into the blinding sun. Her car was covered with dust and the spittle of road oil, but it fired up just fine, and the roar sounded like music. She shifted into gear and sped off recklessly, harboring not a shred of remorse as she watched the last vestige of Bodega Bay vanish in her rearview mirror.

So he was a sleaze, a bum, and a slob to boot. Probably a pornographer or smuggler, too, if not a pimp and a drug dealer. Perhaps they shared a half set of genes, but genes can get mixed up, broken, buried, disturbed. Whatever genes were prominent in his makeup, Katie prayed were recessive in hers. It was clear the opposite was true as well. He was nothing like her, not a shred. Until yesterday, Katie had resented her mother for keeping Vincent's existence a secret. Now Katie saw the wisdom in her restraint and wished Gloria had taken the secret to her grave.

If Katie prided herself on anything it was her ability to brush off disappointment, pick herself up, and stand ready for the next challenge. Life would return to normal, always had. So it goes.

She turned onto the inland route, the safe route, back. Once away from the coast, the road turned lazy, the grades long and gentle, and the temperature skyrocketed.

And then it hit. Struck her windshield with a flash of shadow. Darkened her view, shattered the glass into a million fragments.

She slammed on the brakes and came to a screeching halt inches from the embankment.

The shattered bits of glass hung together precariously inches from her face. A thousand daggers of refracted light pierced Katie's body. She touched the windshield with a single finger and a few square shards wiggled loose and tumbled onto her lap. She picked two up. Cheap jewels.

After a deep sigh she rolled backward onto the safe shoulder, squeezed the emergency brake, and took her first breath. A passing driver honked as he gunned it up the long hill out of sight.

She stepped out to survey the damage and find her bearings. The windshield was one swift gust away from collapsing. Petaluma lay twenty miles ahead. That left one option, Bodega Bay, a few miles back. It was still early, a weekday; someone in town must fix windshields. But she wasn't sure she could handle a few more hours in Bodega Bay and decided on chancing Petaluma.

Then something caught her eye. A small black mass of random motion on the road some thirty yards back. Katie walked slowly toward it, zigzagging to alter her viewing angle, to make better sense of the form. At first she thought it was a blister of road tar heated by the sun. Closer, it looked like a slab of rubber shorn from a tire. But rubber didn't move, not like that.

As she drew closer she understood what had slammed into her windshield like a phantom.

A crow.

She knelt down near the body writhing in pain, a tangled and knotted mess on the double yellow line. One black wing flapped haplessly skyward. The other, pressed against the hot pavement, hardly worked at all. Twisted and broken, the bird's head lay on the road as if listening to a secret message underground. Katie wanted to help her, soothe her, but she could only act as witness to the bird's fluttery spasms.

The crow, unable to grasp the new physics of her injury, struggled to stand and fly. She gazed at Katie with yellow eyes, as if Katie were a goddess with the power to mend splintered bone and crushed flesh. Katie touched a wing, and the crow slapped her away with a flurry of frightened motion.

Katie drew her shadow over the bird to cool it. The crow again valiantly attempted to pick herself up and fly, one final stab at life. She slipped into a series of quick spasms and then, with one last shudder that Katie shared, the crow fell still. Only a breeze to quiver her plume. And then even the breeze died.

Katie stroked her feathers, so black they shined blue. In a whisper Katie assured the bird of a peace beyond, eternal life in whatever heaven awaited creatures of flight. Katie knew it was foolish speaking to a bird, a dead bird, no less, one that had shattered her windshield on a hot road in the middle of nowhere. Still, Katie felt accountable in some strange way, by association if nothing more with humanity and its machines that spare no mercy and offer no solace.

She crouched beside the corpse, never having viewed a bird so closely, marveling over the miracle of its design, even tangled and broken like this.

The bird's wing began to tremble, barely.

Katie shook a tear from her eye to better see. The tremble turned into a twitter. Katie lifted a finger but couldn't find a breeze.

Her heart jumped at the thought of the bird rising to take wing, fully healed and whole. A resurrection, a sign, a miracle.

Then Katie felt the vibration underneath her. It ran up her crouched legs, through her spine, and into her teeth in perfect harmony with the fluttering of the bird's wings.

The truck rounded the bend from atop the hill, silhouetted by a blistering sun behind it, a tall cab hauling a long load of redwood trunks gathered between four metal spikes.

The truck sputtered and spat as the driver forced a downshift. Fumes spewed from the polished exhaust pipes like dragon's breath. The horn bellowed deeply. Once, twice.

Katie tried to scoop up the bird, but blood had adhered one wing to the sweltering pavement and Katie couldn't yank it free.

Three blasts of the horn. A screech of brakes. A glint of grille. The sun.

Katie's nostrils filled with the black scent of burning rubber. She saw the whites of the driver's eyes. The shriek of the brakes pierced her ears.

She scooped up the bird, and in one fluid motion flung the animal over the edge of the embankment. Katie spun full circle and watched the bird arch skyward, reach its apex, and drop like a stone into the brush below.

The truck rushed by with a blast of displaced air so powerful it nearly tipped Katie over. She stood frozen, shoulders shrunk inward, eyes closed, hands cupping her ears, until the departing rumble of the truck echoed and faded. Only then did she feel the adrenaline drain from her body in waves, leaving her depleted and spent, but feeling more alive than ever.

She searched for the carcass in the brush below, but couldn't find it. But she had saved the animal from the trampling of countless tires, and for this Katie felt proud.

As she turned to leave, a single black feather fluttered to the ground beside her. She picked it up, twirled it between her fingers, felt its smoothness, its weightlessness. She stuck it in a loop in her jeans and headed back to Bodega Bay, driving slowly, and with her head poking out of the driver's window so she could see beyond the shattered windshield, ready to collapse in on her at any moment.

'You're lucky,' said the mechanic, as he leaned over the fender.

'I've got my son going to Santa Rosa. He'll pick up a used one. New ones cost an arm and a leg these days.'

He worked cheerfully, wiping each socket clean before returning it to its rightful place in the tray. The shop was swept clean and crowded with red cabinets overflowing with tools. If Katie lived in town, this is where she'd bring her car.

Katie handed back the signed estimate form. 'It was the last thing I was expecting,' she said.

'Happens all the time. I bet I get one every month. People get all bent out of shape because Hitchcock filmed that movie up here. A bird shatters their windshield and they're thinking all sorts of weird stuff. Hey, it would spook me, too, if I didn't see it all the time.'

'It came out of nowhere.'

'They drop from the sky. Wind gusts. You ever fly a kite up in these hills? The wind'll rip it out of your hands. When I was a kid I used to get rope burns on my palms just trying to keep my kites from flying away. I'm telling you, this coast is crazy. Wind gusts, fog. They got sleeper waves around here that'll steal you off the beach and drag you halfway to China. The earthquake of 1906 moved Bodega Bay eight feet to the north, no kidding. This country don't make sense.'

'It's too much of a coincidence,' said Katie.

'What is? You up here filming a movie?'

'No.'

'Good, because they always come up here thinking they can do another *Birds*, but they can't. No one can.'

'Actually, I was here looking for my brother,' said Katie.

'Doesn't sound like a coincidence to me. What's his name?'

'Vincent Jacobs.'

The mechanic's ratchet stopped in mid-turn. 'What are you, some kind of practical joker?'

'What do you mean?'

'Vincent Jacobs? You mean *Vinnie* Jacobs?'

'I don't know,' said Katie.

'Has to be. There was only one Vinnie Jacobs in town. Couldn't be two like him. Haven't heard that name in years.'

'But he lives here, in that junkyard out of town,' Katie explained.

'You mean J&J's, that heap? I never use it.'

'The guy who lives in the back trailer, do you know him?'

'Peter Grow? That asshole is the biggest drunk in Sonoma County.'

'He told me he was Vincent.'

'Did he tell you that? Man, some guys will do anything to get laid. Pardon my French.'

'But he had a driver's license.'

'He's probably got a dozen licenses. I think he was popped for check fraud once or twice.'

'Arrested?'

'*Many* times.'

'You don't think he's Vincent?'

'Was he a mean-looking guy, beer belly, a little scar running across the brim of his nose?'

'That's him.'

'That's Peter.'

'And you say you know Vincent?'

The mechanic wiped his ratchet and slipped it into his pocket. He searched his memory. 'God, I've hardly heard that name since high school. Vinnie Jacobs.'

The mechanic studied Katie, toe to head. 'You're a lot younger, better lookin'. You certainly don't look like his sister.'

'He's my half brother, actually. Please. Tell me what you know.'

'Hey, no problem. It ain't no secret. Vinnie was some rich kid, lived here during the summer, up at Petty's Cove. He went to boarding school or something like that during the winter, smarter than a whip, but nerdy as hell. All the kids used to tease him about his freckles and red hair. It really wasn't so red, come to think of it, more the color of dirty plumbing copper. Whatever, he didn't seem to mind. Nothing fazed him, nothing at all. A nice kid, as I remember. All the time you'd see him on his big Schwinn bicycle. It had a fox tail on the back fender, rubber mud flaps on both tires, and a corny bell attached to the handlebars that all the kids would ring and ring and ring. Maybe we were too hard on him. You know how kids can be.

'Then one summer he didn't show. No one missed him, I'll guarantee you that. People asked about him when they ran out of things to say, but no one knew what happened to him, no one cared. We all figured he just moved away, or his parents bought a bigger beach house up the coast. Years went by and his name wasn't muttered three times in this town, I bet you.

'But then – you see, all the kids had parties on the beaches at night here – beer and pot and shit, you know, high school. Anyway, at one party some of the kids swore they saw Vinnie Jacobs combing the beaches checking the trash cans for food.'

'Vincent?'

'No shit. But not the Vincent we knew. They said he was bizarre or psycho or something. Like an animal. His hair all wild, a crazy look on his face, filthy, wearing ragged clothes, blood sores on his forehead. I'm telling you, there were all sorts of stories. I never saw him, personally. I fall asleep when I get drunk, like my dad. But I got friends who wouldn't lie, to me anyways, and they swear to God it was Vinnie.'

'You said you know where he lives.'

'I said I *think* I know. Up at Petty's Cove, a couple of miles north of here.'

The mechanic spent a good five minutes describing landmarks, estimating distances, changing his mind, and pointing in every direction several times. Katie hardly listened, sure she could find the place with ease.

'Do you think it was really him on the beach?' asked Katie.

'Maybe. I don't know. We were stoned out of our minds most of the time. It's been a long time since I graduated from high school. But every once in a while, someone, not even a local maybe, says they've seen some crazy dude hiding in the crags, lurking about, or sleeping beneath the oak brush at the end of some dirt trail at Doran Beach. Always with red hair.'

The mechanic pulled out his ratchet and leaned over the fender once more. Katie stuck her head under the hood.

'Vincent?'

'Beats me. But I'll tell you one thing. Anytime something spooky happens in this town, everyone blames it on Vinnie Jacobs. I'll be damned. Vinnie Jacobs. He's the certified bogeyman of Bodega Bay.'

CHAPTER FIVE

Katie should have listened more carefully. The route mapped out by the mechanic led her through a confusing series of switchbacks and secondary roads beneath the relentless shadows of tall redwoods and sequoias. Unlike the southern flank of town, where the sun tormented the scorched hillsides, here on the north side the sunlight managed to penetrate only in thin wisps, and even then fell victim to the flickering branches rustled by the slightest breeze. The air felt cool and damp as if the forest greedily trapped the moisture arriving from the coast and smothered it under its thick canopy of leaves.

Following the incident with the crow, Katie felt emboldened. She wondered fleetingly if someone had slipped her some powerful drug without her knowledge, Prozac or steroids or some such concoction potent enough to transform her very nature, infuse her with vigor, courage, and self-confidence, traits as foreign as any to Katie. But the miracle drug lost its potency under these ancient giants. They obstructed her view of ocean and coastal hills and confused her sense of direction, which seemed to be northwest, though for long stretches she drove away from the setting sun, which meant east.

She stopped for directions yet still made foolish turns and errors in judgment. Several times Katie came upon familiar crossroads, sure she had driven herself in circles. Hours remained before the October sun was due to sink, but under the trees it seemed to be setting already. Whatever light remained emanated from no single source but rather fell delicately like electric snowflakes.

Finally she came to what she believed was the place. The only clue given her was a dirt driveway flanked by two short stone walls. Here was the driveway, yet it seemed to lead nowhere other than deeper into the woods. She turned and crept along expecting to find a house beyond every bend, but finding instead only more twisted turns.

Katie thought of retreating. She should have told someone about her destination, a police officer, someone at the magazine, Robert, even Lois. The folly of her zeal had brought her to trouble's door before.

Then she saw the house. A mansion really, carefully constructed with huge, round river stones. Deep eaves threw shadows across the second floor and attic windows, and wisteria vines, thick as arms, crept into every deeply set window. The slate roof was the blue-gray of a stormy sea.

She thought about returning to town or at least to the last gas station to call in her whereabouts. Instead, she rolled to a stop near the carriage house and stepped out to listen for the sound of chatter, children playing, signs of life, but heard only a tall breeze and the crackling of pine needles underneath her feet as she ambled to the front entrance.

The door was thick mahogany, oiled and smooth from age. She lifted the door knocker, a massive brass eagle's talon crafted with frightening detail. She let it drop and the claw tips fell on the brass plate with a ping and a thud.

Katie took a breath and turned to pan the view from the doorstep.

She didn't hear the door swing open behind her.

'Good afternoon.'

Katie whirled around. The simplest greeting escaped her.

'It's you,' Katie stuttered.

'How perceptive.' Madame Charay smiled.

'I'm sorry. Maybe I have the wrong address,' said Katie, though she wasn't so sure.

'Nonsense,' said Madame Charay. 'Come in, please. I so rarely have the pleasure of unannounced guests.'

Madame Charay possessed the agile smallness of a former gymnast, all compact sinews packed beneath tight skin. Katie felt an uncommon strength in the woman's grip despite the most casual of handshakes.

She invited Katie in with such panache that Katie had no choice but to follow the sweeping gesture inside. The woman was elderly but somehow ageless as she floated through the foyer, her chin raised high, her shoulders square and true, and an empty cigarette-holder floating between her fingers.

'I remember you from the flower shop yesterday,' said Madame Charay, extending her hand.

'You do?' said Katie.

'How could I miss such a beautiful face?' Madame Charay said.

Her eyebrows, painted on in the fashion of women a generation ago, raised and fell in concert with her sentiments as she spoke. She wore no other makeup and was remarkably free of wrinkles save for the imprint of crow's feet spreading around the corners of her eyes.

Katie always felt oafish in the presence of petite women and thoroughly uncomfortable before mother figures. She felt doubly uneasy now. 'I didn't mean to intrude. It's just that I—'

'—No need to explain. I'm delighted. Care for a cup of tea? I've just brewed a fresh pot.'

Her accent was American, yet her careful enunciation suggested a hint of British. Facing the woman squarely, Katie beheld the clarity of her blue-gray eyes, the same as the slate roof.

Madame Charay threw open the drapes and a misty light rushed in. From the musky scent of the place, Katie expected to see a room filled with stodgy antiques, dusty and dark. Instead, she found a confusing hodgepodge of styles – modern, Victorian, French provincial, art deco, early American – more an inventory than a decor, as if this were a warehouse of goods awaiting classification and shipment to their proper retail establishments. An ornate buffet stood regally next to a 1960s couch with raucous olive-green polyester cushions. A superbly crafted English oak rolltop desk was accompanied by a scratched-up postwar office chair more befitting a private eye than a wealthy heiress.

Intrigued by the jarring juxtapositions of furnishings, Katie didn't notice the wall hangings at first. Movie posters everywhere, and Hitchcock films, all of them, each framed exquisitely as if they were paintings by Vermeer and Botticelli.

Cary Grant kissing Ingrid Bergman in the one sheet for *Notorious*. 'No risk too great for love so enticing!' read the log line.

A dagger separated Paul Newman and Julie Andrews in the poster for *Torn Curtain*. 'It tears you apart with suspense!'

Cary Grant in a cheek-to-cheek embrace with Joan Fontaine in *Suspicion*. 'Each time they kissed . . . there was the thrill of love . . . the threat of murder!'

Ingrid Bergman and Gregory Peck. 'The magnificence of its cast. . . . The intensity of its emotions . . . will hold you . . . *Spellbound*.'

The Lady Vanishes, *Rear Window*, *Dial M for Murder*, *The Thirty-Nine Steps*, *Rebecca*, *Psycho*, *Vertigo*, *Rope*, *The Birds*, they were all here, and then some Katie only vaguely recalled. *Lifeboat*, *Young and Innocent*, *I Confess*, *The Pleasure Garden*. Katie had watched many of these old thrillers late at night with her mother. And as she studied each poster, her mind flashed on scenes in black and white or technicolor. She recalled snippets of dialogue and muffled soundtracks that lingered surprisingly in the banks of her memory. So strange what one remembers. Then again Katie must have seen *Rear Window* twenty times, *Psycho* fifty.

'Are you a fan?' asked Madame Charay.

Katie felt fidgety, like a schoolgirl addressing the headmistress. 'Oh, yes. Like everybody, his movies really scared me when I was a kid. They still do.'

'Naturally,' said Madame Charay, seeming a bit disappointed by Katie's pedestrian response.

'I mean, he was a great director,' said Katie, feeling the need to prove herself; 'probably the greatest of all time. I see his influence in every suspense movie I watch.'

Madame Charay sighed. 'Alfred was never understood in this country. Commercial success, yes, but the deeper meaning of his work – it was never appreciated. Alfred was so much more than a director, an auteur. These terms don't do justice to his brilliance.'

'How would you describe him?'

'Alfred understood the human psyche like no other. He had the courage to explore it, even its dark side, the side we often choose to ignore yet which so fascinates us. He drew his images from the human reservoir of dreams and fear – his own intensely private dreams – and then he had the courage, the audacity, to record these on film for all the world to see.'

Katie was only half listening, her attention drawn to a line of sealed and softly lit Lucite cases against the far wall, each protecting the most mundane of items.

Madame Charay wrapped her arm in Katie's and led her past the posters, as if visiting an exhibit at the Louvre.

She continued, a priestess reciting liturgy. 'His passion, his vision were unique, yet he practiced with a furious attention to detail and precision, with a masterly control that only true artists achieve. It is a combination one generation in ten is fortunate to experience. And we have fifty-three incarnations of his genius, from his first feature film, *The Pleasure Garden*, to his last, *Family Plot*. There's a certain symmetry to that, wouldn't you agree?'

Katie nodded. She stopped in front of a display case protecting a section of rope.

'What's this?' she asked, unable to hide her puzzlement.

'The rope.'

'The rope?'

'Not just any rope. *The* rope. From his film *Rope*, 1948. John Dall and Farley Granger accomplish the perfect murder but find it necessary to brag about it to James Stewart. Based on the

Leopold and Loeb case, I'm sure you're aware. Who but Alfred had the courage to deal with themes of homosexuality, guilt, and hubris in 1948? John Ford? Please, he was busy making those insipid John Wayne movies. John Huston? *The Treasure of the Sierra Madre* was nothing more than a trifle starring the pretty boy of the day. Frank Capra? The most overrated purveyor of schlock ever to disgrace the screen. No one matched Alfred, none of them.'

Madame Charay led Katie to another case. 'The nylon stockings,' she explained.

'Nylon stockings?'

'*Dial M for Murder*. Another perfect crime gone amiss. Ray Milland hires a scoundrel to strangle his wife, but she kills the killer instead. Perfect plot twist. Alfred simply adored strangulation as a method of disposal, you know.'

Katie thought it was pretty weird, the collection, the obsession, everything. 'You're quite a devoted fan, I see,' she said. 'Did you know him? Meet him in person?'

'Briefly. All too briefly,' said Madame Charay with an expression of nostalgia that reminded Katie of her mother when she read in the paper the passing of an actor of great stature.

'The grand piano over there? From *Suspicion*. Joan Fontaine suspects that Cary Grant wants to kill her. It's a tale of how circumstantial evidence can lead to tragic conclusions. A universal theme. The candelabras? From *Notorious*. The drapes over the front window? *Rear Window*. And the statue of cupid behind you, it's from the foyer of the Bates' mansion in *Psycho*. Need I recount the story?'

Katie turned to the dark bronze statue some three feet tall. 'I saw *Psycho*. I don't remember it.'

'Ah, but that is Alfred's genius. Everything plainly in view, yet unquestioned by the conscious eye. We feel it, perceive it subliminally.'

'Everything in this house comes from a Hitchcock film?'

'A few things. Most.'

Madame Charay led Katie to the couch and motioned for her

to sit. 'Joseph Cotten sat on this couch in *Shadow of a Doubt*. The lamps on the end tables from *Strangers on a Train*, 1951. The bird cage, over there—'

Katie knew the answer to this one. '—the lovebirds in *The Birds*.'

'Precisely. My most arduous acquisition,' said Madame Charay. She poured two steaming hot cups of tea.

'And the teapot?'

'*Suspicion*.' Madame Charay smiled. 'Milk or lemon?'

'Milk.'

Katie scanned the room, appraising every ashtray, knick-knack, and bookend. 'The rooms upstairs too?'

Madame Charay smiled. 'If you only knew.'

Katie leaned back. 'This collection must be worth a fortune.'

'I don't care to put a dollar figure on it; to me it's priceless.'

Katie sipped her tea, careful not to spill it on the relics. She adjusted her bottom so as not to leave an impression on the couch more enduring than Joseph Cotten's. 'May I ask why?'

Madame Charay offered a wistful smile. 'When you appreciate someone as I do Alfred, you spare no expense.'

'You must be his greatest devotee.'

'I would like to think so.'

Madame Charay shifted in her chair. 'Now, enough about me. What about you? I don't even know your name.'

No, she didn't, Katie realized. 'I'm sorry, how rude of me. My name is Katie. Katie Jacobs.'

'Don't apologize. I feel like I already know you. And I suspect a busy girl like you has a reason for being here?' Madame Charay asked politely.

Katie let the patronizing slide. 'I'm looking for someone.'

'And who would that be?'

'My brother. Half brother, actually. His name is Vincent Jacobs.'

Katie watched closely for a reaction, but Madame Charay hardly skipped a beat as she poured a dollop of cream into her own cup.

'Vincent Jacobs,' Madame Charay repeated.

'Yes. Do you know him?'

'Very well. He's my son.'

She said it so matter-of-factly that Katie didn't hear it at first. But it confirmed her suspicions. This was the mysterious woman, according to Grandma, who came with Vincent to visit Gloria long ago and drove off abruptly in the polished car. 'I should have known.'

'And had I known who you were yesterday, I would have introduced myself,' said Madame Charay. 'How is your dear mother?'

'She died last week.'

Madame Charay puffed the illusory cigarette in her empty holder. 'Her smoking?'

'Yes.'

'I'm sorry.'

'You knew her, then?'

'Not well, but well enough to know she couldn't care for Vincent. What do you know of the situation?'

'I know that for whatever reason my mother was never at peace with her decision, that you wouldn't let her see him.'

Madame Charay's brow furrowed in consternation. Then, in an instant, all traces of hostility vanished and the warm smile returned. 'I was *asked* to care for Vincent. Your mother pleaded with me to do so, if you must know the truth.'

'I'm sure that's true. But I'm interested only in Vincent now. Is he alive?'

'Most certainly.'

'And does he live here?'

'He's . . . around.'

'I'd like to see him.'

Madame Charay walked to the window and scanned the forest beyond. 'I'm afraid that won't be possible.'

'Why not?'

'It's difficult to explain. You'll have to trust me.'

'I do, but he's my brother, and every time I think I have found him he slips away.'

'Poor thing,' Madame Charay tisked.

'Are you aware there's a man who claims to be Vincent in town? He's cashing Vincent's disability checks.'

'I'm aware of that.'

'And?'

'Vincent has no need for disability checks. He's well taken care of here.'

'If he's well taken care of, why can't I see him?'

Madame Charay strolled to the gilded cage. She poked in a finger as if caressing an invisible bird. 'Sometimes our explorations turn to disappointment,' she said.

Katie stood to plead her case. 'I have no family; Vincent is it. I need to find him. I have no other motive. Please.'

'What do you know of your brother?'

'Not much. A difficult childbirth, some rumors I heard in town that he's not well.'

'You're a detective at heart,' said Madame Charay with a raised eyebrow.

'No, not in the least,' Katie smiled. 'I'm an art director at a magazine. Believe me, it was pure luck that led me here.'

'There is no such thing as luck, young lady, pure or otherwise, I can assure you of that.'

'Perhaps.' Katie disagreed, but this was no time to argue.

'And if you meet him, what will you do?'

'Introduce myself, see that he's all right, see if he wants to see me again.' That and so much more, but Katie held her tongue.

'And if he doesn't?'

'So be it.'

Madame Charay returned to the couch and gulped down the last of her tea. 'I assume you know very little about mental illness.'

'I know some.'

'Vincent, he's not well. He is . . . perhaps it *would* be best if you saw him. But let me advise you to stop this horrid notion of family. And I must ask of you one promise.'

'What is that?' said Katie.

'If you find that he is provided for, as happy as can be expected in his condition, that you'll leave well enough alone. Leave *us* alone.'

Katie tried to imagine the mysterious circumstances. 'I'm sorry, I don't believe I can make a promise like that.'

'Then I thank you for coming, Ms Jacobs. It was so nice meeting you. I trust you'll find your car without assistance.'

With utter promptness Madame Charay stood and strolled to the foyer. She waited patiently for Katie to join her.

'You can't do this,' Katie exclaimed. 'I'll find Vincent without your help. I'll do what I must.'

'And what exactly does that mean?'

'I don't know,' said Katie. And she didn't. 'I'll call the authorities.'

'Threats are so unbecoming in a young woman, don't you agree? I'm not hiding anything, Ms Jacobs. I'm simply trying to protect my son.'

'And I'm simply trying to see my brother.'

'*Half* brother, as any county judge would be glad to point out. You have no legal recourse here, believe me. I would advise you to accept my generous offer before I change my mind.'

Katie wanted to say no, to walk out in protest, but she felt so close to her brother, and Madame Charay was right: Katie had no leverage here.

'All right, then.'

'That's better. It's getting dark. Would you care to wait until morning?'

'I don't think I can.'

'Are those comfortable walking shoes?'

'Yes.'

'And do you have a sweater in the car? The fog may roll in any moment.'

'No, I didn't think to bring one.'

'I'll find you something.'

Madame Charay vanished, leaving Katie alone with the souvenirs and an anticipation so heightened she could taste it. Whoever Vincent was, at least he wasn't Peter Grow. Still, Katie chose to delay her prayer of thanks until she met him. She explored her belt loop, looking for her lucky feather, but it was gone. Then she heard an odd sound, a scratching, like a mouse caught behind a wall or a small cat asking for entrance.

Before she could locate the source, Madame Charay returned carrying a hideous chartreuse button-down sweater made of some unforgiving material.

'Are you ready?'

Katie swallowed a gulp and nodded yes.

Madame Charay handed Katie the sweater. 'Be careful with it. It was worn by Tippi Hedren,' she said.

'In *The Birds*?' Katie assumed.

'No, not this one. It's from *Marnie*, his most underrated. Are you familiar with it?'

'That is one I missed.'

'Most people have. It's about a skittish young woman with a prostitute for a mother. It's getting late. Let's go.'

CHAPTER SIX

By herself Katie would never have found the path. It began behind the house, a sliver of a trail that within several feet fell under a thicket of cypress and scrub oak.

Madame Charay sliced her way through, skipping across the path but never leaving imprints, dodging with surprising agility the threatening branches and rocks lying in ambush. Katie tripped on a stump and stumbled to her knees. The brittle arm of a dead cypress slapped her face. A droplet of blood fell on Tippi's sweater.

With dusk approaching, the woods were a study in charcoals of brown and gray. The fog rose up like a gas, enveloping the bushes and trees and toying with Katie's sense of gravity and dimension.

Madame Charay slipped ahead and out of sight, leaving Katie unsure of the way. Madame Charay returned and retraced her steps down a trail Katie hadn't even considered.

She felt the light before she saw it, a pink blush cast so softly upon the fog that Katie tried to wipe the color from her eyes. The blush grew richer until the trail ended abruptly at the ocean. Her sudden stop sent spits of gravel tumbling over the cliff and into the angry surf below. A monstrous rock formation jutted into the ocean and bore the brunt of the crashing waves. Katie looked up to face a sweeping sky cycling through shades of coral and salmon.

'Let's keep moving,' said Madame Charay.

The path zigzagged along the cliff, perilously close at times, and moving away at others. Katie shielded her eyes with rigid hands to keep from succumbing to the seduction of a fall. When the path veered near the ocean or dipped low, the stronger waves showered Katie with an icy spray. Katie licked the salt from her lips.

Madame Charay had predicted a short walk, but Katie lost track of time. Ten minutes, half an hour, she couldn't tell. Where was this forsaken place, and how could Vincent be happy living there?

Madame Charay pressed on with brisk economy, and Katie rushed to keep pace. Katie was grateful when the path turned away from the ocean and back into the forest, a surrounding she had just finished cursing.

She looked back to view the sunset, now a violent clash of blood violet and burgundy scored by the crashing surf. She shivered, despite Tippi's sweater, which had torn along the way.

Madame Charay stopped near a log cabin hiding behind a stand of brush. The curtains were half-drawn over darkened windows, and a small ribbon of smoke drifted from a tilted stovepipe.

'Here we are,' announced Madame Charay. She twisted a golden key from her pocket.

'He's locked in?' asked Katie.

'He can open it from the inside.'

With a measured half-turn she freed the lock and stepped in. 'Be gentle,' was her last admonition.

Katie followed and was given only a brief moment to glimpse the threadbare room before the door slammed behind her and the place went dark.

She heard the strike of a match as Madame Charay lit a storm lantern. The light from the flame threw grotesque shadows to dance on the walls.

Katie didn't feel frightened. She felt the warmth of a wood fire in the old cook stove and noticed a certain tidiness to the room. A single set of clean dishes was stored neatly in open crates tacked to the wall. The rough-hewn table had but one wooden chair neatly tucked against it.

The only mess was the jumble of blankets on the unoccupied bed. When they began to stir Katie tripped backward. Surely there was no room under the covers for a human, let alone a fully grown human. They moved again and Katie's hand instinctively found the doorknob, readying herself for flight. Katie waited to see the painted face of a raccoon or the red eyes of a possum.

'Don't be frightened,' said Madame Charay.

Katie thought the advice was for her until she saw a red bush of unruly hair and two inquisitive eyes emerge meekly from the sunken center of the bed.

The look in those eyes. Those *eyes*. Vincent.

He peered from behind his blanket like a child believing he can see but can't be seen. His expression displayed wonderment, fear, uncertainty, and for one brief moment, Katie imagined, recognition.

Whatever features Vincent had inherited from his father, Katie couldn't be sure. But those eyes, surrendering, translucent – those were kindred eyes. The same languid eyes Katie viewed each morning in the mirror. The same eyes her mother used so willingly to deliver contempt. And now those eyes faced Katie once more, lodged in the face of this strange and unusual being, filled with the puzzlement of an animal confronting an unknown entity for the first time and wondering whether to mark it friend or foe.

Vincent's hands gripped the edge of the blanket. His fingernails were filthy and wildly thick, more hoof than nail.

'She won't hurt you.' Madame Charay spoke in a melodic cadence, as if an abrupt inflection would send Vincent scurrying beneath the covers with little hope of him resurfacing.

Madame Charay tried to coax a smile from Vincent with a smile of her own, a flutter of her eyes, a flick of her head, but nothing could peel Vincent's gaze away from the lovely stranger in his cabin.

Katie strained a smile herself, though she knew her trepidation shone through, illuminated by the flame that threw a yellow cast on the three of them.

Was he mildly retarded? Schizophrenic? Deaf? Mute? His expressions, changing and elastic, reminded Katie of the mentally ill she passed so often on the streets of San Francisco arguing with themselves, listening intently to interior voices, debating furiously with apathetic passersby.

'She won't hurt you,' Madame Charay repeated.

Katie nodded in agreement. 'I won't,' she added, as if her assurance carried any weight.

But upon hearing her voice, surprisingly, Vincent relaxed his grip. Inch by inch, with the timidity of the naked, he let down the blanket and revealed his face. It was freckled and kind, twisted teeth and a sagging chin, a few pockmarks on his cheeks, and a snarled nose that looked as if it had been broken several times. But a good face, and Katie sighed in relief.

As mysterious and unknown as Vincent was, Katie felt curiously satisfied. Her sibling, however handicapped, was not a monster. He was not a male incarnation of their biological mother. He was not Peter Grow.

But another part of her wanted more, much more. She wanted to know everything about this enigma, to learn his history, to divine his future. She wanted to confess her sins to him as only siblings can and share the secrets of youth, however lost. She yearned to hug him and smell his breath and see where nature had dabbed on beauty marks. She wanted to giggle with him and feel his hair and drowse lazily under the sun with no thoughts of anything.

'How are we today, Vincent?' Madame Charay asked.

Vincent nodded. He looked to his adopted mother to see if a nod was sufficient under these unusual circumstances.

With pursed lips Madame Charay indicated it was not. 'I want you to say hello, Vincent.'

Vincent fidgeted, and Katie felt his discomfort. She wanted to tell him he didn't have to say anything to her, though selfishly she wanted to hear the music of his voice.

Vincent opened his mouth and made a few futile attempts at sound.

Finally, he found the courage to speak.

'Hello,' he said in a breathy whisper.

Katie's heart thumped with excitement. The conversations they could have, however slow and labored. Based upon that one word, Katie was ready to dedicate her life to coaxing one utterance at a time from Vincent.

'Good, Vincent. Very good,' said Madame Charay. She leaned closer. 'Do you know who this is, Vincent?'

Vincent peered into Katie's eyes for the answer, his gaze, utterly without presumption or judgment, so innocent and honest that Katie imagined him understanding her secrets and fears.

Vincent shook his head, plainly fearful of disappointing Madame Charay. He dropped his chin to his chest.

'No, I don't.'

His words came easier this time, as if, following a long stretch of idleness, the gears of speech were starting to roll again.

All eyes fell on Katie.

She smiled nervously. 'I'm Katie. Katie Jacobs.'

Vincent smiled back.

Emboldened, Katie reached forward to shake his hand, then realized the boldness of the move. Maybe he didn't like to be touched. But she couldn't stop in mid-motion, not now, and her trembling fingers reached out to meet his. Katie was glad to see Vincent's hand climbing to meet hers.

But just as they were about to touch, a small gray rat emerged from Vincent's collar. It scurried down his arm and smelled his crotch. Then with twitching nose, the animal curled itself into a ball on Vincent's lap, oblivious to the visitors in the room.

When Katie recoiled, Vincent scooped up his friend, wondering how such a creature could evoke such a reaction. He shielded the rat under his chin and caressed it protectively, as if Katie might be here for no other reason than to take his faithful companion away. He looked to his mother for reassurance.

'It's all right, Vincent,' Madame Charay said soothingly. 'It's all right. Your friend scared her, that's all.'

Vincent's eyes darted between the two visitors, sensing a pretense he hadn't before, suddenly suspicious of their motives.

'You're safe,' Madame Charay said. 'You're safe.'

Katie berated herself for reacting so suddenly, but the damage was done. She gathered her wits and attempted another smile to reestablish the goodwill.

Madame Charay smiled, too, to assure Vincent, and perhaps Katie as well, that the minor crisis was over. Vincent relaxed a little, accepting his mother's gesture as doctrine.

'Tell Katie the name of your rat, Vincent,' she said.

Vincent took some time before he decided he could trust Katie with the information.

'His name is Tony.'

He worked hard to form his words, yet once they reached his lips they flowed effortlessly in a soothing voice, more woman than man.

'What a wonderful name for a rat,' said Katie. 'He looks very . . . friendly.'

Madame Charay leaned forward to speak into Vincent's ear, whispering to gather his attention.

'Vincent, Katie is your sister.'

Vincent did not respond. He continued to rock steadily in a rhythm that seemed to please Tony to no end. He stole glances at Katie as he grappled with the notion.

Katie felt embarrassed and insensitive. The idea of a sibling had sent her into a spin, yet she never once stopped to think that her brother might be similarly overwhelmed.

Was he proud, relieved, delighted, scared? Katie smiled again, an insipid response for such a momentous occasion, but she couldn't think of anything else to do.

'Katie,' Vincent murmured. He spoke as if learning a word in a foreign language. 'Katie.'

And he smiled.

'Yes, *Katie*,' she echoed, thrilled to hear her name spoken by her brother. Thrilled to see her name evoke a reaction of joy. 'I'm your sister.'

For the briefest of moments, and perhaps it was nothing more than her utmost desire, Katie felt she perceived in Vincent's face a hint of delight, as if it comforted him to know he had a sister, a family. Katie could hardly contain her elation.

'Vincent,' said Madame Charay. 'Katie has come to ask you a question.'

Vincent looked puzzled. What answers could he possibly have? What information did he possess that others didn't?

Katie nodded affectionately. She pulled forward to speak, but Madame Charay usurped her.

'She wants to know if you want to go away.'

'No!' said Katie, startling Vincent.

How could Madame Charay say such a thing, Katie thought. Vincent packed Tony away in his shirt and drew up the covers. He glanced at Madame Charay for reassurance, but she hesitated to give it. Only when his alarm grew close to panic did Madame Charay finally intervene to quiet him.

'No one is taking you away, Vincent. You're safe.'

Vincent seemed only slightly reassured. He viewed Katie with apprehension. She tried harder to appear friendly, empathetic, anything to quell Vincent's fear, but there was little she could do.

She felt she had to speak now, to clarify her stance, to let Vincent know she meant no harm and never would, never could.

'Vincent.' Katie attempted to mimic Madame Charay's intonation. 'I just want to make sure you like it here.'

Vincent seemed puzzled by the oddity of the question. 'Where?' he questioned Madame Charay.

'Here, at Petty's Cove,' she said.

Vincent took a moment to fathom the possibility of other worlds.

'This is my home,' Vincent said softly, as if apologizing for a grave mistake.

Katie knew her concern had been lost in the translation. Translation to what she wasn't sure, to a language born out of Vincent's irregular existence. She searched for words, the right phrase, the neutral inflection. Everything she thought of seemed wrong, inappropriate, threatening.

'Is there anything you want, or need, Vincent? Anything at all I can do for you?' she asked.

Vincent thought earnestly, exhausting quickly his short list of possibilities. He shook his head from side to side in big sweeping movements.

Katie felt frustrated. Why hadn't she prepared her thoughts properly in anticipation of this meeting? What had she been thinking?

Madame Charay seemed restless; she wanted this brief encounter to end. She glanced at her wristwatch and nodded to Katie to wrap things up. Vincent, too, appeared to be losing interest.

But Katie was not ready to leave. Not so quickly.

She didn't know if she could find this place again without Madame Charay. This could be her last chance to speak with Vincent. A handful of awkward words simply would not suffice.

'Vincent, you know you have family. Not much of a family, just me and a grandmother, but it's family that cares about you.'

Katie hoped to fall on the right word, if only by accident and not design.

Vincent lowered his eyes. His concentration strayed, or perhaps the notion of a caring family disturbed him. Whatever the reason, the tenuous connection Katie had made was slipping away. Katie could feel it.

'Vincent,' Katie called. But Vincent decided not to lift his eyes to look at her or at Madame Charay. The audience was over.

'If you need anything – anything at all – you can count on us.' Katie tried to sound like she meant it, but she knew her words didn't ring true, and there was little room for deception in this small cabin.

'I don't need anything,' said Vincent. 'Nothing at all.'

Madame Charay seemed happy with Vincent's performance, and she patted him on the head, then bent down and stroked Tony once across the back.

'I'll be down with dinner soon.' She brushed back Vincent's hair.

Katie stood. The heat from the stove was starting to get her anyway, and she felt herself sweating more than she had on the vigorous hike over. Maybe they were related, but he could never be a brother to her, nor she a sister to him, not in the normal sense. No, the curse on her family was too harsh; it would not allow even that. She had been foolish to think she could barge into someone's life, whatever the circumstances, and form a bond as if they had shared a life for years. Madame Charay was right. One visit would be enough.

'Well, it was very nice meeting you, Vincent. I hope we meet again,' said Katie, extending her hand.

Vincent looked at Madame Charay, then declined to meet Katie's grasp. Katie thought it fitting that she should never touch her brother. Not once. Serves her right for wishing otherwise.

'All right, then. We should be going,' said Madame Charay. 'These unexpected visits tire Vincent so.'

'I understand,' said Katie.

Madame Charay fished in her pocket for the key. It slipped from her hand and fell to the floor.

As she bent to retrieve it, Katie glanced at Vincent.

In that instant he gave her a look so intense she was sure her gasp was audible. Vincent's face filled with desperation, puzzlement, and appeal. He implored Katie, shared secrets with her, cared for her, beseeched her, communed with her – all in one inscrutable look so ardent Katie felt its physical weight pressed against her breast.

Madame Charay stood, key in hand. Vincent's expression vanished, replaced instantly by the dutiful gaze of the simple son Katie had come to know until a moment ago.

'Ready?' said Madame Charay.

'What?' asked Katie, a tremble in her voice.

'Ready to go?' Madame Charay repeated. She sensed the sudden change in Katie and looked to Vincent for explanation.

He smiled back feebly.

'Say your farewells, then,' said Madame Charay.

'Good-bye,' said Katie, her voice betraying her.

Katie glanced at Vincent again, the blank stare restored. She stepped over the threshold into the sky, a palette of dark grays tinged by only a hint of violet. Madame Charay led the way and Katie peeked behind the door one last time as it swung shut behind her.

'Bye,' Vincent whispered with a wave and a wink so tenuous Katie chose not to believe her eyes.

Madame Charay watched Katie drive away from the mansion in her wretched little convertible, dented and sagging, a vehicle fit for a bastard child as Katie surely was, knowing her mother as Madame Charay did.

With the car well out of sight, Madame Charay pulled the ladder from the garage and leaned it against her beloved home. She climbed carefully and hammered shut the thick shutters of a second-story window. Three nails for every one needed. She returned the ladder and tools to the garage, a place for everything and everything in its place, then she walked into the house and up the stairs, making a note to herself to fix a creak in the fourth stair, left side.

At the top of the stairs she made a right turn and stopped at the second door on the left. She cracked the door open slowly, making a chirping sound as she moved in.

She flipped on the light switch and stepped inside to behold her most cherished possession, the living legacy of the man she adored more than any other, a mixed flock of nine hundred crows and ravens, direct descendants, all of them, from the birds that tore the flesh from Tippi's face.

If the crows were a little edgy at present it was understandable. No meal had arrived today, no bucket of birdseed scattered on the hardwood floor like a thousand tiny diamonds. The birds looked at her quizzically, questioning the absence of food. Perhaps they wondered why Madame Charay saw fit to seal off the exterior window, their only gateway to the world outside.

Their edginess brought forth more cackles and screeches than usual. Territorial battles erupted over mere inches of tabletop. A lucky crow in the corner spied an overlooked seed half-tucked under the edge of the worn carpet. He dived on it as his brothers and sisters watched jealously. One envious sibling attacked the lucky one and pecked out a feather.

Madame Charay forgave their uneasiness.

They were hungry, that's all. Birds learn to live with captivity quite readily, but hunger they don't like. Hunger a bird cannot understand, cannot tolerate. And this was a room full of shiny black intolerance.

'Sorry to lock you up, my dears.'

Madame Charay spoke with the soft voice of a benevolent caretaker. She puckered her lips and threw them all a kiss. She locked the door tightly and slipped the key in her pocket to jingle with the key to Vincent's cabin.

'It won't be long. I promise.'

CHAPTER SEVEN

Katie had wanted to question Madame Charay but felt so flustered by the time they reached the mansion it was all she could do to return the ripped and bloodied sweater, apologize profusely for the damage, and drive away without hitting a redwood or an oncoming car. She navigated the winding roads by sheer intuition and considered herself lucky to find the coastal highway at all under the cover of darkness.

Throughout her drive she could think of nothing but Vincent. Vincent's fractured nose. Vincent's mirror-image eyes. Vincent's childish manner. Vincent and the way he looked at her when Madame Charay had turned away. That *look.*

It was her imagination, she concluded. Wasn't it *always* her imagination concocting outlandish schoolgirl fantasies, building solid relationships out of passing glances, inventing evil conspiracies among friends who wished her only good. Vincent's expression meant nothing. And if it wasn't her imagination then it was her empty stomach, the disorienting ride to Madame Charay's, the Hitchcock paraphernalia in that house, or the dizzying heights near Vincent's cabin. Perhaps it was nothing more than the sheer surprise of meeting her brother, or the shock of his red hair.

Even if that look had meaning, chances were it had nothing to do with Katie. It was Vincent and Madame Charay playing a cruel joke on the half sister, that's all, a number they had polished well during occasional visits by social workers, psychiatrists, and neighbors who had strayed from the usual path. Perhaps theirs was a sickening relationship of incest, an affair that needed vigilant guarding and elaborate tales of deception, as do all secrets of forbidden desire. Or maybe it was Vincent alone, maliciously toying with Katie, driving her away for some demented reason, teasing her with a bizarre motive only the insane can fathom, caring little if any for a sister he may have known about all along.

Maybe Katie was reading too much significance into the event altogether. Maybe Vincent's rat had nibbled on his pinky at the very moment the key slipped from Madame Charay's hand. Maybe a flash of Katie's bracelet had blinded him as she stood to leave. Maybe Vincent had simply suffered an attack of gas.

Katie downshifted to negotiate a blind curve. Her headlights prowled in front of her, stealing glances of shadowy trees and wild ferns looking alive and caught in the act.

As hard as she tried to believe, all these theories rang hollow. Vincent's dramatic change of character coming at the precise moment Madame Charay looked away was a sign. It had to be. Wasn't it, after all, Vincent's only moment to communicate genuinely? More than likely he had waited ten or twenty years for such a moment or for such a person as Katie.

And he had brilliantly used the only instrument available to him, his *visage*, as their mother called it, to relay his message. With it, Vincent conveyed a life of misfortune, a heart swelled with fear, a fragile hope hidden under the veneer of simple solitude. Like a skilled actor playing his career role, he silently spoke of a burning desire to break away from his miserable hovel on the shore. Without words he beseeched Katie for understanding, pleaded for help.

Without words, yes, but not without effect. Katie understood. She heard as clearly as if he had whispered in her ear. And she could not ignore his silent petition any more than she could the cries of a wounded animal. Despite the fragile evidence, Katie was willing to do whatever was necessary to help her brother, her half brother. If Vincent's plight fell on her shoulders, so be it. How often had Katie yearned to help a sibling. She would be his savior.

The lights of the village, the few there were, helped Katie relax her grip. Her heart slowed with the return to civilization. The breeze was fresh and filled with the curative scent of salt air.

Katie returned to The Nest, partly because she wanted to avoid the hassle of looking for alternative lodging, partly because Lois meant nothing now. She paid Lois in cash for another night's lodging and climbed to her room, the same one. For the second night in a row she dropped onto her bed exhausted.

But she didn't stay there. After a steaming hot bath and three aspirin, Katie decided to indulge her hunger. She hardly remembered lunch, then realized she hadn't eaten since breakfast, a candy bar and pop from the mechanic's vending machine.

Just to prove that she wasn't nearly as crazy as everyone she had met these past few days, Katie decided to get dressed and take herself out to dinner. There must be a sane person in this town, and Katie was determined to find him or her, even if he turned out to be the waiter.

She pulled on her mauve mohair sweater, dusted off her jeans, cursed herself one more time for not bringing more clothes, and applied a little blush. She fluffed her hair and snapped on a pearl necklace. With one last look in the full-length mirror, she locked her door behind her.

'Going someplace?' Lois inquired, intrigued by the transformation.

'Dinner, if there's anything open.'

'Try The Tides. They filmed *The Birds* there, you know.'

'I know.' Of course she knew; everybody knew. 'Why is everyone in this town still so fascinated with that movie anyway?'

'It brings in tourists, for one,' said Lois.

'And is that why you have all these Audubon prints here?' Katie gestured to the walls.

'Yes and no. I happen to truly love birds. They're quite misunderstood, actually. Take, for instance, the saying "Eat like a bird". Well, birds will often eat twice their body weight daily. *Birdbrained?* Actually, birds are quite intelligent.'

'I see what you mean.'

'And birds share a great resemblance to human nature.'

'For example?' asked Katie. Let this woman chatter, let her reveal her nature through small talk.

'For example, the Australian emu. The female takes many lovers and evades all maternal cares. And while the male tediously incubates the eggs for eight weeks, the female is out doing it again, and again, and again.'

'Very instructive,' said Katie.

'Perhaps that's why the male hornbill of the subtropical jungle builds a clay wall around his wife.'

'To keep her from temptation?'

'Exactly. He feeds her through a narrow opening and breaks the wall only after their egg has hatched.'

'Fascinating.'

'And consider the American cowbird, a local resident. Instead of building a home of its own, the mother cowbird watches for a sparrow or warbler to leave her nest. Then the cowbird slips in and lays a single egg next to the eggs of the rightful owner. The mother sparrow cares for the additional egg, naturally, good mother that she is. But when the baby cowbird hatches, he's much bigger than his false siblings, much hungrier. And even as the mother sparrow tries to feed her young furiously, the cowbird demands all, and the little sparrows starve to death. Pity the poor sparrow.'

Katie did.

'Ah, but the cuckoo,' continued Lois. 'When it comes to cruel villainy, the cuckoo bird puts the cowbird to shame. The mother cuckoo plays the same trick as the cowbird, placing an egg in another bird's nest. But the young cuckoo, soon after it hatches, doesn't wait until its nest mates die of starvation. Oh, no. He simply pushes the unready babies over the edge, one by one. See what I mean? Birds are so much like humans.'

'I think I'll go to dinner.'

Lois smiled and gave a toodle-loo wave. 'Bon appétit.'

The Tides was indeed the only place open. Katie waited for a table by the long bar, polished by the arms of countless patrons. The wide windows at the far end looked out over the docks, crowded with boats waiting for the crab season or tourists for half-day salmon fishing expeditions. At any moment Katie expected a drunk captain to walk in with a curved pipe jutting from his jaw.

On the wall next to her hung a framed black and white still photograph of The Tides in the movie, Tippi trying to make sense of the bird attacks, fearing the end of the world.

'Table for one.'

The dining room was much fancier than the bar, an obvious addition since the film, or maybe the whole place was new. She was shown a seat by the window overlooking the cove, where a creamy moon hung low over the horizon, like a backdrop for one of those corny romantic movies with Doris Day or Rock Hudson.

Katie ordered a glass of wine but changed her mind and ordered the whole bottle. No one knew her in town, and if ever she needed more than one glass, it was tonight.

She scanned the place, filled with couples huddling over their white-linen tables, rubbing cheeks in the candle glow. A few parties of four talked quietly among themselves, breaking into occasional laughter, never raucously or loud. The place was a charmer except for one glaring omission, someone to sit across from Katie. Someone handsome and kind, a tad mischievous, but always a gentleman.

She ordered without paying heed to the prices or her usual self-imposed restrictions on fatty foods. A radicchio salad, fresh clams on the half-shell, a loaf of San Francisco sourdough bread, and for the main meal a bowl of cioppino, which the menu described as 'red, rich, and overflowing with chunks of scallops, shrimps, mussels and snapper'. She was starving.

As she took her first sip of Cabernet Sauvignon, her thoughts turned again to Vincent. Maybe it was all in her mind. Maybe Katie was transferring her feelings onto her subject. Longing and loneliness, desire and fear, these were the emotions Katie roomed with. It wasn't surprising that she ascribed them to Vincent as well.

After all, Vincent was free to leave at any time. The windshield mechanic had said people saw Vincent on the beaches at night. Surely he had free access to town, to medical assistance. He could have contacted the sheriff by now or simply run away if he had wanted to leave.

Oh, for someone to talk to.

Katie tore off a chunk of bread. It was moist and warm, with a yeasty aroma every bit as intoxicating as the wine. She gazed at her reflection in the window, her face aglow with candlelight. She recalled Vincent's face and compared the similarities and differences. But hard as Katie tried, the image of their mother overpowered Vincent's, and it disturbed Katie to think that her mother could haunt her in death even as she had in life.

Katie felt a tap on her shoulder. She jumped out of her deep thoughts and turned.

'May I join you?'

Katie hid the chunk of bread in her cheek. 'Yes. Please sit down, Rob.' Katie gestured.

Her hand slapped the glass and knocked it over. Wine splattered across the starched white linen.

Katie yanked on her napkin to clean up the mess and sent the silverware clanking to the floor.

All eyes turned to the commotion.

The maître d' rushed over, followed by a busboy. Katie froze, sure she would break something else if she moved again.

'Are you okay?' asked Rob.

Katie fumbled to clean up but succeeded only in making

more of a commotion. 'Yes. Oh, God. You must think I'm a bumbling idiot.'

'Not at all.' Rob picked up a fork. 'If it was me, I would have spilled an entire bottle.'

Nice thought, but it didn't stop Katie's face from turning flush red. The maître d' righted the wrong with dispatch and apology, as if the busboy had knocked over the wine. A waiter snapped out a fresh tablecloth, the busboy brought clean silverware, and the maître d' poured a complimentary glass for Katie and one for the gentleman. All eyes turned away. All except Rob's.

'I hope I'm not imposing,' Rob said softly. 'It's just that I don't like to eat alone.'

'No, of course. My pleasure.' Katie carefully allowed her hand to venture near the wine glass, praying she wouldn't knock it over this time. 'Where's Lois tonight?' asked Katie.

'At a meeting, shoreline preservation. She's always going to this meeting or that, involved in everything, very *interested*.'

'She's wonderful,' said Katie, hoping her sarcasm was well disguised.

'Yes,' said Rob, playing with the stem of his wine glass. 'Everybody loves her.'

Was he as nervous as she, Katie wondered.

'Enjoying your stay?' he asked.

'I absolutely love it here. It's so . . . peaceful,' said Katie.

'We don't get many tourists this time of year. Let alone attractive women like you.'

Katie grew embarrassed. She never understood what to do with compliments.

'That is, if you don't mind my saying,' Rob was quick to add.

'I don't mind,' said Katie. Mind? He called her beautiful; she adored it. Maybe it was the candlelight or the ambience, or the moon that refused to abdicate its rule in the sky, but Rob seemed much more handsome tonight. Not that he hadn't seemed handsome when they talked in the lobby, but up close there was a sensitivity, an appealing dreamy shyness in his look. He was attractive yesterday, yes, but tonight Katie felt the energy that fueled it. Intense, intelligent, mature, and definitely male. His shirt was unbuttoned at the collar and a small lapel pin matched the color of his eyes, a steel blue that melted in the candlelight.

'So, let me guess,' Rob said. He placed his fingers on his temples and closed his eyes. 'You're confronting a problem in your life, a career move or a boyfriend perhaps. You wanted some time to get away and think it over alone. So you came up here.'

Katie smiled. 'Not so far off.'

'That's very admirable of you.'

'What is?'

'Confronting your problems. Most people are happier to wallow in their confusion than to embrace any sense of clarity. You should be proud.'

He was full of compliments. Katie was normally wary of too many compliments, but tonight she bought his sincerity, real or feigned, simply because she felt like it.

'I see you're the town psychic, as well as its only psychologist.'

He laughed. 'A psychic I'm not. *Everyone* is frustrated with their job or career. And everyone is scared to give up a sure thing for a dream or a chance of adventure.'

'Or romance?' Katie added.

'Or romance,' Rob conceded.

He swirled the wine in his glass, then took his first sip. 'What's your dream?' he asked.

'Which one?'

'The first one that comes to mind.'

Katie thought, then chose the third or fourth. 'I'd like to start a magazine of my own. Not now, but someday.'

Rob nodded earnestly. 'What kind of magazine?'

'It's silly, really.'

'No, please. I'd like to hear.'

'You really want to know?'

'Sure.' Rob smiled.

'A travel magazine. But not just *another* travel magazine. I'd call it *Romantic Getaways*, and we'd write about great places for lovers to go, with wonderful photo spreads and grand layouts. We'd cover places like Bodega Bay, like Lois's place.'

'Sounds great.'

'You think so?'

'I really do.'

Katie had forgotten how impassioned she was by it all. She leaned forward and freed her hands to better explain.

'We'd have to start small, get some financial backing. It's tough, but I know the market and there's a real opportunity. We would grow slowly, and then . . .'

Her voice trailed off.

For the second time in two days Katie found herself rambling on about something that probably interested no one but herself. Both times, she realized, had been with Rob.

'What's the matter?' asked Rob.

'Nothing. It's silly, that's all; just a dream.'

'It's not silly. It's important to have dreams and goals. Where would we be without them?'

A waiter stopped at the table and delivered a salad to Katie, making her feel even more awkward. Sexist as it sounded, Katie had vowed never to eat alone in front of a man.

'Please go ahead,' Rob said, seeing her uneasiness. 'Don't let me stop you.'

'I'm sorry—'

'For what? I'm the one who barged in on your meal. I'll order when the waiter comes by again.'

'We can share,' offered Katie.

'Oh, no. You go ahead.'

'I insist, really. My pleasure.'

'Are you sure?' Rob asked.

Katie pushed the plate to the center of the table.

'Okay.' Rob smiled. 'Thank you.'

They ate in silence, each leaving the cherry tomato for the other, apologizing when their forks touched unintentionally.

'And what's your dream?' asked Katie. 'Wait, let me guess.'

Katie searched Rob's face and saw more of that blue-eyed dreaminess that was growing on her very rapidly.

'You don't want to be one of those psychologists who cater only to the rich. You want to help even those who don't have the money. For the good of humankind.'

'Sounds like you're the psychic around here.' Rob smiled.

'Me? I'm one of those people who can never figure out the ending of a movie, even though it's obvious to everyone else.'

'Maybe you understand there can be many endings.'

This guy pushed all the right buttons. 'Do you have a specialty?' Katie asked.

'Around here it's pretty much general practice, but I did my thesis on PTSD.'

'PTSD?'

'I'm sorry. Post-traumatic stress disorder. It's what happens to people after they suffer a terrible ordeal.'

'And what does happen to them?' She always had had a fascination for psychology.

'Lots of things,' he began. Now it was Rob's turn to animate, and Katie enjoyed every active gesture that brought him closer to her.

'They might bury their memories. Internalize them. Feel guilty even if it's not their fault. Start abusing drugs or alcohol. Antisocial behavior. Wild mood swings. Thoughts of suicide.'

These were all things that had plagued Katie at one time or another. Maybe she suffered from post-traumatic stress disorder. No, her disorder wasn't so dramatic, she concluded, just a good old case of parental-induced guilt. 'Fascinating.'

'I have one client,' Rob continued, 'whose father was a terrible alcoholic who had terrorized the family. She repressed everything and believed her father to be a saint – idealizing the perpetrator, it's called. Then, two years into therapy, I brought an umbrella into the office, by chance, only because it was raining. But the umbrella triggered a flashback of her father chasing her around the kitchen with an umbrella.'

'Amazing.'

'That's not all. When we brought her mother in for a co-counseling session, the mother remembered the incident very well. But she told us it wasn't an umbrella the father had used that day to chase my client. It had been a butcher's knife. You see? The daughter had repressed the whole incident at first. Then, even as she began recalling bits and pieces, her subconscious played a trick on her and changed the implement of terror from a knife to a much more benign item, an umbrella. Anything to protect the fatherly image my client so desperately wanted to maintain.'

'That's amazing. Shouldn't you be doing research at Berkeley or something?'

'Research was never my strength. I enjoy people. Plus, I grew up here – well, at least until I was twelve.'

'What happened then?'

'I went to live with my aunt and uncle in Oregon.'

'And your parents?'

'My mother died when I was eight. And my father, he's still around, but we never talk, really. He retired from his medical practice about the time I was sent away.'

'Sent away?'

'What?'

'You said you were sent away.'

'Did I use those words? I guess I did. My father couldn't handle me, I suppose. I don't know, really. You can't regret the past; it's just the way it is. I don't analyze it.'

Katie sensed rocky territory and cleared away. 'So what brought you back to Bodega Bay?'

'There was a time I vowed never to return. I don't know what happened. On a lark I returned after college just to see if the place had changed. I found it so peaceful here. Absolutely beautiful. I fell in love with the country all over again, revisited all my old haunts, watched the fog play tricks at dusk. Wait until it rains; everything turns as green as Ireland.'

'You came back home,' remarked Katie.

'I guess so.'

An uneasy moment of silence passed. The waiter took the salad plate, empty but for one cherry tomato.

'You never told me.' Rob broke the spell.

'Told you what?'

'What you're doing here in Bodega Bay.'

Katie had forgotten, and now it rushed back into her head like a strong narcotic.

'What's wrong?' asked Rob.

'Nothing. Something I remembered.'

'It's more than that. I can see it all over your face. You can't hide emotion that strong.'

Katie appreciated his sensitivity but wished he'd save it for another occasion. Then she remembered how just a few moments ago she had wished for someone to talk to. Now here he was, safely engaged to be married, intelligent, empathetic. Katie glanced at him, waiting patiently for her to speak. Be bold, she reminded herself.

'Psychologically speaking,' she started slowly, 'what makes some people survive in the world and others unable to deal with life?'

Rob took time to think, trying to decipher the cryptic meaning behind Katie's inquiry.

'It could be many things. Upbringing, environment, genes, disability, trauma. Why do you ask?'

Katie wavered and Rob saw her hesitation. 'You don't have to tell me if you don't want to,' he said.

'The reason I'm in Bodega Bay is not because of my job or a boyfriend. I came to find my brother, half brother really, whom I've never met and didn't know existed until a week ago.'

'Did you find him?'

'Yes. Today.'

'And?'

'There's something very odd about him. There's something very odd about *everything*, but it's him I'm worried about. His adoptive mother says he's mentally ill. I don't know if it's true or not. But whatever it is, he's so sensitive and sweet, like the world is too much for him to bear. Is there a name for that, psychologically speaking?'

'I've seen cases of people so overwhelmingly perceptive that they had trouble even stepping out of the house. They can't handle all the associations they make with the things they see, hear, or even touch.'

'That's just like Vincent, it seems.'

'That's his name, Vincent?'

'Yes.'

'*Vincent Jacobs?*' said Rob in surprise.

'Don't tell me you know him too?'

'I do, but I thought he vanished after the murder.'

'*Murder?*' Katie repeated.

'I heard my father talking about it a lot. It was around the time he left his practice.'

'Murder?' Katie said, dumbstruck. Why hadn't the windshield man told her? Or Madame Charay?

'What do you mean, murder?'

'You mean you don't know?' said Rob, truly surprised.

'I had no idea.'

'What did Vincent say about it?'

'He didn't say a thing. I didn't ask him. He hardly speaks.'

'Where does he live?'

'Out of town, in a mansion, with his adoptive mother, Madame Charay.'

'That eccentric woman who lives at Petty's Cove?'

Katie's trembling knees shook the table. 'You know her?'

'Vaguely, though I'm not sure from where.'

'Please tell me everything.'

'I don't know much, really. She's a recluse, but that's nothing new around here.'

'And what about the murder?'

'Someone was killed.'

'Who?' Katie couldn't stand the suspense.

'Let me think. It was a girl. A teenager. I can't recall her name. It was so long ago. God, this brings back memories.'

'Please tell me.'

'Okay, it's coming back to me now. It was ugly.'

'Ugly?'

'The girl was hacked to death, or something like that. The body was unrecognizable. I overheard my father talking on the phone. It was gruesome, something about them not being able to identify the body at first.'

'And Vincent?'

'He was the prime suspect.'

'Oh, God,' Katie moaned.

'But it's odd.'

'What's odd?'

'I don't recall any charges being filed. I don't remember a trial or an arrest. A murder doesn't happen everyday here. I can't recall another in Bodega Bay. But it's funny how no one ever talks about that case. Even me. I completely forgot about it until you just mentioned Vincent's name.'

How could she have read Vincent so wrong? A murderer? No wonder he was hidden away up there on the cliff. *That* was the game. But what about the police? Certainly they knew he was up there. You can't keep a secret like that for so many years. You can't get away with murder. Even here.

'But Vincent seems so incapable of harming anything, much less a person.'

'The mind is a strange and curious thing,' Rob surmised.

The stuffed clams arrived, but Katie couldn't even think of taking a bite.

'Plus, he's my brother. We have lots of bad habits in my family but murder isn't one of them.'

Katie glanced at the clams but they made her sick.

'Believe me,' said Rob, 'people aren't always what they appear to be.'

CHAPTER EIGHT

Rob didn't try to fight it when he returned home. He flipped off the lights so as not to watch his body shaking and sweating; the insistent chatter of his teeth was bad enough.

He drew a blanket from the living-room couch and huddled on the floor, head pressed against the carpet shag. The memories, or rather the *memory*, flashed before his eyes no matter how hard he closed them. If he thought Vicoden would ease the pain he would swallow two or three, but he knew four or five wouldn't help. Inebriation with alcohol didn't work either; he had tried that in college. Illicit drugs did little but make him jittery. Sufficient quantities of Quaaludes, morphine, or Demerol succeeded in putting the memory on pause. But the drugs wore off days later, and the flashback resumed at the precise frame of interruption.

On it continued, playing an endless loop, an infinite repetition of a handful of minutes as experienced by a twelve-year-old boy. A private screening in recollection hell, until, for whatever reason, the powers that be decided to draw the curtain down and usher Robbie out into the sunlight until the next mandatory showing, curtain time unknown.

In between showings, Rob pulled it together enough to get through life, or most of it, working night jobs to buy cover for his fatigue, dating casually to allay suspicions, passing exams by sheer luck.

And then, like fading film, the older he grew, the more the episodes diminished, first in intensity, then in frequency. His work helped by diverting his energies. Lois, of course, helped too, a repository for his secret. And if there were other, more permanent consequences of his predicament, Lois was content to ignore them as well.

Rob thought he had vanquished the visions altogether, regained control, succeeded where others needed years of therapy or the grace of God. He foolishly believed his recollections had been stored in some hidden interior vault, under permanent lock and key.

Until tonight when Katie had mentioned Vincent.

Thankfully, she hadn't noticed his palpable shock. He had covered himself well with the scant details he provided along with his cursory clinical assessment. He hadn't lied.

Rob knew this day would arrive. Anyone with an elementary understanding of consequence would know that. But to have the agent of reckoning materialize in the form of Katie, lovely Katie, when he was so unprepared, letting his guard down like that, practicing to be human again, allowing the possibilities to be possible. It was all he could do to finish dinner amicably and wait to reach home before succumbing to the inevitable assault that left him lying under his coffee table watching the loop in his mind.

His schooling had taught him that for every microspeck of organic matter there was a corresponding strand of DNA. He often wondered if every millisecond of time had a similar strand. Time and space are linked so inextricably, they say. If so, he swore to find that snippet of time's chromosome and smash it to smithereens, make it extinct, expunge it from the universe. His universe, anyway.

Rob's first client wasn't scheduled until eleven. He wouldn't sleep tonight, that was sure, not until after the first rays of dawn, and even then only if he was lucky.

It was not until mid-morning that Rob succumbed to fatigue. And through the day he slept, through the overcast haze of mid-morning, through the first occasional splats of raindrops around noon, through the ringing telephone calls of his clients wondering why he had never showed for his appointments at his office in town, through the afternoon downpours that beat the roof hard, through the display of a million rainbow prisms, one for every bead of rain that clung to the needles of the nearby pines.

He slept through all of this and awoke not by any internal mechanism but by an insistent knock at the door just as evening began to fade. Rob heard the pounding in his dreams like a hammer keeping time for a chain gang. He woke and found himself drenched with sweat. The clock said six, but he wasn't sure if it was morning or evening.

He opened the door on an unexpected visitor, and saw it was evening on the first day of rain since spring.

Katie woke to the same overcast sky. Her sleep had taken her to other-worldly landscapes with billowing clouds above and wild white horses galloping by her. She wore long flowing dresses and flower petals in her hair. She moved by will, no engine for locomotion other than the invisible cord that drew her from her chest to any direction she desired. A beautiful sensation of warmth and calm.

A long shower did little to shake off her dreaminess, and she floated down to the lobby to get some coffee.

Lois waited behind the counter as if expecting hordes of tourists at any moment. Katie beelined for the coffeepot and poured herself a steaming cup with a little half-and-half. She took a sip before acknowledging Lois with a polite 'Good morning'. One thing Katie could say for Lois, she made great coffee.

'I see you got in late last night,' said Lois.

Did this woman ever rest? Katie shook off the remnants of her lofty dreams to better operate in this petty world. 'I saw nothing about a curfew in the guest rules.'

Another sip; this one tasted bitter.

'Of course not,' said Lois. 'I just didn't realize anything was open so late,' she added, shuffling papers officiously.

Bills, Katie guessed; that's all this place produced.

'I went for a walk along the docks.' Katie felt no compunction to explain, and surprisingly she harbored no guilt for having dinner with Lois's fiancé. Once the coffee kicked in, Katie would feel duly culpable for the misdemeanor, or the conspiracy, as the case may be.

'So you had a nice evening, then?' asked Lois.

Katie set down the full cup. She'd get coffee in town, however weak. 'I did. And I have a long day ahead of me, so if you'll excuse me.'

Katie headed for the door.

'Sorry to keep bothering you, but will you be staying another night?' asked Lois.

Katie looked around the empty lobby, the full complement of keys dangling on the rack behind Lois.

'Only if you think you can spare the room.'

The offices, or rather the office, of the *Bodega Bay Compass* were located in the town's only professional building, a sober monument to modernity, shared by four tenants: a dentist, a CPA, an attorney, and the thin weekly that had supplied the town news without interruption for eighty-three years.

How the other tenants survived the racket of the printing press was beyond Katie, but when she opened the door she immediately covered her ears. The odor of ink and newsprint brought her back to Sunday mornings in San Francisco, her mother sleeping late, as usual, and Katie racing to the corner store in her pajamas to purchase the fat paper with its eight tabloid pages of glorious color comics.

The press's clamor didn't seem to bother the sole employee, an old geezer fast asleep in a wooden office chair a few feet from the clackity machine, his fleshy chin pressing his chest as he snored. Katie didn't see anyone else.

'Hello,' she shouted, her words no match for the efficient rat-tat-tat of ink slapping on paper.

'Hello!' She tried again in her best stage voice. The aging editor swatted a phantom fly from his nose and fell deeper into slumber.

A swift kick to the counter produced no response either.

Katie thought about leaving when the press started to slow, imperceptibly at first, then cycling slower, slower, until it sputtered, hissed, and fell silent with one last sigh.

The old man's eyes popped open.

He gazed around, confirmed his place among the living, and stretched his arms and legs like a lap cat after an afternoon snooze.

'Hello,' Katie bellowed, not realizing how loud her voice sounded in the fresh silence.

He pulled in his paunch. 'Hello there,' he thundered jovially. 'Been here long?'

Getting up from the chair was a massive undertaking.

'Not really.'

'Because I can't hear over the press; it makes a racket.' He sauntered over to the counter. 'I swore I'd get rid of it, replace it with one of them newfangled digital things. But she's served me loyally, and I can't bear the thought of letting her go. It'd be like shooting the family dog. Know what I mean?'

'I think I do.'

'Rudy Rankin, editor-in-chief. Now, how can I help you?'

'I'm looking for some information.'

'That's our business here at the *Compass*. My father, then me.'

'I'm looking for clippings about a murder or a death that occurred about fifteen or twenty years ago, a teenaged girl. Vincent Jacobs was a suspect, I believe.'

The editor scratched his chin. 'I think I remember. Lily her name was, if my memory serves me right. Chopped to death or some ungodly thing. You a crime writer?'

'Yes, well, no, I work at a travel magazine in San Francisco.'

'Speak up.'

'A travel magazine!' Katie felt embarrassed for talking so loudly.

'Well, this was no vacation, I'll tell you that. Follow me.'

Katie tagged along to a back room where everything was

yellow with age; the water cooler, coffeepot, even the metal filing cabinets. Katie had the urge to find a bucket and some bleach and start scrubbing. A stack of yellowing newspapers leaned precariously against the far wall.

'What's your interest?' asked Rudy. He thumbed through the stack, reading the two lines before the middle fold of each issue.

'Me? Nothing really, a distant relative.'

'Vincent or the girl?'

'Umm, that would be Vincent.'

'Vincent, eh?'

'You know him.'

'Nope, never saw him in my life. Heard enough about him, though. Here it is.'

With a deft twist of the wrist, Rudy slipped out an issue. For one moment the pile of papers teetered, ready to tumble down. Katie rushed to hold them back but they stopped swaying and a smile of satisfaction ran across Rudy's face.

'Never dropped one yet.' He handed her an issue folded in two. 'Here we go.'

Katie unfolded the paper dated Tuesday, April 29, 1980. The front-page banner headline read:

Birds' Director Alfred Hitchcock
Dies Peacefully in His Sleep

Katie scanned the rest of the page for news of the murder but found no mention.

'Deep inside, I believe,' said Rudy.

Katie flipped the pages one at a time until she reached page twelve and a story across from the classified ads, accompanied by a grainy black and white photo of a young teenager smiling demurely. It was one of those school photos that succeeded so well in hiding all personality and distinctive facial qualities. Katie could open any high-school yearbook and find scores like it. She started reading.

Suspect Questioned in Girl's Death

> Police today questioned seventeen-year-old Vincent Jacobs, summer resident of Bodega Bay, in connection with the death of Lily Gronowski, sixteen, also a summer resident. Miss Gronowski was found dead in a private residence outside of Bodega Bay. Sheriff Deming said police have yet to determine the cause of death and an autopsy is scheduled for tomorrow.

Katie jumped to the next column for the continuation, but found another headline instead, announcing the date of the upcoming Butter and Eggs Parade in Petaluma.

'That's it?' said Katie. 'It's a pretty small article for such a gruesome death.'

Rudy shrugged. 'No choice. I pestered old Deming for information but he buttoned up like a clam. Can't write an article if you ain't got material. First law of journalism.'

'It happened the same day Hitchcock died. Any connection?'

'None, so far as I know.'

'Was Vincent ever arrested?' asked Katie, choosing but one of a thousand questions that came to mind.

'Good question. That's a reporter's question, right there. You sure you're not a reporter?'

Katie nodded no.

'No, he wasn't, though rumor has it they had the evidence,' said Rudy.

'Like what?'

'They were lovebirds, those two, Vincent and Lily. The killing happened at some cabin near the ocean, where he lived. He admitted being there the afternoon of the death, blood under his fingernails, open and shut case; least, that's what I heard. Of course, I don't print rumor. Nobody would talk to me if I did.'

'Whatever became of the case?'

Rudy rubbed the back of his neck and closed his eyes, tired still, or trying to draw the memories to the surface.

'Deming said the case was closed. Acting coroner's report said no foul play. There was talk big-city money wanted the case quiet.'

'Why didn't you report that?'

'Report what? I had no arrest, no charges, no investigation. Can't fill column inches with speculation.'

'So it just went away?'

'I suppose if it was a local girl killed, it would have been different, though she is buried up at the local cemetery.'

'Who was Lily?'

'You don't know?' said Rankin with true surprise.

'Should I?'

'Well, if you're a distant relative of his, you must be a distant relative of hers too.'

Katie clenched up. 'What do you mean?'

'Lily was Vincent's sister, or half sister, or stepsister, I don't know which, but she was Madame Charay's daughter.'

'You're kidding.'

'I don't kid. It gets me in trouble.'

'But you never reported it.'

'Didn't need to. Everyone in town knew.'

'How about Madame Charay? What's she got to do with this?'

'That old kook? She just sits up there in her mansion counting her money. I tried talking to her once or twice, but she pushed her nose in the air like I was cow fertilizer. Now is that all, because my ink is drying.'

'Yes, thanks. Can I make a copy of this?'

'Sorry, our copy machine is down,' said Rankin, 'but thanks for coming by.'

He disappeared around the bend to tinker with his beloved press.

Katie examined the photograph, searching for some evidence in the dead girl's face. Pretty smile, turtleneck sweater, blondish hair in that year's style. The photo revealed little.

Katie turned her back to the door so Rankin couldn't see her. She thought about ripping out the photo, then folded the newspaper and laid it on top of a filing cabinet. She walked from the room and slipped past Rankin, bent on his knees fixing some sort of jam in the press.

At the front door Katie turned back. 'One more question. Where is Sheriff Deming now?'

Rankin looked up, his fingertips covered in ink. 'That ol' fart? If he's still living, you'll find him out at Green Manors on Bellagio Road. It's one of them old people's homes where they go to wither and die.'

'Thanks,' said Katie.

'And, hey,' called Rankin.

'Yes?'

'Thanks for not ripping my newspaper.'

'You're welcome.'

The moment Katie stepped from the building a single swollen drop of rain burst across the bridge of her nose and splashed against her cheeks. She looked up, stretched out her palm, waited. But not another drop fell from the sky.

As soon as she arrived, Katie wondered why she hadn't put her mother in a place like the Green Manors Assisted Care Home for the Elderly. There was a shuffleboard game in progress, albeit slow progress, and plenty of competent-looking staff mulling about. Residents, bundled up in blankets, occupied wheelchairs leaning gently on the slope of the central green. Then Katie remembered why; it was easier living with her mother than the guilt of not providing for her. Too late now, anyway.

Katie closed her eyes and tried to imagine Vincent in the violent throes of a murderous act, slashing his sister with whatever implement he had used. Katie couldn't envision such a thing. Not Vincent.

An orderly directed Katie to Sheriff Deming, who sat so still in his wheelchair Katie feared he was dead. He faced a window with only the slimmest view of the ocean beyond the parched hills. When the orderly announced Katie by first and last name, a corner of Deming's eyebrow raised slightly.

'May I sit down?'

Deming nodded almost imperceptibly, as if conserving his movements for fear of running out. Katie hadn't noticed it at first, but the man had a hole in his neck from a tracheotomy. She had seen her fill of tracheotomy patients on her mother's ward those last few days.

Katie spoke in measured words, explaining who she was and what she was looking for.

After a long pause Deming lifted his finger to block the hole. His voice sounded like an alien's might, diffused and mechanical.

'Damnedest murder I ever saw.' He pulled his finger away and labored to fill his lungs with air.

'Why?'

'The body. Never seen nothing like it.'

He spoke quickly, since each word kept him from the next breath. 'It took the acting coroner two days to figure out if the killer was human or animal.'

He conserved his words like his movements. Right to the point and stop. 'And what were his findings?' she asked.

'He said animal, I say human. She was clawed to death – her body torn up like road kill.'

Each time Katie inquired about the murder the details grew more gruesome. Katie wondered if she would ever reach a point where she would not want to hear more.

'But you didn't arrest Vincent,' said Katie.

'Could have. He confessed to the murder.'

'Confessed? Then why didn't you arrest him?' Katie witnessed the man shrinking in front of her. How many more breaths did Deming possess? She sensed not many.

'Long story,' he snapped.

'It's because he didn't do it, isn't it?'

Deming took a long series of deep breaths, returning a hint of color to his face. His eyes peeled away from the view and fell on Katie for the first time. Milky white, they stared right through her as if she were a ghost. Then Katie understood. He was blind.

'You've never lived in a small town, have you?' he asked.

'No. Always the city,' Katie said apologetically.

'When you're sheriff in a place like this, there are influences you can't ignore.'

'What do you mean?'

Deming paused again. His breaths were short and staggered and did little to satisfy his craving for oxygen. He turned back to his beloved ocean view that he couldn't see. His breathing found a satisfactory rhythm and he spoke again. 'Do you believe in heaven and hell, Miss Jacobs?'

'Yes, I guess I do.'

'It's all crap to me.'

An orderly walked up, as if on cue. He placed his hands on Deming's wheelchair.

'Ready for your nap, Sheriff Deming?' said the orderly.

'Please. I'm getting tired.'

The orderly wheeled the chair down a hallway. Katie walked alongside, clutching the chair's arm.

'Please help me.'

Deming faced straight ahead as she spoke. 'I've never understood the overwhelming compunction to confess before you die. It's for the feeble-minded. Don't you agree?'

The orderly picked up speed. Katie broke into a jog. 'Who killed Lily? Who?' she pleaded.

They reached a door to a private room. The orderly stretched out his key ring and unlocked the door. He rolled Deming inside and swung him around to face Katie one last time.

'Please,' she begged.

He waved her away. 'It's too late now. Go home.'

'For Vincent's sake.'

Deming turned to the orderly. 'Get me out of this chair before I shit in it.'

The door swung shut on Katie's face.

She heard a sharp cry of pain from behind the closed door, followed by Deming's muffled voice.

'The only hell I know is here on earth.'

The cemetery leaned like an old tombstone itself on a hillside under the shadow of sad oaks outside of town about three miles. Katie stopped at the office, a squat cinder block building with small windows covered with bars, but it was locked. She strolled until she spotted dirt flying out of a grave, one shovelful at a time.

'Excuse me,' asked Katie.

An elderly digger's head popped up, sweaty and grimy. He wiped his brow and flashed a crooked set of teeth as yellow as corn. 'What can I do you for?'

'I didn't know they still dug graves by hand.'

'They don't. My backhoe's down, and I got a funeral in the morning. Anyway, I need the exercise. You get out of shape doing nothing but pulling levers.'

The digger leaned on his shovel, eyeing Katie's casual attire. 'You ain't from around here.'

'No. I'm looking for a plot.'

'All sold out; have been for years. And it don't look like we'll get more anytime soon. No refunds, if you know what I mean.'

'It's a *used* grave I'm looking for. Lily Gronowski.'

'Here, give me a hand.'

The digger extended his arm to Katie. Katie helped him out of the hole, then discreetly wiped her hands on her jeans.

'Lily, nicest grave in the place. It's over there, under the eucalyptus.'

'Thanks.'

'You're in for a treat.'

'What do you mean?' asked Katie.

'The flowers.'

Katie hustled to the shaded site. A neat row of painted white stones skirted a grave topped with a tall headstone of polished marble granite. The engraving was an illustration of two doves taking wing, each holding in their beak a corner of an embroidered blanket. The blanket floated like a prayer shawl over the inscription.

Lily Gronowski
1963–1980

Below the name, four lines of verse had been inscribed in script.

Truth, crushed to earth, shall rise again,
The eternal years of God are hers;
But Error, wounded, writhes in pain,
And dies among his worshippers.

Katie noticed something else. It was a fresh bouquet of orchids. Madame Charay's orchids in transformation. From white, the petals turned slightly pink, rich red, and then they engorged themselves with hues of ruby and scarlet and finally a luxurious purple full of warmth and tone, the most beautiful purple Katie had ever seen. Before her eyes the purple began to drain, slowly at first, then with a rush, leaving behind a rusty, withering hand of petals, lifeless and spent.

Now Katie understood why they were called the *immortals*. The truth of that purple was immortal. The truth of anything able to fully reach its potential, to manifest itself so purely, that was immortality, no matter how brief the moment. For the first time Katie realized that immortality was not a consequence of time, but of truth.

She returned quickly to the grave digger, hard at work back in the hole.

'Madame Charay was here.'

'You just missed her.'

'She puts the flowers on the grave?' asked Katie.

The grave digger wasn't following Katie's line of thought. 'Who else?'

'But their last names, they're different.'

'Since when do parents and children have to have the same last name? Anyway, Gronowski is that old lady's name. Or was when she signed the papers. Charay is her first name or maiden name or stage name; I can't keep that stuff straight anymore. Someone wants to be called something, that's fine with me, just don't keep changing it like the seasons.'

'Are you sure?' asked Katie.

'I got the records inside. You can't lie on a cemetery plot application. It's against state law.'

'What else do you know about Madame Charay?'

'Not much. She bought that plot and two beside it. Paid cash. Gives me a generous tip at Christmas.'

'Two other plots? Who are they for?'

'I assume one's for her. She's getting up there in age, after all. Even the rich gotta die.'

'And the third plot?'

'Could be the devil himself. You don't ask questions in this business. Just nod your head and move slowly.'

'Does anyone else ever visit Lily's grave?'

'There's a guy comes about once a year. Doesn't stay but five minutes and leaves.'

'Do you know who? Is his name Vincent?'

'Lady, I don't mourn alongside them. I just lay them to eternal rest.'

CHAPTER NINE

The eagle-claw door knocker felt even heavier this time as Katie slapped it against its plate. The brassy thud echoed off the tree trunks and returned to startle Katie, but failed to draw any attention inside. She lingered politely before clutching the massive knocker again and throwing its full weight against the door.

Madame Charay had apparently gone out for the afternoon or was not interested in playing host. Katie drifted over to the carriage house to see if a car was gone.

The windows had been painted black. With her key, she scratched away a little paint, just enough to see what the skylight might illuminate.

There was a powder-blue Austin Healy, dwarfed on either side by two much larger automobiles. On the left a green Jaguar or some such vessel favored by royalty, and on the right an impeccably maintained late-1950s Ford Fairlane with Arizona license plates ANL-709. Another space was empty.

Katie squinted an eye to look around inside. There wasn't much. A sagging wooden shelf struggled to hold up a load of paint cans and cleaning supplies, a dusty saddle and its tack hung on a stake, some farm implements, an aluminum ladder in the rafters, two fifty-pound bags of birdseed, and a trash can or two.

Katie returned to her car, her good sense telling her to leave before Madame Charay returned. But the forest seemed exceptionally quiet, and Katie felt sure she would have no trouble hearing an approaching vehicle several hundred yards away, giving her plenty of time to dash back to her car if necessary. She couldn't fight the compulsion to investigate, to sneak a peek, just a little one. A quick tour around the outside of the house, that's all.

She started at the north corner, hugging the wall, feeling her way around the smooth river stones with her palms, until she reached the first set of windows, set so high Katie was forced to stand on her tiptoes merely to set her nose on the sill.

The sheer size of the room stunned her. It was a library, with tall towering built-in shelves filled with leather-bound books. More than the square footage, it was the tall ceiling that perplexed Katie, taller, it appeared, than the house itself. She stepped back to reassess the exterior, which upon inspection still seemed incapable of accommodating such a room.

And then there was the grandeur of the interior. Unlike the jumble of styles in the sitting room, the library was decorated in but one style, Louis XIV. Ornately carved knobs and balls adorned every foot, arm, and corner of each chair, armoire, and divan. Each pompous piece was upholstered with luxuriant fabrics. The broad wooden desk was more simply stated, with its wide leather blotter and matching brass statuettes perched on marble bases. A grand chandelier of wrought iron and gold leaf hung from the ceiling, and massive faux-marble pillars stood sentry on either side of the French interior doors.

It hit her suddenly. *Notorious*. Ingrid Bergman is forced to marry an ex-Nazi played by Claude Rains, but she loves Cary Grant, the steely U.S. agent who can't admit he loves her, and has since the moment they met and she passed out drunk in his arms.

If these were original set pieces, as Madame Charay had suggested, the expense and effort were unimaginable.

Katie crept along the wall until she reached the next set of windows. Again she was forced on tiptoes to look inside. This room was a cinch to identify. Postwar modern, efficient, masculine, *Rear Window*, complete with checkered carpet, Venetian blinds, bottle of whiskey, and two ready glasses.

A pair of high-powered binoculars, a zoom camera, and an old-fashioned flashbulb unit had been arranged neatly on the small table next to a wheelchair, as if James Stewart was due to limp in on crutches any moment with proof that Raymond Burr had truly killed his wife and packed her in a trunk.

Katie turned the corner and moved on to the next window.

She peeked in on old mother Bates's bedroom, lovingly preserved in *Psycho* by her demented son Anthony Perkins, and preserved just as lovingly here.

Katie moved on, kicking up dust as she sidestepped through the dry flower-beds along the house's edge to the final set of accessible windows. She peered in on the destroyed kitchen of the unfortunate chicken farmer in *The Birds*, whose eyes were gouged out during his slow death. The room had been reproduced in exacting detail, as far as Katie could tell, down to the shattered teacups hanging from the eye-hooks underneath the hutch pantry. Only the eyeless body of the tortured farmer was missing. Then Katie remembered: he died in his bedroom.

Katie turned the final corner and rushed back to her car, her head swimming with the sickness of the obsession.

She stopped and listened for the grumbling of an approaching automobile, but heard only the gentle rustling of trees. Madame Charay was far away, Katie could sense it.

And Vincent was alone.

Appearances are deceiving, Katie tried to convince herself. Rob had reminded her of that again last night. What did she know of Vincent other than the secondhand gossip of the townspeople and what she had learned during one brief meeting with him, fully chaperoned. He was a suspected sister killer, and Katie was a sister. But she couldn't feel this much for someone evil.

She pricked her ears one last time, then hustled to the back of the house. She found the trail with ease and wondered why it had appeared so hidden yesterday. She plunged under the brush and hurried down the path, using yesterday's footprints as her guide, mimicking the quick steps and compact moves of

Madame Charay. The brush encircled her, and in seconds she was in the darkness. As she passed the snagged thread from Tippi's sweater, her footsteps surprised a flock of nesting terns. They rose instantly, in unison, a hundred flashes of dark wings inches from her face. Instinctively, Katie froze and blocked her eyes with her arms, ready for the sure attack. But the birds lifted and scattered quickly to the refuge of the trees above.

Katie emerged from the woods to face the ocean, the second time in two days it had surprised her. This time she battled back her fear and ventured a downward glance to see a sliver of a crescent beach surrounded by wild formations of craggy rocks.

A single thread of smoke rose from the chimney. The curtains were tightly drawn. Katie knocked gently – she didn't want to scare Vincent. She didn't need that.

No answer. Could he be with Madame Charay? Had she whisked him away rather than face any risk Katie might pose? Katie turned to face the ocean, contemplating her next step.

And there she saw him, peacefully still in a lotus position at the edge of the bluff, gazing upon the wide expanse of water. Strange, Katie hadn't seen him there when she walked up.

She called to him, but he didn't turn.

She deliberately scraped the pebbles with her feet to give him advance warning of her approach. When she got a few feet behind him, she stopped, frightened by his stillness.

'Vincent?'

Vincent crinked his neck.

'It's me, Katie. I came by to say hello.'

Vincent nodded ever so slightly, or perhaps it was Katie's wishful thinking. Perhaps he was waiting for her to inch just a little closer so he could snatch her up and rip her to shreds, the first victim to come along since Lily.

Turn and leave now. Last chance.

Her heart pounding, she took a seat beside him, not too near, and crossed her legs in the same peculiar fashion as he, sharing his silent view of the ocean, as gray as gunmetal under the gathering clouds.

She braved a sideways glance, her first look outside the dim light of the cabin. He was taller than Katie remembered, long spine, the lithe body of a long-distance runner. His wiry hair wasn't the red of carrots but rusty red. His eyebrows grew in accidental tufts, and his upper lip and chin sprouted a two-day stubble, though he couldn't grow a full beard if he tried. A few pimples dotted his adolescent face, frozen with the perplexed expression of a teenager.

She wondered how many sunsets Vincent had seen. How many passing ships, wild storms, migrating schools of whales. How many stranded visitors and unidentifiable beasts. How many strange and rare occurrences that happen only at meeting places of great forces, like here, where ocean and earth collide.

Vincent smiled, or so Katie thought. It may have been a display of nervousness, a wince of pain, but it provided all the incentive Katie needed.

'Beautiful view,' Katie said.

'It's going to rain,' said Vincent.

Katie was relieved to hear such an ordinary response, relieved Vincent hadn't grabbed her by the throat and snapped her neck in two.

'May I sit down?' Katie asked, a stupid question considering she already was.

Vincent nodded blankly. Where was the Vincent of that vivid expression? The Vincent with so much to say and only his visage to say it with? Not here today.

Katie had come all this way, had spent three days tracking Vincent, had risked her life by coming here today, yet she could hardly think of a thing to say.

'You remember me, Vincent?'

Vincent nodded again. 'My sister.'

This time Katie was certain that Vincent smiled, and it filled Katie with joy to know that her existence pleased him, enough to launch her into a short discourse.

'We have the same mother – birth mother – and no other brothers and sisters, as far as I know. Madame Charay is your *adopted* mother, though it's obvious she cares for you tremendously.'

Was she explaining too much or too little? She presumed he understood terms like birth mother and adopted mother, but these may all have been intangible abstractions to him. She stopped to see if any of it made sense.

'Gloria,' Vincent said.

'Vincent, you *know*.'

Katie fought the urge to hold his hand, still unsure how he might react to physical contact, a milestone not yet reached between sister and brother.

Vincent leaned her way, which Katie interpreted as a sign of affection. 'Do you love her?' he asked.

Katie was caught off guard. She had contemplated the question many times without arriving at a definitive answer.

'I think I did. Most of the time.'

'Does that mean she's . . . dead?'

'Yes, Vincent.' Katie felt a fool for not telling him earlier. It was, after all, his mother who had died too.

'She died last week. I'm sorry you never got a chance to meet her.'

Vincent grew sad. 'I remember Gloria. I am sorry she is gone.'

He had met her, of course. Grandma had talked about that day Vincent came to visit. He remembered.

'She was always sorry she couldn't care for you, Vincent. If that's any consolation.'

Vincent nodded. He plucked a shoot of grass and twirled it in his fingers until it was a blur of motion. Was he contemplating the meaning of life and death, the tragedy of lost motherhood, or simply watching the blade twirl round in his hand?

Katie picked up a blade too. It felt ready to disintegrate in her hand, so devoid of moisture it was.

'Have you ever loved anyone, Vincent?'

Vincent's fingers stopped in mid-twirl. He shifted uneasily in place.

'Madame Charay,' he answered. He glanced sideways at Katie to see if the response was acceptable. Languid eyes full of regret.

Katie nodded. 'She's very nice. And she loves you too. Anyone else, Vincent? Anyone else you loved?'

The waves crashed below.

They sat in silence for a long while, until Katie could no longer control her curiosity. 'I understand you had another sister once.'

Vincent peeked at Katie. 'A long time ago,' he said.

'What was her name?' Katie asked as innocently as possible.

Vincent worked hard to formulate his response. 'I forgot.' His attempt at deception was as transparent as a child's. Katie nodded and smiled.

'I heard her name was Lily.'

Vincent began to tremble slightly. He looked at her directly for the first time, and she saw the pain in his eyes.

Katie suddenly felt cruel for mentioning the name. Here she was, five minutes with her brother and already making him suffer.

'Vincent, I am your family. Do you know what that means?'

Vincent shook his head no.

'It means I would never do anything to hurt you. No matter what happened in the past. I only want to help you. Do you believe that, Vincent? Please believe that.'

Vincent's changing facial expressions mirrored his interior dialogue of uncertainty. He flicked the blade of grass over the edge of the cliff.

'I don't care what happened,' Katie continued. 'I care only about you. Vincent, you have to believe me.'

The intensity of waves increased. Katie glanced along the shore to the crescent beach she had discovered earlier, but it seemed much thinner, displaced by the rising tide.

'Vincent, I have to ask you a question. And no matter what you answer me, it's okay. I'll walk away, if that's what you want. I'll come back always, if that's what you want, or never come back again. I just have to know, Vincent, for myself. For my own peace of mind.'

Vincent did not stir.

Katie sucked in a breath of sea air. She had to ask. 'Vincent, was it you? Was it you who hurt Lily?'

The trembling increased. Vincent wrapped his arms around his midsection in a futile attempt to hold himself steady. His chin burrowed into his chest. Katie saw a hint of a tear in his eye.

'Please tell me, Vincent. I'm your sister.'

Vincent mumbled something. The crash of a wave drowned his words.

'What, Vincent?'

He mumbled again, covering his mouth with his dirty hand.

Katie peered under his brow. 'Please, Vincent, speak up.'

'Yes,' he voiced in the frailest of whispers.

Vincent slouched forward and stared at his knees, ready for his punishment.

'Yes? Was that a yes?' But she knew it was, and she felt a deep anger now, not directed at Vincent, rather at the cruel combination of circumstances that conspired to force this gentle soul to murder.

Vincent bit his lower lip. 'Yes,' he blurted out. '*I* killed her. *I* killed Lily. It was *me*.'

Vincent broke into sobs.

Katie placed her arms around him, touching her brother for the first time.

And she cried, too, cried because she had wanted so badly to believe it wasn't true. Her body swelled with emotions: regret for coming here, anger at Madame Charay for whatever part she played in this wretched affair, hatred for her own mother for delivering Vincent into this world and then abandoning him to this ruthless fate.

The two stayed there, brother and sister, lamenting on the cliff, listening to the waves pound the rocks, until first Vincent and then Katie stopped crying, and together they lifted their heads and looked to the sky as it imposed its grayness on the ocean.

'Why did you kill her?'

Vincent shrugged in bewilderment. 'I don't know.'

Katie placed her index finger over her tightened lips. 'Your secret is safe with me.'

They held hands, silently, together for a long time. Then Katie kissed Vincent on the forehead. Vincent's eyes, sad and blue, peered back as vulnerable as Katie had ever seen a pair of eyes, more vulnerable than hers.

'Are you going?' asked Vincent.

'Would you like me to come back and visit you again?'

'Yes.'

'I will then, Vincent.'

Vincent smiled.

Katie smiled too. 'Good-bye for now.'

'Good-bye,' said Vincent.

Katie kissed him once again and rose to leave. The crescent beach was gone, swallowed by the tide, replaced by a violent surf that smashed against the rocks like a jealous beast. Katie looked back one last time.

Vincent waved, then returned to his lotus position facing the west, meditating on whatever Vincent meditated upon, a sorrow, Katie was sure, she could never begin to fathom.

She walked the path back to the house trying to swallow the lump stuck in her throat like a pit. It grew two sizes when Katie saw Madame Charay near the house shoveling a dead crow into a thick, green plastic trash bag.

'What happened?' Katie asked as nonchalantly as she could, not sure how Madame Charay would react to her presence.

'Bird slammed into the house, died instantly.'

'Sounds very Hitchcockian,' said Katie.

'It happens quite often, actually. Not just here, but all along the coast.'

'The air currents, I understand,' said Katie.

'Apparently.' Madame Charay tied the bag in a double knot.

'Visiting your brother again?'

'I hope you don't mind,' said Katie sincerely.

Madame Charay looked over the top of her dark sunglasses. 'Did you think I would prohibit you? Though I must say I'm from the old school and prefer visitors to announce themselves.'

'I'm sorry. I truly am. It wasn't my plan to visit Vincent. Actually, I came to visit you.'

Madame Charay flung the bag over her shoulder and hauled it to the carriage house. Katie followed, breaking into a near jog to keep pace.

'And to what do I owe this pleasure?' asked Madame Charay.

'I came to ask you a question.'

'And what question is that?'

'Why didn't you tell me?' asked Katie.

'Tell you what?'

'About the murder. About Lily.'

Madame Charay pushed her glasses to the tip of her nose and gave Katie a rumpled brow of consternation.

'And what did Vincent tell you?' Madame Charay said. She closed the carriage house door, locked it, and began the stroll back to the house.

'He told me he killed her.'

'I see.'

'If that's true, why didn't you turn him in?' asked Katie.

'One goes to great lengths to protect one's children.'

'Even the murderer of your daughter?'

'You don't have children, do you, Miss Jacobs?' Madame Charay asked.

'No.'

'Perhaps you'd understand if you did.'

'Perhaps Vincent didn't murder anyone,' said Katie firmly.

Madame Charay dumped the bag into an aluminum trash can and closed the lid tightly. 'You think he's lying, then?'

'I don't know what to believe, but I don't think he did it. Not Vincent.'

Madame Charay closed and locked the carriage house and walked Katie to her car before responding. 'Perhaps you're right.'

'He was never charged with the crime.'

'This is true.'

'But never exonerated either,' said Katie.

'And that matters to you?'

'Very much.'

'Then I suggest you go to the police. Have the case reopened,' said Madame Charay.

'Maybe I should.'

'Please do. As long as you realize what would happen to Vincent in prison or a mental ward, *if* he were able to survive the ordeal of an investigation, reporters, handcuffs, not to mention a lengthy trial.'

Katie couldn't disagree. Whatever shady deals Madame Charay had made to keep Vincent here were far better than exposing Vincent to the outside world.

'Would you care to come in for some tea?' asked Madame Charay.

'No, I think I should be going.'

'To the authorities, I should hope,' said Madame Charay.

'Perhaps I will.'

CHAPTER TEN

The first drops of rain splattered on Katie's windshield moments after she turned off Madame Charay's driveway and onto the secondary road. They fell upon her face, fat and warm, and Katie thought about pulling over and putting up the convertible top. But after a long summer and early autumn of dryness, the rain seemed preposterous, and Katie was sure she could beat its onslaught to the hotel.

Two miles up the road, the rain beat down in sheets. Katie's windshield wipers labored helplessly to sweep the deluge away. She stopped along the road, drenched, and struggled to flip up the top. But the release had jammed, or so it seemed; Katie could hardly think or see straight in the deafening rain.

She giggled at her predicament. The rainwater moistened her skin and traveled in warm rivulets down her arms and legs. She looked down and saw her shirt glued to her body. She didn't mind; nobody was there to see.

Her only material concern was her car, a traveling vessel collecting water by the bucketful. It only got worse when Katie left the protection of the giant trees for the coastal highway.

Along the way she spied the shelter of a lone service station. A 'closed' sign hung in the door, but there was a roof over the pumps, and she rolled to a stop gratefully to collect her thoughts. Her body steamed like a heated coil. Katie shook out her hair and wiped her face with her hands. She snapped her shirt away from her breasts just in case someone showed up.

From desert to jungle in minutes – the mechanic was right,

the coast was unpredictable. She tried the car top again. She had lifted it a hundred times without a problem, yet despite her best efforts of brain and brawn, it would not budge.

Katie made a dash for the phone booth unprotected by the overhang at the far end of the lot. She felt compelled to call someone, anyone, though she wasn't sure who.

The booth fogged quickly, and Katie almost didn't see the car rolling into the station. It was the sedan's dull headlights that caught her eye. She wiped away a circle of steam but still could scarcely determine make or model.

A hearse of some kind? She looked closer. No, just a black Cadillac, an aging Coupé de something with shark fins and tinted windows and the gurgling bass line of the exhaust.

Katie was glad for the help at first, but she didn't like the way the driver cut the engine, the way the car squeaked and bounced as it coasted over speed bumps, the way it stopped so close to the phone booth Katie could spit on the hood without fear of missing.

No hubcaps, antenna bent, rusting chrome. Katie wedged her foot against the booth's folding glass door. She rubbed the steaming glass more, enough to see a man step from the car and saunter toward the booth unfazed by the rain.

Katie's knees buckled.

It was that junkyard dog, Peter Grow.

She wedged her foot tighter and raced through the thin phone book for Rob's name.

She pulled change from her pocket, coins spilled to the floor. She bent, found a quarter, and dialed Rob's number.

Peter's hands flexed into fists. Fat raindrops bounced off his head like marbles.

One ring. Two.

Pick up, Rob.

Peter shielded his eyes for a look inside.

Please, pick up.

Katie pressed her knee until it ached, protection against the steamy nightmare outside the glass.

Oh, God, answer, please, Rob.

Peter pounded the window.

Save me, Katie pleaded.

He pounded again.

Thank you, God. 'Rob? This is Katie. Please help me, you've got to help me.'

'—I'm not in right now, so please leave a message after the beep.'

Beep.

Dammit.

Peter shook the door. Katie's foot held firm.

'Go away!' she cried.

He leered with the eyes of a predator. He wiped away the rain and squashed his face against the glass.

Katie slammed down the phone. She ripped out the page with Rob's address.

Peter circled the booth. Pounded again. She could smell his greasy aroma.

Trapped, she felt so trapped.

No.

No, she wasn't going to let herself feel that way. Not anymore. She took a deep breath, opened the door, shoulders squared, feet apart, the toughest look she could muster.

'What do you want?' she grumbled.

'It's *you*,' he said with surprise.

'What are you going to do about it?' Katie demanded.

'Nothing. You finished with the phone?'

'Yes, I am.'

'Good, 'cause I got a flat and I ain't go no spare.'

That was all? Katie thought.

A flat tire? A mere coincidence? Maybe not, but Katie wasn't going to argue.

'Stand back.'

Peter moved away and Katie stepped from the booth, her hands in front of her karate-style as she drew a wide berth around him.

Peter took her place by the phone and jiggled change from his pocket. 'Still in town, huh?'

Katie backpedaled to her car. 'Looks that way.'

He dropped a coin in the phone. 'You won't be for long.'

'What's that supposed to mean?' Katie said.

'Nothing. How about a ride to town?'

'Gimme a break,' said Katie in her best gangster rap.

'That's what I thought.'

The convertible had trouble starting at first, but it fired up, and Katie gunned it into the attacking rain, checking her rearview mirror every few seconds, clenching the soggy page with Rob's address. She took a deep breath and marveled over her display of courage, but it did little to stop the shivering made worse by the rain turned cold.

Neither the shower nor the shivering let up until Katie found Rob's place down a series of bumpy roads. She squeezed water from her shirt, combed her hair back, and tried to shake Peter Grow from her mind. She knocked on Rob's door, part of her hoping he wasn't home, another part wanting nothing more than to race into his arms.

The Tudor-style farmhouse was like many Katie had seen these past few days. An inviting front porch stocked with two wooden rocking chairs. Out front, a creek coming back to life with rain meandered through a small orchard thick with apple, fig, and pear trees.

She knocked again with no reply. Why should he be home? She had just called ten minutes earlier only to reach an answering machine. She was foolish to come, even if the incident with Peter gave her a ready excuse. She didn't like pushy or needy women, and arriving at his doorstep in this condition smacked of both. Then there was last evening's dinner, which had ended oddly. Once they got talking about the murder, Rob turned distant, even aloof. Katie couldn't blame him. Who in his right mind wanted to chat with a murderer's sister? And here she was, not twenty-four hours later rapping on his door.

Why had she dialed Rob instead of the police? Why hadn't she returned to her trusted mechanic to unjam her convertible top, or traveled back to the shelter of The Nest for warmth? She knew why. It was more than needing protection from the elements or Peter Grow. Much more.

Katie turned to leave, relieved the encounter wasn't to be. But when she reached the bottom step and heard the door jolt open, her heart skipped a beat. She twirled around with an unforced smile.

The smile vanished the moment she saw Rob hiding behind the door, squinting against the gray daylight. His eyes were bloodshot, hair tussled, cheeks covered with stubble. His face was lined with wrinkles Katie swore weren't there last night, but the clothes were the same.

'Are you okay?' asked Katie.

He pulled back into his darkened house. 'I had a bad night, that's all,' he murmured weakly. 'I couldn't sleep.'

'You look awful,' said Katie. 'I'm sorry. I didn't mean it like that.'

'No, you're right. It must have been something I ate.'

He rubbed his eyes and took his first good look at Katie. 'And what happened to you?'

Katie glanced down on her drenched clothing. 'Oh, the rain. My car top got stuck. I was wondering if you could help me fix it.'

Her reasoning sounded feeble now, and Katie winced at the lame rationale.

'I'd be happy to,' he said, rather unconvincingly.

Katie retreated a step, feeling so wrong for having come. 'I'm sorry. Maybe I should go.'

'No, no,' Rob protested. 'Please come in and get dry. We'll take a look at your car. You'll just have to excuse me and the house; it's a bit of a mess.'

'You sure?'

Rob insisted with an assuring nod. 'Let me get you some dry clothes.'

He led Katie into his library and dashed off into a back bedroom, leaving her alone with stacks of books everywhere, books on psychology, philosophy, art, sociology, architecture, film, religion, mysticism, and well-worn editions of literature.

If she wasn't soaked, Katie might have indulged her urge to pull out a book and nestle down in the green leather reading chair tucked in the corner. As it was, she felt terrible for leaking water all over the Persian rug, so she huddled in the spot where Rob had left her so as to contain the mess.

He returned in a jiffy in fresh clothes, shaved and combed, looking a thousand times better than moments before, though his eyes still showed traces of red.

'I hope these will do.' He handed Katie two soft towels, a hairbrush, sweatpants, and a clean and pressed button-down cotton shirt, one of his own.

'Thank you,' said Katie. 'I'm so sorry to get everything wet, to disturb you like this.'

'Please. No apologies. Let me show you the bathroom. I'll make some coffee.'

Katie emerged feeling fresh in Rob's shirt, unbuttoned to her cleavage. She rolled up the sleeves above her wrists and knotted the long shirttails across her belly. She felt clean and fresh and slightly dangerous.

She found Rob in the living room, adding logs to a small fire. A cup of dark coffee awaited her on the table. She was pleased to see him looking his old self again, or at least the Rob she had come to know.

She told him about the harrowing experience with Peter Grow, but only when she mentioned the murder did his full attention turn on her.

'I found some things out,' she said, sipping her coffee.

'Like what?'

'The girl who was killed, her name is Lily Gronowski. Does the name ring a bell?'

'Now that you mention it. How did you find that out?'

'A little investigating. Do you know who she is?'

'You tell me,' said Rob.

'She's Madame Charay's daughter.'

Rob turned and paced away from Katie. 'Small world.'

'And I visited Vincent. Alone.'

'And?'

'I asked him if he killed her.'

Rob closed his eyes. 'Busy day. What did he say?'

'Yes.'

'He did?'

'You sound surprised,' said Katie.

'No, no, that's what everyone thought all along. I'm just surprised he confessed so easily.'

'That's why I don't believe it,' said Katie.

'Then you think he was lying?'

'Maybe he was just trying to please me. Maybe he thought that's what I wanted to hear. Maybe he was mistaken.'

'Mistaken? How can you be mistaken about murdering someone?'

'You tell me. You're the expert on memory and psychology. It can happen, can't it?'

'Highly unlikely.'

'It's not just me who thinks so. Editor Rankin doesn't believe Vincent is the killer, even though he won't admit it. The ex-sheriff is rotting sick with it.'

'They didn't say anything, did they?'

'No, but they didn't have to. Plus, I know in my heart Vincent didn't do it. He's no murderer. And Madame Charay knows that too.'

'You sound pretty convinced after just a few hours poking around.'

'It's my heart talking, I'll admit it, but not without some corroboration.'

'What did Madame Charay say?'

'She says he won't survive an investigation.'

'She's right,' said Rob. 'And even if he could take it, why stir things up?'

Katie thought the answer was fairly obvious, but maybe not. 'For Vincent's sake.'

'You told me yourself he likes it there. And even if he doesn't, what's the alternative? Believe me, I've seen my share of psychiatric hospitals; it's enough to scare you to death. Maybe Vincent is better where he is. Ten years ago I may not have said that, but I can say it now.'

'Better the way he is? Feeling guilty about a crime he didn't commit? Believing himself to be a killer?'

'You don't know that.'

'And what if he isn't the killer? Then a murderer is running free.'

Rob stood and paced the floor. 'Jesus, you're talking about something that happened years ago. If there's a murderer on the loose, he's long gone, or in jail, but certainly not murdering anyone in this town. There hasn't been a murder in Bodega Bay since Lily.'

Everything Rob said made sense, almost. 'All right, I'll accept everything you say. Just answer me one question. Why would Madame Charay protect the killer of her daughter, her own flesh and blood?'

Rob didn't respond. He twisted a poker into the fire and set free a flurry of sparks. 'Secrets run deep in this town,' he said. 'You told me yourself, she's crazy.'

Katie shivered at the thought of Madame Charay and her bizarre obsession. She told Rob about the rooms in the mansion. He listened intently with a quizzical expression, but he didn't speak.

'Why do people revere the movies so, and actors, actresses, and directors?' Katie asked.

'I don't know. Maybe it's because we lack courage, all of us, and we're drawn to those who have it. And with every adventure, or romance, or tragedy we see our stories played out on the big screen.'

'Temples of our desire,' Katie added.

'And temples of our fears too. The images are larger than

life in every sense of the word, demigods locked in battles or passionate embraces, possessing traits we only wish we possessed.'

'Now I think I understand,' said Katie.

'Understand what?'

'My mother a little better, why she tried so hard to be an actress. It was her odd way of insisting that she was good, worthwhile. She tried to be an idol rather than emulating those people she admired. She never realized that mothers are idols, too, even if the audience is small.'

'If you were a client, I'd say you just achieved a breakthrough.'

'At this point I'd much rather understand Madame Charay and her infatuation with Hitchcock. It's pretty unusual, don't you think?'

'Actually, not really.' Rob took a seat on the corner of the coffee table. 'You know the house in *The Birds*, the Brenner place across the bay?'

'Yes.'

'Shortly after the film was released, people started flocking there like it was some sort of shrine, as if they expected to see a miracle. At first they just gawked, but then they started taking pieces of the house as souvenirs, just to have a part of it. In no time they were ripping the place apart, board by board, nail by nail. Then one night the house went up in flames. No one ever figured out why or who. But even then, when only the burned-out frame survived, they came. And they came after the town bulldozed everything and hauled the debris away. And they still come, the curious, the devoted, every day they come to commune with a bare patch of concrete where a built-up old shack once stood for something in a fictionalized movie about events that never happened and never could.'

'But there have been plenty of movies made, in plenty of locations. Why here? Why Hitchcock?' she asked.

'You know what Hitchcock said? He said fear is an emotion people like to feel when they know they're safe. I can tell you from experience, fear is the only emotion many people feel. He was a master at bringing them close to their emotions. Isn't that what an artist is supposed to do, tap the subconscious?'

Suddenly it all came clear to Katie. All the pieces were right here, all the necessary talents. Why hadn't she thought of it before?

'Did you say subconscious?'

'I did,' said Rob.

'I know how we can help Vincent.'

'What do you mean?'

'And you're going to help me.'

'Me?'

'That's right.'

'How?'

'Hypnotize him,' she whispered.

'*Hypnotize him?* Are you crazy?'

'No, I'm not. You're a psychologist. You've been trained, haven't you?'

'In theory, perhaps, but it's more complicated than that.' Rob stood up.

'But you could do it, if you had to.'

'There's more to it than you think. It's a complicated procedure. I don't have a client history. I have no way of knowing the severity of his condition, or even what his condition is.'

'So?'

'So, he could be on psychosomatic drugs. He could lapse into an epileptic seizure. Hypnotizing him could harm him psychologically or physically. It could kill him.'

'But it's highly unlikely, isn't it?'

'Perhaps. But besides that, it's a breach of professional ethics. I have no authority whatsoever to provide treatment, no signed releases. It's a blatant violation of every ethical vow I've taken.'

'No one would find out. No one would need to know. Just us.'

'Just us? What if he confesses under hypnosis? I would be

required by law to report it. Then what? The police would be involved, an investigation. He'd be hauled off to jail. He wouldn't survive there, much less make it to his trial date.'

'But what if he didn't kill her, Rob? What if he's innocent and trapped up there? Think of what this will mean for Vincent.'

'You can't take someone who's been living one way for thirty years and change their lifestyle. You don't want that, take my word.'

Katie tried to hide her disappointment, but she couldn't. Maybe he was right, maybe she should return to San Francisco, come back every other weekend with a bag lunch to share with Vincent by the sea. 'You're right.'

'I guess so,' said Rob, this time without much conviction.

Katie heard the waver in his voice, saw the opening.

'You're not convinced, are you?'

'I don't know.' Rob lowered his head.

She studied him hard. 'You *want* to go up there.'

'*Want* to go?' Rob chuckled. 'That's not how I'd describe it.'

'But you will,' said Katie, leading with her optimism – or was it her intuition? She wasn't sure.

Rob sighed. Every strand in his body recoiled at the notion. But there was no fighting it. The time had come to face the pain, the truth – whatever the repercussions to Vincent, to himself, to Katie.

'Here's what I'm willing to do,' he started. 'We'll go up there, together. We'll assess the situation, talk to Vincent, evaluate our options.'

'And hypnotize him?'

'I don't know. We'll see, one step at a time.'

'Are you sure you want to do this?'

'No.'

Katie didn't mean to, but she couldn't help reaching up and kissing Rob's neck. He held her tight. It felt good, so secure. Maybe this was what Katie had come here for, one moment of comfort.

Rob's jaw tensed. He pulled away. 'How should we do it?'

'You tell me,' said Katie.

'We could get there by car, but we run the risk of being seen. If we come in by foot that would take us past Madame Charay's. I think our best bet is by ocean.'

'Ocean?'

'I have a motorboat.'

'But it's a rocky shore with rough surf. I almost fell off the edge.'

'I know the beaches. They come up at low tide. You can bring a boat in, but there's not much time.'

Katie saw a fire in his eyes.

Rob glanced at his watch. 'It's low tide now. We have two hours, maybe three left. We'll do it tonight.'

'Tonight?' Katie said in disbelief.

'Go get ready. Meet me at The Tides in half an hour. Can you do that?'

Katie looked into his vulnerable eyes. 'Yes, I can.'

She wasn't ready for the kiss, but she wasn't surprised.

His fingers ran up her back and released in her a bothersome flush that rushed through her body. Dressed in his shirt, held in his arms, warm in his house, it felt so good to be kissed by him.

Their tongues met and Katie pushed him back gently.

'No,' she said. 'Lois.'

'Lois,' Rob repeated.

The rain had stopped outside. Despite Katie's prediction, the sky was clearing on the west, and a shimmering blue made the clouds look silver.

Rob fixed the car top with little problem.

'Now get going,' he said gently.

'Rob.'

'Yes?'

'I know it's not for me that you're doing this.'

'No, it's not.'

'And it's not for Vincent.'

Rob nodded his agreement.

'And it's certainly not for Lois.'

'No.'

'That leaves one person,' said Katie.

'Half an hour,' he said, kissing her on the cheek.

'Half an hour.'

Rob started shivering even before Katie drove off. For a split second his mind flashed on the torn-up remains of Lily Gronowski. He closed his eyes and tried to will the vision away, but he couldn't. Perhaps that's why he had agreed, to rid himself of the recollection once and for all. Looking down the throat of the devil himself was better than the prison of memory.

He walked to the creek, dry until today, and touched his toe in the water long enough to feel the wetness filter through his laces. The time had come.

Rob strolled back to the house thinking of all he had to do in the next thirty minutes. Still, he couldn't help but crawl back under the blanket and hide beneath the coffee table for the few precious minutes he could spare.

CHAPTER ELEVEN

Fade in. The bay marina at early dusk after a rain. Streams of sunlight sharper than crystals cut through wisps of fog.

Katie watched the skiff approach, its low outboard motor churning a widening wake in the glassy waters. Rob skippered the boat along the far shoreline, by where the Brenner place used to be, then north, skirting the swampy cattail flats, and swirling finally to arrive at Katie's feet. Following the rain, Rob's was the only boat on the bay, and the expanding ripples from its wake landed at the dock at the same time as he.

He wore thick brown hiking boots, a denim jacket buttoned to his collar, and a baseball cap shading his eyes. The fingers of a pair of rough leather work gloves protruded from his jacket pocket. He cut the engine and stood to give Katie a hand. She hopped in, wobbled momentarily, forgetting how precarious aluminum boats can be. She sat down to catch her balance, thankful she hadn't spilled over the edge.

Rob handed her a leather jacket. 'It'll cool down as soon as we get beyond the bay.'

Katie wrapped the jacket around her shoulders and immediately felt its warmth. 'I brought a blanket from the hotel. If we need it.'

It was her contribution, all she could think of, all she had, and she had promised herself she would repay Lois if the blanket was ruined or lost.

Rob pushed off and shifted the boat into gear. The engine responded briskly as Rob maneuvered through the narrow channel markers. The drone of the engine echoed off the low hills and returned slightly altered.

At the Brenner place, sure enough Katie saw a few tourists out of their cars, cameras slung around their necks, mulling about, not knowing what for, as if one of Alfred's cuff links might appear on the ground.

Rob remained silent, keeping a steady hand on the throttle arm, his eyes peeled in front of him, never wavering from the channel. He hoped Katie didn't notice his slight shivering, or, if she did, she would attribute it to the boat's vibration. The waters ahead he had traveled many times, but this journey was into territory he had vowed never to trespass again.

The murmur of the boat made Katie sleepy despite her excitement. When the channel widened, Rob throttled up with a blast of speed and headed into open seas. The boat slapped the water, sending cold shards of ocean spray across Katie's face. It felt good and helped her wake from her trance.

Once away from shore, Katie was able to comprehend the length and beauty of the coast. At each promontory point, monstrous rock formations stood sentry – tortured vestiges of outpost castles, a thousand Manderleys reduced to piles of rubble by the battering waves.

She spotted a small island to the right. 'What's that?' she asked.

'Bodega Rock. Shipwrecks and seals.'

Rob turned the boat north, and they rode by a white sand beach spread out on the coast like a dazzling necklace. 'Salmon Creek Beach,' he said.

The beach ended abruptly, replaced again by rugged shoreline with no hint of mercy. 'We'll dock at Duncan's Point, then continue on foot.'

Katie kept an eye peeled for a phantom beach on which to land but found none.

Rob gauged the sun, checked his watch, identified landmarks along the shore with his squinting eyes, skirted the waves like a dancer. Suddenly, he cut the engine and swerved inland, letting the waves push the boat slowly to shore.

Katie looked for a landing beach but spotted only the tiniest sliver of sand. Rob waited patiently for the waves to move them closer to the beach. When the boat drew close, he throttled once quickly for a burst of speed, then killed the engine and pulled it from the water. A single cresting wave was all the momentum needed to glide the boat gracefully onto the soft sand.

Rob hopped out, and with the aid of the next wave pulled the boat on shore. He unfurled a thin rope and wrapped it around a rock, making a quick expert knot. Katie stepped out and helped push the boat up even further.

'How do you know this place?' she asked.

'I used to dive for abalone here when I was a kid. Follow me,' Rob said.

He started up a steep trail of moist sand, slick with the recent rain. The trail snaked past colonies of purple mussels and gnarled cypress trees that leaned perpetually east, trained by the marine winds. Katie followed as best she could, but the smooth bottoms of her sneakers were no match for the slippery sand. Her fingernails filled with dirt as she struggled from hold to hold.

On top of the bluff Rob clasped Katie's hand and pulled her into the forest. They moved among the tree shadows like criminals searching for cover from the cops or whoever might be chasing them. Katie felt alive, alert, every pore open, every sense working at capacity.

Rob stopped and checked the calibrations known only to him. 'We're getting close,' he whispered.

He led Katie to a worn trail that looked familiar. She saw the green polyester thread twisting in the breeze, and turned west to see a string of smoke from Vincent's cabin.

'Shhhh,' Rob whispered, yanking Katie to a crouch.

'That's Vincent's—'

'Shhhh!' Rob covered her lips with his hand. '*Look*,' he mouthed.

To her horror Katie saw Madame Charay emerge from the cabin door. Balancing an empty tray of food on her palm, she pulled the door shut behind her and began the march up the trail, right toward Katie and Rob.

Rob pulled Katie off the trail and hid her behind a thick redwood. 'Now, don't move.'

Rob pressed his body against hers. Cheek against cheek, chest against chest, their breath and fingers mingling. Silently they listened to the quick little crunch of Madame Charay's feet as she approached. Katie held her breath, squeezed Rob's hand. She pulled in her stomach, pressed against the tree until she felt the bark rippling against her back, anything to allow Madame Charay to pass without spotting them.

The footsteps reached a crescendo. Katie squeezed Rob's hand tight and shut her eyes. Then, without a hitch in step, Madame Charay passed by.

Katie swallowed a few short breaths. After a wait she peeked around the tree to watch the small figure travel up the path.

At the exact same moment Madame Charay spun around. Katie froze in the beams of a hazardous gaze. Madame Charay sniffed the air, listened to the changes in the breeze, appraised the light and shadows, then she turned back and continued up the path out of sight.

Rob and Katie stayed pressed against the tree a few minutes more, longer than they needed to. Then Rob took Katie's hand and stepped onto the trail again.

They reached the cabin as the sun touched the ocean, a writhing sphere of heat extinguished by the rippling water.

Katie tiptoed to the cabin and rapped twice softly. 'Vincent?'

She tried the knob, and it released with a sharp click. She listened for a reaction inside, a shuffle, a shiver, a hello. All she heard was the squeak of the hinge as she let herself in.

The last rays filled the room with an ethereal gold light. Vincent sat up in bed, feeding bits of apple to Tony. Vincent smiled when he saw Katie.

'Hello, Vincent.' She held back Rob, not knowing how Vincent would react to a stranger, a man.

'Hello, Katie.'

'May I come in?'

'Yes.'

The rains had released a musty smell of the sea from the cabin walls, and the slanting sunlight struck Vincent's face at odd angles.

'You were right. It did rain.'

Vincent nodded.

'Vincent, there's someone I want you to meet.'

Vincent's face filled with concern.

'He's a friend.' Katie smiled. 'For me, please?'

Vincent nodded his consent with hesitation.

Katie pulled Rob inside and wrapped her arm in his to show that he was a trusted friend.

Vincent twisted in alarm. He swept up Tony and dropped him into his shirt, then sunk deeper into the hole in his bed.

'He's not going to hurt you, or Tony. He wants only to help, I promise you.'

Vincent seemed only slightly assured.

'My name is Robert. We met once, a long time ago. Do you remember?'

Katie looked at Rob. He hadn't told her. Vincent picked up on Katie's bewilderment and edged deeper under the covers.

'I . . . I don't remember,' Vincent stammered.

'That's okay, Vincent. It was a long time ago. You probably forgot. I hardly remember myself. I was a little boy, and you were older. But we can be friends now. Vincent, would you like that? I would.'

Vincent softened a little.

'Good. Because I like you, Vincent, and Katie likes you. She tells me wonderful things about you.'

Vincent waited, still unsure of the purpose of this visit.

'Rob just wants to ask you some questions. Some very simple

questions, just to make sure that you're all right. He's a *doctor*. Is that okay with you?' asked Katie.

Vincent studied this alien being with dark hair. Rob removed the cap so Vincent could see him better.

Vincent nodded yes.

'Thank you, Vincent.' Rob drew the lone chair closer to Vincent's bed, always mindful of keeping a respectful distance. How Vincent had aged, Rob thought, since the day of the murder.

Katie sat Indian-style on the barren floor. 'Here, I brought you something. I almost forgot,' she said.

Katie gave Vincent a Hershey bar. His eyes shined with delight as he unwrapped it feverishly. At the smell of chocolate, Tony emerged from the shirt and began sniffing about. Vincent shared tidbits with him – one chunk for Vincent, one crumb for Tony – until the candy bar was consumed and the foil crushed into a ball for Tony to nudge around with his nose like a circus seal.

'Vincent, will you look into my eyes for a moment?' said Rob. 'So I can see their color.'

Vincent obliged and Rob checked his pupils for dilation and asymmetry. No problem there, but Vincent's eyeballs trembled rapidly. What it meant, Rob wasn't sure. He *wasn't* a doctor. But he had enough training to know it was significant.

'Good, Vincent. You look very healthy. I can tell from your breathing. You breathe well. Do you know that? It's a gift to breathe well. Listen to your inhalation, see how deep it is? And your exhalation, it's so clear and strong. Inhale, exhale. Very good, Vincent. Breathe in, breathe out. In, out, like the waves. In, out, sometimes light, sometimes strong. In, out, sometimes pulling, sometimes pushing. In, out, sometimes crashing, sometimes silent. In, out, in, out. Now close your eyes, Vincent. In, out. Good.'

The lids of Vincent's eyes slowly closed and his breath turned slow and rhythmic.

'Now fill yourself with your breaths. In, out. Expand with

your breath. In, out. Expand your breath to your fingers, your toes. Take it higher, higher. Fly with your breath, hum with your breath, sing with your breath.'

Vincent's inhalations grew deep and firm, his nostrils quivered. Tony lay asleep in his lap.

'And now you're floating. Floating on the waves. Floating on the water. Floating on the waves in the sun on a warm day. Up, down; in, out. You're floating, Vincent, on the water, breathing in, out with the waves. In, out; up, down; floating. It's so peaceful on the water, breathing in, out on the waves. In, out. Good. Your arms are floating on the water, floating beside you on the water, chest high, in, out, on the water.'

Katie could hardly hide her amazement when Vincent's arms rose magically and undulated in the air as if floating on the gentle waves Rob was describing.

'Floating feels so good, doesn't it? Floating on the water. In, out; up, down. Good, Vincent. You're floating. Lower your arms now, back to your sides. Breathe in and out. Lower your arms. Good.'

Vincent's arms sunk back to the bed. What surprised Katie now was not Vincent, but Rob's intense demeanor.

'Now, Vincent, I want you to open your eyes. And I want you to focus on that knot in the wood on the ceiling. Do you see it? By the chimney flue, third board up.'

Vincent's eyes opened and locked tight on the knot. His eyeballs trembled no more.

Rob nodded. 'That's it. It's funny how shapes change when you look at them. Don't you think so, Vincent? They stretch and blur. They change color. Sometimes they are ringed by a halo of light, sometimes darker than night. Look at that knot and tell me what you see. Talk to me about the changing shapes as you look into the knot, your target. If your eyes wander, bring them back to the target. Always the target. Look now and concentrate on the knot, feel the knot, become the knot, understand the knot. Let your mind fall in on itself as you search the knot's meaning, your meaning, the target.'

Rob quieted to a whisper. Katie noticed his own breathing matched Vincent's. They sat still, Vincent locked on the gnarl and Rob locked on Vincent, breathing together, a dual engine of the altered state.

'Now use your breath to fuel your thoughts. And tell me, Vincent. Tell me what you see, what images flicker in your mind as you look at the target?'

Vincent sat up, brightened. 'A ship,' he singsonged.

'A ship. That's good. A ship where, Vincent?'

'A ship in the sea, *silly*.'

Vincent was no longer the adult Vincent, but a frolicsome Vincent. A child Vincent.

'And what is the ship doing?'

Vincent's gaze ventured further into the knot. 'It's sailing.'

'Sailing where?'

Vincent turned pensive with a new perception. 'Sailing here.'

'To Petty's Cove?'

'To Petty's Cove.'

'How old are you, Vincent, at Petty's Cove when the ship is sailing here?'

'I am eight and a half. One hundred and thirty two days until my birthday. Lily taught me to count backward from 365, 366 in leap years, but this isn't a leap year.'

'Vinnie. What is happening around you at eight and a half years old?'

Vincent's face animated with interior images, the same contortions and constructions Katie had seen the moment of her first farewell with her brother. Only now the emotions, the expressions, were subtler, milder, a million miles away, the thousandth reflection.

Vincent pouted. 'Mummy has my hand, and she is taking me back.'

'Back where?'

'To the house, the big house. Mummy holds my hand. It's warm in the sun. *May I stay outside, Mama? May I please?* "No", she says. "We have to go. We must."'

'Go where, Vincent?'

'To the basement. The room in the basement. The dark room. I pull away, but Mama has me good. "Stop being a wicked little boy," she yells. She's hurting my wrists. I don't want to go. I want to play outside. But I walk down the stairs nicely, so she doesn't push me. "Now put this on," she yells.'

'Put what on?' asked Rob.

'The dress. That old lady's black dress and knit shawl. The ones Mummy always tells me not to get dirty. And the wig. Mummy gives me the gray wig, and I put it on because she'll hit me if I don't. "Now put on your shoes," she says. I am putting on the shoes, those ugly witch shoes with high heels.'

Vincent fidgeted, sealed his eyes tight, buttoned his lips.

'What is it, Vincent? What's happening?' Rob asked.

'*Please, Mummy, no*. She is painting my face gray with ashes. *I don't want to look like a skeleton, Mama*. "Sit still!" she yells. "Do as I say." I am sitting as still as I can. *I don't like this, Mummy*. "Shut up," she yells. "Now, play dead. Play dead." I sit still in the creaky chair, so still it hurts. "Now say your line," she tells me. "Say it with feeling." *A boy's best friend is his mother. A boy's best friend is his mother. A boy's best friend is his mother*. I repeat it, and repeat and repeat forever.'

'Then what happens?'

Vincent cocked his head ever so slightly to the left, as if remembering for the first time.

'Then she lets them in.'

'Them? Lets who in?'

'The sailors,' Vincent said calmly.

'What sailors?'

'From the ships.'

'The ships that you saw?'

'Yes.'

'What are the sailors doing?'

'Having a party.' Vincent smiled. 'We're all having a party.'

'And what are *you* doing at the party?'

'Playing games.'

'What kind of games? What are you playing right now, Vincent?'

'Jacks. I drop the ball and pick up two. Drop it again and pick up three.'

'Jacks. Are you winning?'

'They *always* let me win.'

Vincent paused, thinking to himself for a long time.

'What's happening, Vincent?'

'They're leaving.'

'The sailors?'

'The party's over. I wave good-bye. Mummy says, "Take off that dress. You got the shawl dirty again. You embarrassed Mummy. You're always embarrassing Mummy," she yells. "You're *psycho*." But I don't care what she says because I am free to go. I pull on my shorts and run out to play. Oh, the sun feels so warm.'

'Where are you now?'

'In the courtyard with—' Vincent paused. A look of sublime delight painted his face.

'Who are you with, Vincent?'

'Lily.' He beamed.

'Lily who?'

'Beautiful Lily.'

'What is Lily doing?'

'She is singing. We are singing together. *Mother, Mother, I am ill. Send for the doctor over the hill. "Mumps," said the doctor. "Measles," said the nurse. "Nothing," said the lady with the alligator purse.* Lily puts flowers in my hair and caresses my ear.'

'You like Lily?'

'Oh, yes. My sister. She cares for me. Lily.'

Suddenly Vincent's face changed again, filling with great urgency, panic. His voice changed too.

'The knot is changing,' he cried. 'Changing.'

'What is it now? Tell me.'

Pure horror across his face. 'A truck.'

'What kind of truck?'

'With cages. *No, Ma, no!*'

'How old are you?' Rob asked urgently.

'I am thirteen.'

'What is happening, Vincent?'

'The men are getting out.'

'What men?'

'The men in white. *Don't let them take me, Mom.* They grab my wrists. *Don't grab my wrist, you meanies.* They are putting me in the back of the truck. *I'll be good, Mother. I promise.*'

Vincent flayed his arms in a savage struggle with the imaginary men in white. Katie feared Vincent might hurt himself. She looked to Rob, but he would not depart from his questioning.

'Where are they taking you?' he asked.

'To the hospital. Mummy says, "Teach him a lesson, boys." *Get your hands off of me. Mummy, help!*'

Katie touched Rob's arm. She couldn't bear to see Vincent like this anymore. 'Stop it,' Katie whispered in Rob's ear.

'Not yet.'

Suddenly Vincent's face transfigured to woe. 'It's changing,' he said.

'What's changing?'

'The knot.'

'What is it now, Vincent?'

'A stain.'

'A stain of what?'

'A stain of blood,' he moaned.

'Where is the stain of blood?'

'In the hospital.'

'How old are you, Vincent?'

'I am fifteen.'

'Whose blood is it, Vincent?'

Vincent started crying.

'It's mine.'

'Why are you bleeding?'

'They hit me. They hit me across the face. *I'm so cold.*'

'Who hit you?'

Vincent's eyes filled with hatred.

'Them. The orderlies. They always hit me.'

'Why did they hit you?'

Vincent wept with waves of pain.

'Rob, please, *stop* him,' Katie pleaded.

Rob ignored her. His face seethed with intensity. 'Why, Vincent, why did they hit you?'

Vincent's body shivered.

'Tell me,' pressed Rob. 'Why did they hit you, Vincent? Why?'

'Please, stop it.' Katie tugged at Rob's arm.

Rob shrugged her off.

'Tell me why they hit you, Vincent. Tell me why.'

'Stop it!' Katie screamed.

Vincent halted his sobs long enough to speak in a sheepish voice of pure shame.

'Because I wet my pants,' Vincent cried.

Katie grabbed Rob by the chin and turned him to face her. 'Stop it, now,' she demanded.

She wasn't ready for his expression, filled with a fiery intensity, a negative of everything Katie had come to know about him. He was a fire-breathing dragon with bursting veins in his forehead and the wild gaze of a predator.

'Rob, what is happening to you? Stop it.'

Rob looked at her, through her.

'Stop it. You're scaring me.'

But Rob wasn't hearing, wasn't listening, wasn't here.

Katie slapped him across the face sharply.

'Stop it!'

The strike shook Rob from the spell. The veins recessed, and his gaze returned to civility. His breathing slowed.

'I'm sorry,' he said, shaking himself from the trance.

'Are you all right? What happened?' Katie asked.

'I don't know.'

He turned to Vincent and in a calm voice continued. 'Vincent, I want you to look at the knot. Once again look at the knot.'

Vincent refocused.

'*I'll* tell you what it is now, Vincent. It's a balloon. A big, hot-air balloon. You're stepping into it, Vincent. Into the basket of the balloon. And it's taking you away. Away from the hospital. Away from the blood. It's taking you away from the past. You're traveling up, up into the sky. Higher than the trees, higher than the clouds, higher than your worries. It's so peaceful as you float up, float away from your troubles. You're floating, Vincent, floating to the present day, to the *now*. And you're coming down. Coming down in your cabin. You're landing now, setting down, softly, slowly, peacefully. No fear. Just the here and now, and you, Vincent. Together again. Home.'

With that, Vincent's eyes shut and his head slumped on his shoulder.

He began to snore.

Rob gently laid Vincent's head on the pillow. Tony woke and crawled into Vincent's shirt.

'Is he going to be okay?'

She turned for an answer and saw the pain in Rob's face, a terrible, sorrowful pain. She didn't understand it, but she couldn't question it, not while Rob trembled like this.

She pulled up the covers around Vincent's neck and tucked him in. She kissed him on his soft cheek, and felt the warmth of his skin.

'Come on, let's go,' Rob whispered, wiping the sweat from his brow. 'He'll sleep well tonight.'

CHAPTER TWELVE

She didn't ask him on the boat ride back, not right away. Not while he stoically piloted the boat, piercing the night sky with his stare, pretending to keep a keen eye out for other vessels, obstructions, sudden rocks. But there were no such threats. The water was calm, the moon full enough to illuminate two worlds, and the shore safely several hundreds yards off. Katie pulled the jacket collar up around her neck and waited silently.

After leaving Vincent's, they had hustled back down to the beach where the tide was already lapping the boat's stern. Another few minutes, a half an hour maybe, and the beach would have been swallowed by the sea, the boat lost or crumpled against the rock like the foil from Vincent's chocolate bar.

Skipping along the swells, Rob tried several times to bring up the throttle, but the little outboard churned water as fast as it could and no faster. Not until they reached the cradle of the bay and were cruising safely in the narrow path of the channel did Rob relax. And Katie picked her moment.

'What happened back there?' Katie asked.

Rob emerged from the grip of his deep thoughts. 'Vincent recalled some very painful childhood memories.' He spoke with the detached voice of a clinician. 'It's not easy going back in time. It takes a tremendous amount of courage, even under hypnosis. I'd say it was an extremely productive session, though I'm somewhat concerned about the randomness of his recollections. That's highly unusual. Psychologically speaking.'

'I mean, what happened to *you*, Rob?'

Rob took his eye off the straight course home. 'Me?'

'Yes, something happened to you. You changed there. Became another person.'

'You're right. I haven't conducted a hypnosis session in a very long time. I'd forgotten how emotional they can become, for the hypnotist as well as the subject. It's a well-documented phenomenon.'

'It was more than that. There was some connection between you and Vincent.'

'Purely clinical, I assure you.'

Katie wasn't convinced. They rode past the Brenner place. A single flashlight, wholly inadequate for the job, scanned the site in search of whatever it was the faithful searched for, whatever it was that Alfred had touched in their subconscious, and touched still with every screening. But it wasn't there, and Katie wanted to shout out to them. Whatever they were looking for, it wasn't there. Not now, not ever.

She turned back to Rob. 'You said you met Vincent once. You never mentioned that to me.'

Rob slowed the boat to a crawl and started the final wide turn to the docks. 'We did meet briefly once. I knew he wouldn't remember me, but it gave me an opportunity to test his veracity, an important criterion when hypnotizing someone. A trance doesn't always produce the truth, you know. People can lie under hypnosis.'

The flashlight at the Brenner farmhouse flicked off. Katie heard the roar of an engine and the glint of metal as a car pulled away from the vanished set.

'And you never saw him again?'

'Maybe once or twice. It's a small town.'

'Once or twice.' Katie tried to sound innocuous. 'You knew your way up there pretty well.'

'Any boy growing up along the coast knows every beach and bluff north and south of here. That's what young boys do, explore. Lord knows there's little else to do in this town.'

He had all the answers.

Katie saw the docks loom nearer, and she knew her time with Rob would soon be up. 'We have to go back, for Vincent's sake. Don't you think?'

Rob shook his head vigorously. 'Absolutely not. It's not worth the risk.'

'The only risk is that we'll never know the truth about what happened the day Lily was murdered – if Vincent was even there. And if he wasn't there, that tells us everything we need to know.'

'Twenty minutes ago you were urging me to stop hypnotizing him, and now you want me to go up there again?'

She watched the channel markers pass by them as they chugged into town. 'I was scared, and now I'm not. Doesn't that ever happen to you?'

'Yes, it does,' Rob said. 'But it's not the point. He could fake it under hypnosis. He could accuse an innocent person.'

'Do you think he was faking it tonight?'

Rob aimed the boat for an unoccupied slip. 'No. No, he wasn't.'

'Then will you do it? To find out the truth? For Vincent's sake?'

'I don't think so,' Rob said softly.

'But why?'

'Did you see his eyes before I put him under? The way they shuddered ever so slightly like there was a small earthquake in his head?'

'I did.'

'The medical term is nystagmus, if I remember correctly. It's an indication of cerebral damage to the portion of the brain that controls balance and coordination. He must have suffered some sort of head trauma or other injury in his childhood. It could be congenital, I don't know. But the fact is, once I observed it, I should never have gone ahead with the hypnosis. It was foolish. I took a chance. Who knows what could have happened? A seizure, a coma, a psychotic reaction. There's no telling. I was lucky to bring him out of it. If I hypnotize him again, we may not be so lucky. And then I'd have a very hard time explaining to my peer review board why I hypnotized a high-risk patient, without consent, no less. So you'll have to excuse me if I decline. But I can't risk it, for Vincent or for me.'

Katie saw the silhouettes of the romantic diners in the large windows of The Tides. They held hands, kissed over candlelight with not a care in the world. She heard the sound of fishing boats rubbing against the docks. 'Rob, why won't you tell me?'

'Tell you what?'

'Tell me what happened between you and Vincent years ago. Tell me your involvement in all of this.'

He maneuvered the boat into the thin slip no wider than the boat itself, almost magically, without touching the sides.

'Nothing,' he whispered. 'Believe me, Katie. Nothing happened at all.'

Frustrated, Katie looked up to the lights of town. She followed the blue and red of a police car as it weaved through the narrow streets and made a few familiar turns.

'Isn't that The Nest?' Katie asked.

'Where?'

'Right there, where the police car just parked,' said Katie.

'Oh, my God. Lois.'

Lois frowned. She preferred getting the clean laundry into the rooms earlier than this, but the day had been filled with so many errands – the bank to secure the loan to keep the place going, the laundromat for the sheets she should have washed days ago, the grocery store for the jams and breads for guests that didn't come. Guests who resisted straying too far from the main highway. Guests who loved day trips but preferred staying in San Francisco or Santa Rosa, where shopping malls and movie theaters served as ready distractions. If it were not for the brief summer season and long holiday weekends, The Nest would have been locked up long ago. Lois wondered how long she could live like this, from summer to summer, weekend to weekend, scrimping and saving, borrowing money in the winter to pay for the lights, only to pay it back with her summer profits. At least Rob's income was stable; she could look forward to that.

She thought of all these things as she approached Katie's room with sheets and fresh towels.

Fumbling for her keys, Lois noticed the door unlocked and slightly ajar. Her management research had indicated that security was a top concern among the upscale clients she hoped to attract. Consequently, the doorknob had been set to automatically lock on closure, unless overridden inside. And Lois had instructed the workmen to adjust the hinges so that the door would gently swing shut on its own.

So Katie was fidgeting with the locks and doors, was she? Or could she really be as absentminded as she appeared? No, Lois guessed Katie had simply lost her key. That was a fifteen-dollar additional charge and Lois was glad to collect it, thank you.

Lois tried to shut the door behind her but found a corner of the rug tucked in the jamb. Oh, so this breach of security was intentional on Katie's part? Who was this Katie anyway? What did Lois really know of her?

Lois took a sidelong glance up and down the hallway. She prided herself on the privacy she offered her guests, but this was different. Katie was different.

Lois tiptoed into the room and set the sheets and towels on the bed right next to the shirt.

She did a double take. A blue-cotton *man*'s shirt.

Funny, Rob had one just like that. Lois brought it to her nose. Underneath Katie's cheap perfume, Lois smelled Rob's unmistakable musky scent. The bitch.

Lois's hesitation vanished. She went about the business of snooping with the precise efficiency with which she approached all her duties. She opened the dresser drawers, not sure what to look for or what she might find but determined to find evidence of something.

She found nothing but the little balls of dust she had asked Lucinda to clean time and again. She flung open the armoire.

Three wire hangers dangled from the bar. She pulled out the drawer of the nightstand and saw only the Bible placed there by the Gideons and barely disturbed since.

She fingered her way into Katie's only piece of luggage, a torn vinyl overnight bag, rescued from the litter bin, Lois was sure. A few T-shirts, a sweater, all in need of a good washing.

Lois picked up the towels and headed for the bathroom. If ever there were clues to be uncovered about a woman it was in the bathroom. The light had been left on. She hated guests who wasted electricity.

She sniffed the vanity for signs that this girl was anything but a pauper masquerading as someone respectable. She found a small compact of rouge, a toothbrush, toothpaste, and a hairbrush with synthetic bristles. How primitive. Lois was glad Katie had paid in cash.

She heard a shuffle in the bathtub, behind the shower curtain.

What was Katie hiding? A dog? Lois detested pets. They chewed up everything, cut the rugs with their sharp little claws, and left a foul smell, which their owners swore didn't exist. Now *this* was against house rules, and Katie would have to go.

Lois ripped back the curtain.

He struck fist-first, a blow that split Lois's lip and sent a spray of blood across the ceramic tile.

The second punch sent Lois crashing against the wall. She slipped on a thin puddle of water turning pink with her blood and fell face-first on the floor. Going down, she had only a moment to see the intruder.

He was gloved and masked in black, all black. He pinned Lois's neck to the floor with the heel of his thick black boot.

From the corner of her eye, gasping for breath, Lois saw a short metal pipe dangling menacingly above her head.

'No! Please don't hurt me. I'll give you money. I have money downstairs.'

At the sound of her voice, the stranger released his foothold. He spun Lois around to face her. He lifted the metal pipe to strike, then brought it down slowly to his side. Breathing like a bull, he pushed the bloody hair from her eyes and studied her face.

Lois locked her knees tight and brought them to her chest. 'Take anything you like. Just please don't hurt me. Don't *touch* me.'

'You're not her,' he said.

'Not who?' asked Lois.

He didn't answer.

Instead, he fled from the room like a wounded animal.

Lois pressed an ear to the cold bathroom floor. She heard him take the wooden stairs in three sudden leaps, heard the front door slap open and shut, heard his footsteps race away on the granite slabs of the front path.

She lay panting, her lip swelling, and the blood drying in her hair.

And she cried. Cried because he almost touched her. Cried because of this cage she had built for herself that sucked every fiber of gladness from her marrow. Cried for Rob's shirt.

She cried only for a moment. Then she drew strength from the smell of ammonia on the floor and dragged herself up to call the police.

Because nobody does this to Lois Mandible.

Deputy Berwick was well into his inquiry when Rob and Katie raced in. They entered with such a commotion that Berwick rested his palm on the butt of his revolver until he determined these were friends, not foes.

'What happened?' asked Rob. He raced to Lois, who sat at the dining-room table clutching a handkerchief, a fat lip distorting her classic beauty.

'Looks like Ms Mandible had a burglary here,' Berwick grinned, proud of his detective work. He was a large, strapping farm boy not two years out of college, or high school, or from wherever they recruited them now, and squeaky clean in his smartly creased brown uniform.

'A *robbery*,' Lois corrected him.

Rob stroked back a lock of Lois's hair that had escaped from her tight wrap, still wet from a shower. Katie's skin crawled at the sight.

'Now, don't go jumping to conclusions,' said Berwick. 'From what I can tell it was a burglary in progress. Typical B and E. We've had lots of them lately down in Bolinas and as far up as Sea Ranch. Looks like a professional job. Shanked the lock clean open.'

'But he had a mask and a lead pipe,' Lois argued.

Berwick waved the suggestion away. 'Standard MO. The last thing a burglar wants is to get caught, so he brings a mask. He didn't have a gun, right? If he were intent on robbery he would have brought a gun, don't you think? You can buy 'em nowadays cheaper than a Monday-night dinner. But they don't like to do that, see, because then it's *armed* robbery if they're caught. So they bring a pipe.'

'Let me get some ice for your lip,' Katie offered.

'Which room was hit?' Rob asked.

Berwick glanced down at his report. 'Room sixteen.'

Katie stopped in her tracks. 'That's my room.'

Berwick tipped her a hat. 'I'm glad you're here, then; you can take inventory. Tell me if anything is missing.'

'But I . . . I didn't really have anything to steal.'

'Even if they didn't get anything, it's a burglary nonetheless. The law's the law.'

'A *robbery*,' Lois corrected him again impatiently.

'Whatever you want to call it, the question is, what can we do about it?' asked Rob.

'The usual. Check for fingerprints, look for tire markings.'

'He ran away on foot; I heard him,' said Lois.

'Well, one less thing to do, then,' Berwick said. 'And if you say he wore gloves, there isn't much use in taking prints. I'd have to call a detective from Santa Rosa for prints. With budget cuts and all, they don't like to come out on simple burglaries, especially this far. If they dusted every burglary they'd spend all their time chasing down cheap jewelry. Doesn't make sense in these times of high crime.'

'But he *hit* me. That's a crime,' argued Lois.

'I've got that right here in the report.'

Lois stomped her foot. 'This isn't fair. I pay my taxes. This is my home. My business. Rob, *do* something.'

Rob struggled for words, then said: 'Well, what did he look like?'

Lois's eyes rolled in her head. 'I told you, he was wearing a mask. But he was caucasian. And I saw his eyes. They looked like . . . like *Katie*'s eyes!'

Lois squinted and pointed a finger at Katie. 'Like *hers*.'

Katie felt guilty. 'Me?' she stammered.

'Yes, you. Your eyes. *Those* eyes. That color. And he said something to me, now I remember. Something strange. He said "You're not her." *Her*. He was looking for Katie. Oh, how could he mistake me for *her*?'

'Me?' said Katie, pointing to herself.

'Anyone out to get you, Miss Jacobs?' asked Berwick. 'Are you running from a boyfriend in the city? We've got strong new rules on domestic violence in Sonoma County.'

Katie looked to Rob for help. But his hands were tied with Lois's.

'No. Not one. I mean, I have boyfriends, but none who would chase me. I live a very boring life, believe me.'

Berwick's rumpled brow indicated that his investigation was taking a new direction. 'Are you on business up here midweek? Because we don't get very many visitors up here midweek.'

'Well, yes and no. I was told I have a brother who lives up here, but I couldn't find him.'

'What's his name?' asked Berwick.

Katie cringed. 'Vincent. Vincent Jacobs.' The moment she blurted out his name, Katie regretted telling the truth.

'Hmm, Jacobs,' mulled Berwick. 'I don't know a Jacobs.

Of course, there are the Jacobsons on Valley Ford Road, but they're well over ninety and never had any kids. No, I don't know a Jacobs, but that don't mean much. I've only been in the west county for a few months.'

A wide-eyed look of recognition filled Lois's face. 'That's it! That's who the attacker was. Vincent Jacobs.'

'You know him?' asked Berwick.

'Not personally,' said Lois. 'But I saw him once, down at the beach at night. It was horrible. I remember his face, those eyes. It was Vinnie Jacobs who attacked me. His eyes. Katie's eyes.'

Rob jumped from his seat. 'That couldn't be,' he said resoundingly.

'And why not?' Lois demanded.

'Because. I know Vincent Jacobs from my practice. He suffers from severe schizophrenia. Now, that's confidential, deputy, I shouldn't be telling you this. But he's incapable of committing such a crime. It couldn't be him.'

Despite Rob's testimonial, Berwick pondered the possibility. 'Where does he live?' he asked.

Rob risked a glance at Katie.

'Up at Petty's Cove,' Rob mumbled.

'Oh, yeah. With that eccentric old lady. They told me about her.'

'But it couldn't be him,' Rob continued, impassioned. 'Take my word for it. My professional word. Not Vincent Jacobs.'

Lois planted her hands on her hips. 'Are you calling me a liar, Rob?'

'No. I'm just saying you must have been mistaken. You were frightened, that's all. He had a mask. You said so yourself.'

'I *know* what I saw.'

Rob turned to Berwick for judgment. 'Believe me, deputy, it couldn't be him.'

Berwick squinted his eyes in thought, proud to play King Solomon. 'Well, Dr Du Maurier, maybe it couldn't be him. I don't doubt your professional opinion. But tell me why, then, did Katie say she couldn't find her brother? After all, you know him and know where he lives.'

All eyes turned to Katie. Christ, she always got caught when she lied. Her mind raced with lies, threats, confessions, fears, not the least of which was that it truly could be Vincent. She stammered, pleaded for a miracle.

Rob intervened. 'I'll tell you why, deputy. She's protecting him. His psyche is very fragile. A visit from a police officer could tip him over the edge.'

Thank you, Rob.

'Everybody's scared of the police, doctor,' said Berwick. 'Maybe I need to take a ride up there, see for myself.'

'No!' Rob shouted.

'Rob, what has gotten into you?' Lois demanded.

'Please don't, deputy. There's no need to,' said Rob.

'I'll make that decision.'

'Wait, there's more,' said Rob. He turned to Katie. There was nothing else he could do, and Katie knew it. 'We were just up at his place.'

'Rob,' Lois scolded him. 'What is going on?'

'I put him under a sedative, to sleep. There's no way he could get here. It would take him a hour to walk to town *if* he were conscious. And he doesn't drive, believe me. Lois is simply mistaken, deputy. It wasn't Vincent Jacobs. You have my word and I'll testify to that in court.'

'That's right,' Katie added proudly.

Berwick took turns sizing up the three players before him and seemed to come to a new conclusion concerning the dynamics of the situation.

'Well, I'll let you three figure it out. Meanwhile, I'll file the report without visiting Vincent *for now*.'

Katie's sigh of relief coincided with Rob's, leaving Lois all the more incensed.

Berwick picked his massive body up. 'Well, that'll do it for me. Miss Jacobs, would you please call in the morning with the inventory of missing items? Meanwhile, lock your doors, all of you, though the safest time is after a burglary because you know they're not coming back. Good evening.'

'Good evening,' Lois grinned.

She waited for Berwick to leave before she turned to her fiancé with eyes of fury. 'Robert, we need to talk.'

Katie moved quietly toward the stairs. 'Maybe I should leave you two alone.'

'No!' shouted Lois. 'I think it's confession time around here. Wouldn't you agree, Rob?'

Rob lowered his eyes.

Katie slunk back to the table.

Lois seethed. 'I don't know what you two are up to, what little games you're playing. But I think Rob's got something to tell you. Go on, tell her, dear. Don't keep her hanging.'

'What are you talking about?' asked Katie.

'Don't play innocent with me, Katie. I saw Rob's shirt in your room.'

Katie turned red. 'There's nothing going on, I assure you,' she stammered. 'Rob's helping me with some family business, that's all.'

'I don't disbelieve you for a second. If I didn't know him better, I'd be jealous. Let me ask you, did he kiss you, Katie? Did he come on nice and strong and sensual, and then silently rejoice when a minor disturbance or objection pulled him away?'

Katie was stunned by Lois's alacrity. 'And what if he did?'

'That's my Robbie,' Lois smiled. 'Ask him. Ask him to tell you one of his little secrets. Then maybe you won't be thrilled to come home in one of his shirts.'

'Rob, you don't have to tell me anything,' said Katie, though she was dying to know.

'Oh, yes, he does. Come on, Rob. It's not fair to the female gender to keep it a secret. Let's see how much she cares for you after you tell her. Be a man. You see, Katie, Rob thinks women like him for his brains, his looks, but that gets tiresome, weary, after awhile. I keep telling him, *women these days . . .*' Lois flung up her hands in mock gesture.

'All right!' said Rob, lifting his head. 'Okay. I'll tell her if that makes you happy. I'll tell her. And then you won't have anything to lord over me anymore.'

'Go on,' said Lois with a smile of pleasure.

'Rob, stop,' Katie interrupted. 'I don't need any explanations. I don't deserve one. You've done enough to help me.'

'No, I want to tell you.'

Rob clasped his hands in his lap. He started a few times before stuttering to a stop. Finally he said, 'I have a condition. A male condition.'

'Oh, don't couch it in medical terms,' said Lois impatiently. 'You always do that when your back is up against the wall. Let me tell her. Give me the pleasure. I get so few.'

Lois turned to Katie with the relish of juicy gossip. 'Do you know what his *condition* is? It's funny really, considering how worked up they get about it. He's impotent, Katie. As in *cannot-get-it-up*. It's not so unusual, I guess. Men always sense failure before the act and women afterward. Except with Rob it's not a temporary thing. I don't think he's ever actually *been* with a girl. Not in the real sense. And women today, they've gotta have it. All except me. I'm the only one who will have him. The only one to share his little secret. Well, the three of us now, quite an unusual ménage à trois. But I don't mind his *condition*. Suits me fine since the pleasures of the flesh never did much for me. Rob and Lois, call it a match made in heaven. So don't get your hopes up, dear girl, because this boy's coming back to Mommy.'

'I'm sorry, Katie.' Rob melted with remorse, a little boy caught in a petty crime, believing it a felony.

Katie stood up, enough of Lois's petulance. 'Sorry for what? We all have our weaknesses, our deficiencies, our haunting pasts. I won't even ask what you were doing up in my room, Lois.'

'Nothing!'

'Rob is willing to admit his failings. How about you, Lois? What are you hiding? What little secrets drive you? No, don't tell me. I don't want to know. I don't want to have to feel pity for you. I'm sure you have plenty for yourself.'

Katie walked over to Rob and wrapped her arms around his shoulders. And she stood there, rocking him, feeling his pain, wanting so badly to kiss it all away.

CHAPTER THIRTEEN

As soon as she awoke, Katie called Deputy Berwick to inform him that nothing was missing from her room, hoping the news would help shuffle the burglary report to the bottom of the pile.

It couldn't have been Vincent, Katie told herself. Lois had been wrong in her hasty identification, plain and simple. Nevertheless, Katie studied the brochure map and was not comforted to discover that Petty's Cove was much closer to town than she had thought. Vincent could easily have cut inland by foot and beaten them to The Nest.

Katie refused to entertain such a notion, fully aware that her gullible heart had steered her wrong before. But if it wasn't Vincent, who was it? An anonymous burglar, as Berwick had suggested? Peter Grow? A coincidence? If Rob hadn't been with her, Katie might have suspected him too.

The evening had ended with Rob making a quick exit, preceded by a petition from Lois for him to stay the night. How could she, Katie thought, after all she had put him through. Rob didn't stay, thank God. For any other crime Katie could forgive him, but not for crawling back to Lois's arms after the way she humiliated him.

Tossing and turning in bed, Katie had sworn she'd take it up with Lois again in the morning. She thought of a million clever rejoinders she wished she had thought of in the heat of the moment. But a restless sleep had zapped much of her gumption, and in the morning light she shuddered at the thought of having to face Lois again.

To her relief, she didn't find Lois roosting behind the counter as usual. The B&B was under the provisional management of a woman with the most alluring almond eyes Katie had ever seen. Her name was Lucinda, she said, and in halting English with an abundance of *I'm sorrys* explained that Lois was *indisposed.*

That was fine with Katie. She smiled profusely, settled up, and strolled into the morning, fresh from the rain. She flipped up the convertible to let in the warmth of the sunshine and peeled away happily from The Nest, hoping never to return.

The day was squeaky clean; the houses, the streets, the leaves – everything gleamed. San Francisco seemed like history now, a shadowy dream too distant to recall. Funny how a few days can turn a reality into a dream. If only dreams could be turned into reality with such ease.

She drove the short few blocks to town thinking about Rob and his revelation. She didn't believe it, first of all. Not that it wasn't true presently, or had been in the past, or when Rob was with Lois. But Katie refused to believe it was a permanent condition, if that was the right phrase for it. No, Rob was too sensual by nature not to feel emotions of love, desire, arousal. It had to be something else, something psychological, something revocable. Katie wouldn't have it any other way, not in her dreams.

She wondered if she could enter into a lifelong relationship with such a man? Certainly there were alternative ways of conceiving children, and that's what mattered most, Katie told herself. She felt guilty for even thinking that intimate relations mattered when one was truly and deeply in love with someone.

She parked alongside a pickup truck with a frisky pig tethered in the back. He snorted with great interest as Katie searched the short block for Village Hall.

It took her far longer to find than expected. The government office was hidden in a slim storefront sandwiched in between a bait shop and a souvenir store. She had made the mistake of looking for a stately building with columns, or some such architectural clue of bureaucracy at work.

She walked in making the same mistake again, looking for a mighty bronze plaque or emblem proclaiming this to be the official post of the Village of Bodega Bay. Instead, she found a tiny walkup counter with a warped Formica top and a rusty desk bell.

'Excuse me. Is this where they keep the records of birth and death?'

The village clerk wore the weary expression of career civil servants holding out for retirement and nothing else. Katie saw a pack of menthol Newports on the woman's desk, a cigarette sticking out ready for the next break.

'Some of them.' The clerk groaned off her chair and met Katie at the counter. 'They started taking them to the county office in Santa Rosa in '82. More room there. But we still have the records from before then. People come here mostly to pay taxes or grumble about them. Every once in a while we grant a building permit.'

'I'm looking for a certificate for a Lily Gronowski. That would be April 29, 1980.'

'Birth or death?'

'I'm sorry. Death.'

'Because the birth certificates are much easier to find. We keep them up front because people need them when they lose their driver's license or apply for a passport. But death certificates, well, once their owners are gone and buried, there's not much interest in them anymore – the people or the paper.'

'Sorry for the inconvenience,' Katie said. 'But I'm sure this is death.'

'Okay, but it will take me a minute.'

'I'm in no rush.' Katie smiled.

The clerk picked up the cigarettes on the way to the back room. A few minutes turned into fifteen before she returned, reeking of smoke but wearing a smile. Who was Katie to judge the pleasures that drove people to their deaths? Sometimes Katie wished she had one or two.

Katie had hoped an autopsy report might be attached, but the certificate was a single legal-sized sheet of paper. Katie had also foolishly envisioned something along the lines of parchment with scripted lettering. But the document was as perfunctory as could be, more like an application for a job or auto insurance than a document to certify an event as monumental as the death of someone's child. Once in her hands, Katie realized she had no idea what she was looking for.

She started at the top. Lily's date of birth was listed as July 1, 1963. Madame Victorine Charay was listed as her mother. Ferris Gronowski her father, deceased. Katie skimmed the legal gibberish until she came to cause of death. *Predatory animal attack, possibly brown bear or mountain lion. An exact determination is not possible due to the severity of the injuries and the inability to identify and capture the animal.*

Animal attack. Just as editor Rankin had said.

'You done?' asked the clerk. 'Because I got the file drawer open in the back and I don't like to do that. Smoke kind of gets in there and I get in trouble.'

Katie wished she wasn't done, but she couldn't think of anything else she could learn from the document or even why she had been compelled to review it. Perhaps it was to confirm Lily had really been killed, that this entire affair wasn't a bad dream or a cruel joke. 'Yes, I'm done.'

Just as Katie handed back the document, something caught her eye. A name. At the bottom of the page. Under the title of acting coroner. Katie yanked the certificate back and read the typed name out loud.

'Dr R. Du Maurier.'

Du Maurier. That was Rob's name. Katie examined the scribble that passed for a signature. Her hands trembled. Dr R. Du Maurier? Dr *Rob* Du Maurier, she mumbled to herself. How can that be? Rob was a boy when the murder occurred. He said so himself, twelve years old. Oh, my God, an ageless vampire.

Katie showed the signature to the clerk and echoed her fears. 'Is this Dr Rob Du Maurier?'

The clerk took the certificate back for a look. She chuckled with a raspy smoker's voice that for an instant reminded Katie of her mother.

'I know Dr Rob. He treated my teenaged daughter, my youngest, when she fell into a depression after her thirty-year-old boyfriend dumped her. Thank God he did, the bum. No, that signature isn't his.'

'Then whose?'

'That's Robert's father. Dr *Richard* Du Maurier.'

Katie nearly swooned into a faint. 'His father?'

Of course, his father was a doctor. Acting coroner, the document said. If the elected coroner had been on vacation or unavailable, the police naturally would turn to the local doctor, Dr Richard Du Maurier. 'May I make a copy of this?'

'Sure, but it will cost you twenty-five cents. City's on a budget too.'

'No problem.' Katie reached in her pocket and plucked out a crumpled twenty-dollar bill but no change. She had left it all on the dresser as a tip for the maid. 'This is all I have.'

'Well, since it's only one copy, I guess I can give it to you for nothing.'

Katie waited impatiently while the clerk took it to the back room. For the first time in her life she craved a cigarette, and she understood her mother just a little bit more.

The stream in front of Rob's place flowed swiftly, but the house was still. Katie knocked, though something told her that after last night Rob was not taking visitors.

How could he keep something like this from her? Did she know him at all? Were all the men in this little town bred for strangeness?

She knocked again. No answer, of course. Men didn't answer their doors around here; they waited for women to barge in.

The front door was locked, so Katie marched around back and up a short staircase leading to the kitchen. She let herself in without a qualm. Quite a bad habit she was picking up in Bodega Bay.

'Rob?' Katie called softly.

The darkness was stifling, and Katie pulled up the blinds over a stack of dirty dishes. She tiptoed into the dining room, which looked like it hadn't been used in years, and through a swinging door into the dark living room.

She felt around for a light switch without any luck. The only window in the room was on the far wall. All she could make out in the darkness was a pile of blankets on the floor.

'Rob?' she called softly. She started across the room.

Halfway across, suddenly a hand shot out from underneath the blankets. It grabbed Katie by the ankle and twisted her down to her knees. She tried to flee, but the hand held her like a cuff.

Katie clamped her hands together. She closed her eyes and with all her might slammed her fists down on the moving mass of covers.

'Ouch!' a voice returned.

Rob's head emerged. 'What the hell are you doing?' He let free her ankle.

Katie caught her breath from the fright. 'You grabbed me.'

'Of course I did. I thought you were a thief or something.'

'I'm sorry,' said Katie.

'A little late for that.'

Katie fretted over the damage. She had never hit anyone in her life, not like that. 'Let me get you some ice.'

Rob touched the bump quickly forming on his forehead. 'That's okay. What are you doing here?'

'The back door was open.'

'Oh, so that gives you every right to just waltz on in. What do you want?'

'The truth.'

Rob shook off his stupor and looked into her eyes. 'Last night wasn't enough for you?'

'No, it wasn't,' said Katie. 'Look at this.'

Katie handed him the copy of the death certificate.

Rob took a cursory glance and handed it back. 'You beat me up for this?'

'Look at the signature at the bottom.'

It took a moment for Rob to focus. When he saw the signature he jumped to his knees.

'That's my father!'

'You didn't know?' asked Katie. She studied him for every minute reaction.

'Know? How could I?'

'How could you not? Your involvement with Vincent. Now your father. Every time we're together there's a new revelation. What is going on here?'

Rob handed the certificate back to Katie. 'You're crazy,' he said.

'Me? Look at *you*. You're sleeping in your clothes in the middle of the floor. Your reaction to Vincent yesterday. Your condition. You're not telling me everything. And I want to know, Rob. I need to know.'

Rob shrugged his shoulders and sighed. 'Honest to God, this is the first I heard of this. What can I say?'

'Start with your father.'

Rob sat up and licked the sleep from his teeth.

'My father? Now, there's a story. Where do I begin? The way he drove my mother to her grave with his insane jealousy and drunken affairs? Or with my earliest memory of him? Forcing me into a closet for the crime of giggling when he happened to walk by. He terrified me when I did something wrong, found fault when I did something right. But why am I complaining? I guess I was luckier than most. He didn't smack me around or abuse me, just ignored me mostly, the great American dad.'

Katie felt a wave of empathy, a small wave. 'Not all fathers are bad.'

'Yeah? What about yours?' asked Rob.

'He was a Hollywood producer. He left when I was young. I have vague memories, no more.'

'Consider yourself lucky.'

'I do, but let's not change the subject. Why did he conduct the autopsy? What's he got to do with this?'

'I don't know,' Rob said.

'Yes, you do.'

'I don't.'

'Rob, you're lying.'

'I'm not, God damn it!'

Rob jumped from the blankets and pointed to the door with a trembling finger. 'I'm not. And if you think I'm lying you get out. I never asked you to come. I never asked to be part of your little adventure with Vincent. I never asked you to step between me and Lois. Get out and don't come back. I'm sorry I ever set eyes on you.'

'All right, I'll leave, and I won't come back. But you know what? Lois was right. All your fancy talk about art and psychology, it means nothing. It means nothing because you don't have the courage to look inside you. You don't have a fraction of the courage that you ask your clients to summon every day when they're sitting in your office trying to piece together their shattered lives. You bet I'll leave, and you can crawl back to Lois, if that's what you want. And I'll find the truth about Vincent on my own. I don't need your help.'

Katie huffed to the door, shaking with the sting of her words. It felt good finally to speak the truth without worrying about the consequences, if he'll like her later, or if she'll regret it forever. It felt good to burn a bridge.

Alone, that's the way it had been always and the way it was going to be, the sooner she accepted it the better. No better time to start. She marched down the porch steps without any inclination to turn around.

'Katie,' he called softly. 'Wait.'

Katie stopped out of politeness, but she refused to turn. She couldn't falter, not now. 'I have things to do.'

'No, wait. You're right, Katie. Everything you say is right.'

'Don't patronize me.'

'I'm not. I mean it.'

'Well, that's fine, and I'm flattered, but it doesn't matter anymore.' Katie took a step toward her car.

'Stop! Please come back. Come back and I'll tell you everything. Just don't go.'

Katie wanted to continue, but she couldn't. She swung to look at Rob, his pleading eyes filled with sincerity. 'I'm listening.'

'Please come back in. And I'll tell you everything. But don't say I didn't warn you. It's not pretty.'

Should she believe him? No, but she was willing to give him a chance. One. The first hint of deceit or trickery and she was gone.

Katie followed him inside and sat on the edge of the couch, arms crossed, legs crossed. Rob plunked down on the armchair and wrapped a blanket around his head and body so only his face showed. Even then, the brim of the blanket shadowed his eyes from Katie's unyielding glare.

'First of all, I didn't know about my father's signature. I honestly didn't. Today is the first I saw it. That whole period of my life is a haze. You have to believe me. But it makes sense now why he signed it. It only confirms my suspicions.'

'What suspicions?'

'I have something to tell you, something I've never told anyone, not even Lois. And you're right, I haven't been fully truthful with you. I guess this is confession week, though not by my choice. The truth, the whole truth? I'll give it to you plain, but I'll need your understanding. Can you promise me that, a little understanding?'

'I'll try.' Katie wiped the sweat from her palms.

'Don't leave until I tell you everything. And above all, don't jump to conclusions until I've finished.'

Rob slipped the blanket off his head. He found a half-empty can of coke and took a swig. He swished the soda around in his mouth and grimaced before swallowing a mouthful.

'I don't know why, but I have this memory. And it keeps recurring like a bad dream. Only it comes of its own accord, day or night, asleep or awake, and it stays for days, like a bad habit or an unshakable addiction. I have no recollection of why I was up there, or how I got there in the first place. But my memory takes place at Vincent's cabin. The mind can play strange games. Lord knows I've seen my share of messed-up people believing things they couldn't have done or swearing innocence over clear acts of guilt. Maybe I was there, maybe I wasn't. I don't know. But the vision, this image is so clear, so crystal clear, that I can't believe it's a figment of my imagination. Katie, I was there. I was there the afternoon Lily was murdered. In my mind I was there.'

Katie caught her breath. 'Go on.'

'And in my vision, I see Lily. I see her being killed. No, that's wrong. I don't see *her*, I see shadows through a half-closed window of the cabin – the window behind Vincent when we hypnotized him, you remember? More than that, my memory is of hearing her being killed. Hearing her screams of terror from inside the cabin, hearing her moans of pain as the beating drones on endlessly, hearing her final cry of madness, hearing the pounding, the beating, the tearing of flesh that continued for minutes, hours after her last cry. I don't recall how long it lasted. How can you measure time when reality is in question? All I know is, it was near dark before it was all over. And that's when I braved a peek in the window, when I saw Lily lying there, every inch of flesh ripped from her body, a red mass of tissue and bone, hardly human, let alone female and beautiful, like Vincent describes her. And that's the memory that runs through my head, the endless loop that starts and stops of its own accord, my twilight zone.'

Katie rested her hand on his. 'You were a young boy who wandered upon a terrible scene, a murder.'

'No, wait. I'm not done. Save your pity. You may not need it. There's more.' Rob pulled his hand away. He leaned back, closed his eyes and swayed slightly as he spoke.

'Sometimes I try so hard to recall, to remember who was with her in that cabin. Who spent the afternoon ripping her to shreds. Who killed Lily a million times over after she was already dead. Was it Vincent? I thought so for a while. It could still be. I don't know. Was it someone else? Possibly. I can't rule it out. But sometimes, just sometimes, when I'm in the darkest throes of the vision, unconnected from this world in every way, deep in that hell inside of me, I think I know. I think I know who it was.'

'Tell me.' Katie's voice quivered.

'Me.'

Katie muttered something unintelligible even to herself. She eyed the door ready to flee, unsure of the madness in front of her.

Rob gazed up at her. 'Puts things in a different light, doesn't it?' he said.

'I guess it does,' Katie confessed.

'So now you know why my father lied on the death certificate. And I do too. To save me. And now I know why he sent me away quickly after the murder. So no one could find out, before I could do more damage. It all makes sense now. And it confirms my greatest fear.'

Rob took another swig of flat soda. 'Do you despise me now, like I despise myself?'

'No,' Katie said, though she wasn't sure how she felt.

'Now you're lying. Look, why don't you go to the police, get it over with. I don't care anymore. If it stops the memories, I'll be happy to spend the rest of my days in prison.'

Katie weighed the option, and all the others that came to mind.

'I have one question for you, Rob.'

'What?'

'When you are awake and thinking clearly, in a sound state of mind, do you think you did it? Do you really think it was you?'

Rob sighed and looked Katie straight in the eyes. 'I don't know. I honestly don't know.'

'Well, then, it's clear what we have to do.'

'What?'

'You think you killed Lily, Vincent thinks he killed Lily. You can't both be right. True?'

'True.'

'Let's solve it.'

Rob chuckled. 'And what's your plan this time – hypnotize myself?'

'Talk to your father.'

'Oh, no.' Rob shook his head vigorously.

'Don't you see? He knows the truth. He knows what happened. You have to go see him. *We* have to go see him.'

'I told you. Go to the police, do what you must, but I'm not going to my father.'

'Why not?'

'Because I just can't. You don't understand him. Us. It's not a normal relationship between father and son, parent and child.'

'Yeah? Well, one day I'll tell you about my mother and we'll compare notes. But we have to see him. Rob, please do this for Vincent, for you.'

Rob considered the suggestion for a moment. 'And if he confirms my suspicions, what then?'

What could she say? She took a gulp of the flat soda and tried not to look optimistic.

CHAPTER FOURTEEN

They drove south in Rob's Jeep, out of town past the last gas station. These barren hills that had appeared alien to Katie days ago now seemed so natural, as if she had always lived here or had been born down the street. She reminded herself not to feel too comfortable; she was, after all, driving to God knows where with a guy who didn't know himself if he was a murderer or not. Was he going to throw her out of the car at high speed, or strangle her in a frenzy?

They made a left turn at a road sign that pointed to Bodega, and Katie was happy to find a pretext for conversation.

'Bodega? I thought we just came from Bodega?' asked Katie.

'That's Bodega Bay. There are two towns a few miles apart.'

Katie saw the old schoolhouse on the hill, a lonely, gloomy structure with its tall arched windows and antiquated bell tower, looking just as ominous as it had in the film. Katie remembered the scene well. Inside the classroom Suzanne Pleshette leads the children in song while outside Tippi Hedren smokes a cigarette and waits for class to end, oblivious to the flock of crows amassing on the jungle gym behind her.

'I thought the schoolhouse was in Bodega Bay,' Katie said.

'He used both towns and made it seem like one. Editing and splicing, the tricks of film.'

'Not unlike the tricks of the mind,' Katie said.

Rob took a right down a dirt road, then a left down yet another dirt road.

'Look, I don't know what we're going to find. He could be dead for all I know. More than likely nothing has changed, nothing in a million years.'

Rob was interrupted by the sound of gunshots. Two in quick succession, enormous blasts that filled the valley with echoes.

Katie turned to Rob to confirm her alarm. But Rob hardly flinched.

'Birds and small animals. His hobby.'

Katie nodded politely while her stomach turned. With life so fragile and death inevitable, it always sickened Katie to think people killed for pleasure.

The road quickly deteriorated into a deep set of tire ruts that whipped the Jeep around like a ride at a carnival. Katie was glad to see a chain draped across the road, marking the end.

She waited for Rob to stop, but instead he veered sharply and climbed a steep embankment around the chain. The maneuver tipped the Jeep precariously and drove Katie's fingernails into the soft dashboard. So that's how he was going to do it? Crush her in a car wreck.

When she opened her eyes the Jeep was on level ground on the other side of the chain, rumbling over an overgrown driveway.

'Do you do that often?'

'Lock is rusted shut. It's the only way.'

The house was a stately Virginia mansion fallen into disrepair, encroached on all sides by overgrown thickets of brush. With its facade of civility it looked entirely out of place in this wilderness, as if it had been picked up whole from some charming Southern hamlet and dropped here accidentally, or perhaps intentionally as banishment for sins unknown.

A stout little dog barked insistently and wagged itself in circles at the end of a short chain.

Rob parked and let the dog free. 'A blue heeler. Buster. I'm surprised he's still alive.'

The dog sprinted to a muddy puddle for a drink. He didn't stop until the water was gone and he licked nothing but mud.

Then he returned to Rob's side and licked his hand in a bid for affection.

Rod's father emerged from the bushes, mud boots up to his knees and a double-barreled shotgun slung across his chest. His hair was as white as salt and cropped in the uneven manner of someone who cuts his own. Katie felt his eyes look right through her as he marched toward them with a steady gait. He was a handsome man, and the resemblance between Rob and his father was impossible to miss. This was Rob in thirty years.

'Hello, Dad,' Rob said without emotion.

'Well, look what we have here. Is this your wife?'

'No, this is my friend, Katie. Katie Jacobs.'

The old man looked her up and down. 'Jacobs, eh? I see the similarity. Is she a slut like her mother?' he said.

Rob pulled Katie by the arm and started toward the Jeep. 'Let's go. We're getting out of here.'

'No, Rob,' pleaded Katie. She turned to his father. 'You knew my mother?'

'Everyone knew your mother. At least, all the men.'

Rob eyed Katie with astonishment. 'Your mother lived up here?'

Katie hadn't told him; it never seemed relevant. 'I'm sorry,' she said, the wrath of father and son upon her. 'She was up here briefly, during the filming of *The Birds*.'

'Long enough to rattle a few marriages and dirty the town with syphilis,' said Dr Du Maurier.

'That's not true,' Katie shot back.

'Let's go,' Rob insisted.

'He can say anything he wants. It doesn't bother me,' said Katie.

'A tough one,' said Dr Du Maurier. 'I'm surprised, Rob. I thought you'd choose a doormat.'

Rob squeezed Katie's arm. 'I said, let's go.'

Katie pulled away and scolded Rob. 'Don't you see what he's doing? He's driving you away again. Don't let him, Rob. Not this time.'

'She's right. I need to talk to you, Dad.'

Dr Du Maurier strolled toward the house. 'We all have our problems. Leave me alone.'

Rob followed close behind. 'I think you owe it to me.'

Dr Du Maurier laughed. 'Owe you? Are you still on that? *Big bad daddy screwed you all up.* Is that how it goes?'

'Not anymore. This time it's father be damned while son finds out the truth.'

Dr Du Maurier pointed an imaginary gun at his son's face and squeezed the trigger. 'You get out of here,' he said coldly.

He marched to the house and slammed the front door, but not before Rob shouldered his way in. 'You're not going to scare me away this time.'

Dr Du Maurier ignored the company as he walked through the unfurnished living room and into the den, a room filled with the overstuffed heads of dead animals peering down from the walls. Against one wall a massive glass-enclosed gun cabinet proudly displayed twelve or fifteen shotguns and rifles, more than Katie cared to look at.

Rob's father poured himself a shot of Johnnie Walker Black. He downed it and poured another.

'So what is it you want? Ask me and get the hell out.'

Rob wasted no time. 'There was a death many years back. April 29, 1980, to be exact. Lily Gronowski.'

'Madame Charay's daughter.'

'You know her?'

'Don't tell me you don't remember?' said Dr Du Maurier.

'Remember what?'

'You are in pitiful shape. Forget it.'

'Forget what?'

'I said, forget it.'

Rob unfolded the certificate and handed it to his father. 'Look at this. You conducted the autopsy. You signed the death certificate.'

Dr Du Maurier fumbled for his reading glasses and scanned the document.

'Animal mauling. I remember.'

'How many autopsies have you performed?' asked Rob.

'Two, three. What is this, an interrogation?'

'It was a murder, Dad, not an accidental death. Not an animal mauling.'

'Don't dare talk back to me, boy. You don't know what you're talking about.'

'But you're going to tell me. What happened up there at that cabin?'

Katie saw the muscles flex in Rob's face. She watched the strength rising in him, the power of his purpose.

Dr Du Maurier poured himself another drink. 'What happened? Just what I said in the report, that's what happened.'

'You're lying.'

'I don't have to defend myself against this drivel.'

'You were hiding something then and you're hiding something now.'

'Hide from you, son? I don't hide from anyone.'

'So what is it that keeps you a prisoner up here, and keeps me a prisoner of my past?'

'Is that why you came here? To shame me?'

'You retired right after the murder. You sent me to Oregon. It all happened so closely together. Didn't it? It's funny how things seem to a child. Those events felt years apart to me. But it was days, hours between them. Boom, boom, boom, all in a row, all connected, cause and effect. Why? That's what I want to know.'

'I told you, it wasn't a murder. It's there, in the report. Animal mauling.'

'Why was I there, Dad? Why was I up at that cabin where Lily was murdered? Why do I remember it so vividly?'

'I stand by my report. Period.'

'Is it because I did it? Because I killed that girl? Is that it? Did you cover for me?'

Dr Du Maurier slapped Rob across the face.

'I've never heard such foolishness. Now, you listen here.

You take your harebrained ideas and your tramp and you get off my property. And don't you ever come back.'

'You can't shut me out anymore, Dad. Did I kill Lily? Tell me, for God's sake. Give me that much.'

Dr Du Maurier calmly opened a desk drawer. He drew out a polished revolver, popped open the chamber and spun it around like a lottery wheel, making sure both guests saw it was fully loaded.

'You know something, son, you've always been a royal pain in the ass.'

He aimed the gun at Katie's eyes and drew the hammer back with his dirty thumb. 'Now, I said get out.'

Katie tugged at Rob's sleeve. 'I think we'd better go.'

Rob eyes filled with anger. He pointed a finger back at his father. 'It's not over, Dad. It's not over because you're a coward, and cowards always lose. Believe me, I know.'

'You don't know shit, boy.'

Katie tugged on Rob.

'I'll be back,' said Rob.

His father laughed. 'Who are you, Schwarzenegger?'

Rob lunged, but Katie pulled him back.

'You'll see,' said Rob. 'You'll see.'

Outside, Buster clamored to jump into the Jeep, but Rob shooed him away and slammed the door.

The rebuff didn't stop Buster from chasing the Jeep down the driveway, his little legs cutting full speed through the clouds of dust and exhaust. With each backward glance, Katie saw him trail a little further, until she looked back and he was gone.

Rob spoke without looking at Katie. 'You know, sometimes I think we're all in our own private traps. As much as we struggle or pray, curse out loud or wish otherwise, we remain entangled forever. Forever trapped.'

As recently as a few days ago, Katie might have agreed with him but no more. 'If the trap is of our own making than isn't it true that we must also pose as the key? I have to believe that we can free ourselves, though it may take all our might and all our lives and even then the scars will forever serve to remind us of the unhealed wound inside.'

Rob wasn't listening to her quaint sentiment. He pulled his foot from the accelerator and let the Jeep roll to a stop.

Katie looked at him quizzically. 'What is it?'

'Something he said.'

'What?'

'We have to go back.' Rob slammed it into reverse and spun the vehicle around.

'What? Tell me,' Katie asked again.

'A word he used. The way he said it.'

Rob picked up speed. They passed the dog trotting back to the house, his mouth frothy from exertion, his expression filled with confusion over the comings and goings.

'What word?' Katie could not recall any unusual word, let along one strong enough to turn Rob back to face his father.

'Shame,' said Rob. He screeched to a stop at the house. 'You stay here.'

'No, I'm coming with you.'

Katie followed Rob into the den, not knowing what they were looking for, what they would find.

She stopped cold at the threshold. 'Oh, my God.'

The body lay sprawled behind the desk. A halo of blood surrounded his face, and the muzzle of the revolver was still in his mouth. The crown of his head had blown off like a hat in the wind, and his eyes were rolled upward in their sockets, as if inspecting the carnage above.

'Good Lord.' Katie buried her face in her hands.

'I should have known,' was all Rob said.

Deputy Berwick was not so cavalier in his assumptions this time around. Nor did he hesitate to bring in detectives from Santa Rosa, three of them.

Rob went over the story a hundred times, the same one he had practiced quickly with Katie before the police had arrived.

'I hadn't spoken to my dad in a few weeks,' Rob explained

to Detective Thurman. 'And the last time we did speak, he sounded distraught. So I drove up here this morning. My friend Katie was in town, and I asked her to come with me. We talked to him briefly and left after a few minutes. But I felt something was wrong, and we raced back to this.'

The story sounded simple enough. But when Detective Gaffney pulled Katie aside and asked her to repeat it, her guilty skin burned like gasoline.

'How long did you talk to the doctor?' asked Gaffney.

'Oh, five minutes, maybe ten. I'm no judge of time.'

'What did you talk about?'

'His state of health, mostly. Diarrhea.'

'Did he seem distraught?'

'Sort of, I'd have to say, yes.'

'Then why did you leave?'

'Well, because . . . you see . . . we didn't think he would *shoot* himself. There's a big difference between being upset and suicide.'

'And you determined that in five or ten minutes?'

'Look, I don't know. Rob's the psychologist. It's his father. I'm just here visiting.'

'Why?'

'Why what?'

'Why are you visiting?'

'All right, you caught me. To get away from a boyfriend in the city. He beats me nightly with a stick.'

'You don't look beat up.'

'I've got good skin. Like my mother.'

'What's she got to do with this?'

'Everything.'

After a few minutes Gaffney left Katie to study the way Dr Du Maurier's fingers wrapped around the trigger. Thurman spent his time estimating the distance the good doctor was blown back before his skull broke free from the force. Benjamin followed the line of blood spatters arcing over the wall and ceiling, then poked at the fleshy periphery of the wound with his pen.

The three lawmen talked it over in a corner for a good half-hour before breaking and strolling back wearing poker faces.

Surely they had seen through Katie's flimsy responses. Surely they were going to slap handcuffs on both of them. Katie rubbed her wrists and readied a confession, contemplated a life in prison.

Benjamin spoke for all three detectives. 'Looks like suicide all right. I guess you two can leave,' he said.

'That's it?' asked Katie.

'Unless you have something else to tell us.'

'No,' said Katie, wide-eyed.

'You can always change your story.'

'There's nothing to change.' Katie smiled. She felt her legs pumping, ready for a sprint.

But Rob wouldn't leave. Not until he completed the details by phone with the mortuary over in Petaluma and confirmed that a plot had been reserved in the local cemetery. It seemed like he was on the phone for hours, making many of the same provisions she had for her mother days ago. Katie sat in a corner of the living room watching the business of death. The photographs, the unraveling of the body bag, the endless reports to be filled out.

Maybe Rob was right. Maybe we can try with all our might to change our miserable little lives, but in truth we are simply running a treadmill in a cage we can't see, fighting a futile battle against forces too great to be reckoned with.

Rob returned looking spent.

'Rob, I'm so sorry.'

'Me too. Let's go.'

It wasn't quite dusk when they left the house. Rob let Buster into the Jeep this time. The dog spent the ride at the window catching the scent of freedom with canine determination. The shadows had grown long and a breeze kicked up the dust. Katie felt a chill run through her bones. She didn't complain. It was punishment for her part in the death of Rob's father, for not telling Rob about her mother, for disturbing so many things.

She shivered at the thought of Dr Du Maurier's words about her mother. No one understood her mother. It wasn't the men that mattered. They were a means to an end. A foolish means to a worthless end, maybe, but at least she had a dream. She sacrificed everything for a few brief seconds of immortality on screen and a mention on that swift credit roll at the end of every picture that nobody ever stuck around to watch. Katie admired her mother for her tenacity. And she regretted not telling her while she was alive.

They stopped at Rob's place only long enough to drop off the dog and grab some gear. Then they headed to the wharf, where Rob's little boat bobbed gently in the waves. They worked silently like a team, not needing to exchange words or glances, understanding fully the task at hand, their roles to be played, the dangers ahead.

Rob started the engine, and Katie pushed the boat away from the pier. As they cut across the bay Katie glanced across at the Brenner place. She understood a little better the small congregation of the faithful gathering at the altar of their fears.

CHAPTER FIFTEEN

They came upon Vincent from the south. He sat by the rocks of the cliff, watching a pair of egrets fly low across the water, their wings always in danger of touching the swells but never doing so, as if some sixth sense divined the water's intent. He sat erect, legs crossed, twittling a piece of grass in his fingers while gazing upon the setting sun, its exaggerated palette of colors now so familiar to Katie.

Rob walked a few paces behind Katie, evaluating Vincent's demeanor, happy to see him cognizant. She crunched a twig underfoot, a warning to Vincent that visitors were approaching. Vincent didn't seem to notice.

'It's us again,' Katie called loudly.

Not a twitch.

Katie approached slowly.

'Vincent?' She leaned over his shoulder, peering down on his pockmarked cheeks, his rusty hair.

'Go away,' he muttered.

'Vincent, why?' asked Katie, saddened by the rejection.

'Madame Charay doesn't like you here. Go away.'

Katie shot a glance at Rob.

'She knows?' Rob asked.

Vincent nodded yes.

'You're right, Vincent,' said Rob. 'We shouldn't have come. And we won't come again unless we ask her. Okay? But we're here now, so can we stay? Just a few minutes?'

Vincent flung the blade of grass over the edge, but it didn't drop. Instead it rose higher with a gust of wind until the gust died and the blade fluttered to the sea like a lost feather.

'Okay,' Vincent said.

But it didn't seem okay, not to Katie, and she never wanted to ask Vincent to do something against his will.

'If *you* want us to leave, Vincent, we will. What would you like?'

'Stay,' he said.

Rob took a seat next to him, shared the vista, emulated his posture, synchronized his breathing.

'We were here last night, Vincent. Do you remember what happened?' Rob spoke calmly, fatherly.

'We talked.'

'That's right. Talked about what?'

'Tony. Chocolate.'

'We did. Do you remember anything else?'

Vincent took time to explore the question. 'I don't remember.'

'Do you remember anything about sailors?'

Vincent's face turned quizzical. 'No.'

'Do you remember going to town last night? Did you try to visit Katie in her hotel room?'

Vincent gazed at Rob and Katie with a blank stare, unsure of the meaning of the question or perhaps playing dumb, Katie didn't know which.

'That's okay, Vincent, you don't have to answer.'

Rob scanned the horizon. His eyes stopped on a ship, a tanker of some sort, so far out it looked like it wasn't moving at all.

'You see that ship in the distance? Vincent, I want you to stare at that ship, that target, just like we did yesterday. And I want you to breathe again, deep breaths. In, out. Just like yesterday.'

Katie glanced up the trail, fighting a suspicion that someone was watching from the shadows of the trees.

'That's good,' said Rob. 'In, out. In, out.'

Vincent complied, and soon he was unable to drag his eyes from the silhouette of the tanker that moved but didn't.

Katie gulped down her fear. As much as she wanted the truth, she understood the dire ramifications of the moment. Police, renewed investigations, arrests, accusations, trials, all these were possible. Worst of all, barring some unforeseen circumstance, Vincent or Rob might be forced to spend the rest of their lives behind bars or in an insane asylum.

A wisp of fog materialized out of nowhere and the egrets flew around it, through it, happy for the camouflage in their never-ending search for sustenance.

Rob spoke in measured words and Vincent followed the rhythm. 'Now, Vincent. I want to take you back in time, to a very specific date. It is April 29, 1980, a warm, spring afternoon following a week of rains. The earth is moist, the grass is sweet and green, and the flowers are in bloom. Breathe in, out. In, out. And tell me, Vincent, what you are doing today?'

Vincent took some moments before arriving at the date, then his face sprang to life. 'Caressing her cheek,' he said.

'Good, Vincent.' Rob closed his eyes, and Katie understood that he was returning in time as well, tuning himself to the same temporal frequency as Vincent.

'Whose cheek?'

'Lily's.' Vincent touched an invisible cheek in front of him, as if Lily was with him now.

'You like to caress her cheek?'

Vincent smiled sheepishly. 'Yes.'

'Where are you?'

'In my cabin.'

'And what are you doing in your cabin?'

'Lily is lying on the bed. I am sitting next to her.'

'Tell me more.'

'She takes my fingers and licks them one by one. Then she puts my hand on her cheek and she giggles. She is so beautiful, Lily.'

'What happens next?'

'She says. "Vincent, you've grown since last year; you've become a man."'

Vincent's face contorted with befuddlement.

'What is it, Vincent?'

'I'm not a man. I don't feel like a man.'

'Go on,' said Rob.

'Lily licks my lips with her tongue. She giggles. I hear her breath. I smell her like roses. She is kissing me with her lips, her tongue. Blood is rising inside me. I need air. I pull away. I can't be with Lily. I can't.'

'Why not?'

Vincent's face became anguished, fretful. 'Because she is too good for me. Too beautiful.'

'But you want to be with her, don't you?'

'No. Yes. It feels good, very good, I don't know. I'm so confused. She says. "Why won't you kiss me? Aren't I pretty enough?" *I think you're beautiful. Honest to God, Lily. The prettiest girl in the world.* Lily smiles. She licks my finger. "Did you kiss the girls at the hospital?" she asks. I don't want to tell her. I can't tell her.'

'Tell her what, Vincent?'

'I never kissed a girl before. I don't know how.'

'Go on.'

'She wraps her hand around my neck and pulls me to her, pressing her tongue into my mouth. Oh, I'm scared. I'm so scared.'

'Why are you scared?'

Vincent began panting in short, bothered huffs. 'Scared she'll laugh at me. *Don't laugh at me, Lily, please.*'

'Does she laugh, Vincent?'

'No.'

'What happens next?'

'Lily takes my hands, both of them, and lays them on her breasts. My heart is pounding. I've never touched a girl's breast before. I pull my hands away, and she puts them back. I leave them there because that's what Lily wants.'

'And you like to please Lily.'

'Yes. She lays her hands on my hands. She moves my hands about, massaging her breasts until they are flat and I feel her nipples grow harder. She unbuttons my shirt, one button at a time. I'm embarrassed, frightened. It feels good. I want her to do it, but I don't. *I don't know. I don't know.*'

Vincent's face turned flush red, engorged with his anguish.

'Keep going, Vincent.'

'She licks her finger and runs it down my chest, tickling my belly button. "Don't you like it?" she says. *Yes. Yes, I do.* "Me too," she says. She slips off my shirt and I try to put it back, but she won't let me. She kisses me hard. Her tongue burrows into my mouth. She smells so good, her lips are soft. I pull away and she laughs at me. *Don't laugh, Lily.* "Are you frightened?" she asks. "I bet I know why. You're a virgin, aren't you?" *Yes, I am.* She giggles. *Don't laugh.* "That's okay, Vincent. I am too."'

'Go on.'

'She says. "Have you ever seen a girl's breasts before?" I nod my head no. She smiles and says. "Would you like to see mine?" I nod yes. "Close your eyes and don't open them until I tell you," she says. I shut my eyes tight, real tight, and I count. *One, two, three, four, five, six, seven, eight, nine, ten, eleven, twelve.* "You can open them now." I open my eyes. I see her skin and her shoulders. Her nipples are brown like Tootsie Rolls.'

Vincent became flustered, disturbed. He pulled his knees together.

'What is it?' Rob asked.

'I don't know. I'm wetting in my pants, like I do in my dreams or when I touch myself. It comes in throbs and feels like buckets, like waves running through me, like the sun, like a dream. I look down and I see it.'

'See what?'

'The wet spot. A tiny wet spot on my pants. *Oh, God.* Lily sees it. *Don't laugh, Lily.* Lily laughs. "You silly boy," she says. *Don't laugh at me.* "You wet your pants and you didn't even touch my breasts. You *are* a virgin." Then she says. "Here, Vincent, touch my breast. Kiss it with your lips, right here." She points to her nipple and I kiss it hard. She giggles, and she touches me there, down there by the wet spot.

'She presses my head, my lips to her nipple. I kiss it because she wants me to. Then she unbuttons her pants and slides her hand down there. She starts groaning and moaning. Am I doing something wrong? Am I hurting her? I try to pull away to keep from hurting her, but she presses me forward. "Don't stop," she says. I push harder, kissing her nipple, fumbling to keep it in my mouth as she squirms on the bed. She groans loudly. I feel her body throbbing.'

Suddenly Vincent gripped his knees tightly. A look of alarm ripped across his face, sending shivers through Katie's fingers.

Katie searched the darkening woods for the pair of eyes she felt certain was staring them down. Did Vincent see something?

'What is it, Vincent?' asked Rob.

'We hear a noise,' Vincent whispered. 'A noise outside the cabin. "What was that?" Lily asks. "Is it *him*?" She pushes me away and buttons her shirt frantically. "Button your shirt," she scolds me. But I can't. I fumble; my fingers aren't working. *Work, fingers, work!* She panics. "Hurry. Do you know what he'll do if he finds us? Do you know what he'll do?"'

Katie squeezed Rob's hands. His eyes were fixed on Vincent, on the single question that consumed him.

'Go on, Vincent, tell us what happened next.'

Vincent's fear reduced his voice to a whisper. Rob closed his eyes and synchronized his memory to Vincent's, a soundtrack to a silent picture, the final screening.

'The door. Someone is opening the door. Lily hides her bra under my pillow. "Hurry!" she yells. But I can't; my fingers aren't working. *Oh, God, no.* The door creaks open and the light blinds my eyes. I am trapped in the sleeves of my shirt. "Hurry!" Lily yells.'

'Who is it, Vincent? Is it—' Rob stumbled on his own name.

'I can't see. The sun is shining in my eyes. I can't see. But he is angry, I can see it in Lily's face. She tells him: "We were only *playing*. Vincent's a *boy*, a boy, that's all." He slaps her across the cheek. *Don't hit Lily*, I yell. He turns to me. "Retard," he says. He hits me in the face with his fist. *Mama*. Blood runs into my eyes. "Leave him alone," Lily yells. She jumps from the bed to protect me.'

'Who is he, Vincent? Who?'

'He catches her and throws her against the wall. I hear the thump of her head. Her hair is caught on the bark. *Leave her alone!* I shout. I jump on his back and tear my fingernails into his face.'

'Who is it, Vincent? Tell me.'

'He grabs me by the hair and pulls me off. He punches me in the face. Again and again. I fall to the ground. Blood flows from my nose. I can't breathe. He pulls out a pipe and hits me in the knee. I hear a crack. So much pain. "Stupid retard," he says.'

'I *command* you, Vincent, to tell me who it is.'

But Vincent cannot stop responding, a captive to his vision.

'He grabs Lily's arms and shakes her. She screams. "Let me go! Let me go!" She bites him and kicks him. *Don't hit Lily. Hit me*. I try to stand, but my knee buckles.'

Vincent paused. His mouth fell open in horror.

'What is it, Vincent? What is happening?'

'He pulls it out of his pocket.'

'Pulls what?'

'The eagle claw.'

'What eagle claw?'

Katie knows.

She had touched it, commented on its weight and mass. 'The brass door knocker from the big house,' she said.

The image of the instrument flashed in Rob's mind too. He knew it, remembered it, visualized it clearly. And it filled him with dread.

'What does he do with it?' Rob's voice trembled, his whole body a quivering stream of anticipation.

Vincent closed his eyes, no longer needing the horizon's ship to see into the past.

'He hits her with the claw. Across her face, across her cheek. It rips her cheek. *Oh, Lily.* She bites and claws, tries to get away. My knee won't let me stand. *Oh, Lily.* He strikes her again. *No.* Blood. *No!* Lily's face. *Lily.* She struggles so hard. *Beautiful Lily.* "Vincent, help me," she cries. She reaches out to me. "Vincent, help!" *Hit me.* He rips her shirt off. I see her breasts, the breasts I just kissed. She tries to cover them but he pulls her arms away. *Hit me.* He strikes her breast with the claw. *God, no. Hit me.* He strikes the other breast. Claws it. *Hit me!* Hacks it until it starts shredding. *Lily, God, Lily. Me. Me. Hit me!* She falls, lifeless, limp. Her eyes stare into nowhere. *Oh, Lily.* What has he done? He keeps hitting her with the claw. Ripping, shredding, tearing. *My Lily.* And then he turns her over and rips more, rips more.'

Vincent collapsed into sobs.

Rob jumped to his feet, his mouth frothing, a wild stare in his eyes. '*Who*, Vincent? Who is killing Lily? Tell me now.'

'It is him. *Him*,' Vincent said, so obvious to him.

'Who is *him*? Who is it, Vincent?' Rob demanded.

'Him. Our brother,' he said softly.

'Whose brother?'

'My brother. Lily's brother.'

'What's his *name*, for God's sake?'

'Peter,' Vincent whispered through his sobs. 'Peter.'

'Grow,' Katie filled in the last name. 'Peter Grow.'

Vincent wept.

Peter Grow. Not Vincent, not Rob. Peter Grow. Katie covered her face.

'Why does he kill her, why?' Rob asked.

Vincent whimpered. 'Because he loves her too.'

* * *

Rob released Vincent's shoulders. He stumbled back, light-headed, dizzy.

A flood of memories tumbled into Rob's mind. The door knocker. Of course he knows it. He had seen it with his own eyes. He knew the door well. It had slammed in his face many times, leaving him outside to his own devices while his father and Madame Charay giggled over clinking glasses in the drawing room.

That's why he had been up at Madame Charay's that day. It wasn't abalone diving or exploring the coast like boys do. It was another jaunt to the peculiar house with the eagle door knocker. He was there to wait out the sordid little affair between his father and Madame Charay.

The images returned in torrents. The bizarre furniture that he saw when he peeked into the windows. The grotesque sight of his father slobbering and pawing over her. The stuffed birds, the movie posters, the smell of Madame Charay's perfume when she took the time to tussle his hair before patting him on the rear and telling him to run along. It all came back in a rush.

But he couldn't recall having seen other children. Not Vincent, nor Lily, nor Peter. No, not until that spring day during school recess when they came to find Madame Charay wailing with grief. Now Rob remembered. *They've taken my Alfred. My Alfred's dead*, she sobbed.

'Scoot along,' said his father.

My Alfie, she cried.

That's when Rob saw a flash of Lily behind a tree, pretty as a flower. Yes, he remembered now. She didn't see him. Rob followed her, dashing from tree to tree to keep his cover as she meandered down a path Rob had never found before. The path to Vincent's.

Rob remembered now. Remembered feeling ashamed for spying on this girl who looked like a movie star or a model, the most beautiful creature he had ever seen. He couldn't help but follow her, entranced, wanting her. Each time she stooped to pluck a flower, he wanted her more. Lusting for the first time in his life, entertaining thoughts of touching her in the private places he knew men craved, a deep-down aching to be with her that drove him wild.

That's when she entered the cabin. That's when he spied her through the window and saw the shock of red hair belonging to Vincent. That's when Rob bent his ear to listen to the sounds of love. And that's why his eyes were closed when Peter Grow entered the cabin. When the sounds turned to murder.

Now Rob remembered it all, everything that happened that day, every frame in time. Now he understood his feelings of guilt all these years.

'Rob, are you okay?' asked Katie.

'Yes, yes.'

He felt so many things. Relief, rapture, elation. But he also felt unsure how to handle the reprieve, how to orient himself without the burden of guilt weighing him down, uncertain how to proceed without the weight of shame, like a prisoner granted unexpected exoneration, a blind man given his sight.

Katie tugged at Rob's arm. 'Rob, where are you? You're scaring me.'

'I'm sorry. I just remembered something, that's all. Let's bring him out of it. I'm all right, everything is all right. It's over now.'

Rob took a moment to catch his breath.

'All right, Vincent. It's over. I want you to look at that ship and breathe easy.'

But Vincent didn't look at the ship. His fingers stiffened and dug into the ground.

'She's coming!'

Vincent bolted upright.

'No, Vincent. No more. It's over.'

'She's coming!' continued Vincent.

Katie turned again to see if Vincent was speaking of this moment in time, not back then, not the day Lily was killed. She saw nothing in the darkening forest. 'What's happening?'

'She's coming!'

'I don't know,' said Rob.

'Stop him,' Katie cried.

'Vincent, I want you to breathe deep. In, out. In, out.'

'She's coming,' he cried. '*Please don't, Mama. Please, no.*'

'Rob, what's going on?' Katie fretted.

'I don't know. There's more, he's continuing. Vincent, let's come out of it now. In, out. In, out. Breathe in, out.'

'*Mama, no,*' Vincent wailed.

'Rob, help him!'

'He's not responding. Look into my eyes, Vincent.'

'*Mama!*' Vincent shrieked.

'Oh, please, Rob.'

'I can't stop him. Who's coming, Vincent?'

'My mama.'

'To the cabin?'

'Yes.' Vincent trembled. '*Oh, God, no. Please don't let her find me here. Please, no.*'

'What is it, Vincent?'

'The door flies open. It *is* her. *Mama, no, it wasn't me.* She steps in and sees Lily on the bed. "My baby," she cries. "My baby," she wails. I want to run, but my leg hurts so badly. *Don't hurt me, Mama, please, no.* "First Alfred and now my baby," she says. "What have you done to my baby?" she cries forever, then she turns to Peter and slaps him across the face. "Look what you've done! You fool. You've ruined everything. Go wash up, and go away. Run, you stupid boy." Peter runs. He is free, and I am left with Mama. *Mama.*'

'Please stop him,' Katie pleaded.

'No,' said Rob. 'He has to finish.'

'He's in *pain*,' Katie said.

'Go on, Vincent.'

'She walks to me, stands over me like she does. Twists my ear. She says. "*You* did this. *You* did this." *No, Mama, it wasn't me. It was Peter, not me. Peter.* "No, you!" she says. "It was *you.*" *No. Not me, Mama.* She grabs my arm. "Come on, we're going." *No, Mama, not there, not to the room.*'

'What room? The basement?' asked Rob.

'The black room. I try to run but my leg hurts so badly. She holds me tightly, telling me over and over, "You killed her. Do you understand? You killed her." *No, Mummy!* She drags me to the house, to the room, upstairs. "You killed her, and you're not coming out until you say you killed her, Vincent." *I killed her. I killed her. Just don't put me in the room.* She says. "Nice try. Now go, you fool." She opens the door. *No, Mama, no!*'

Vincent's face grew contorted with horror, his arms flailed and fought.

'What is happening, Vincent? What is happening in the black room?' asked Rob.

Suddenly he stopped fighting, stopped flailing.

'What is happening, Vincent? Tell me,' Rob pleaded.

His arms dropped, his face grew blank.

'What's going on?' Katie cried.

'I don't know,' said Rob. 'Vincent, listen to me. Nod your head if you can hear my voice.'

Motionless, expressionless, Vincent stared ahead, beyond words, beyond the ship, beyond space.

'Can you hear me, Vincent?'

No reaction.

Rob waved two fingers in front of Vincent's eyes. 'See my fingers?'

Not a blink.

'Oh, God,' said Katie.

'Vincent, I want you to concentrate again on the ship,' said Rob. 'Look at the ship.'

But the ship had moved, and Vincent stared at where it had been.

'Vincent, dammit! Listen to me. Come back!'

But Vincent was beyond it, above it, on another plane, transcendent.

Rob stepped in front of him, pressed their foreheads together.

'Vincent, look into my eyes. *My* eyes, Vincent. Look into my eyes.'

'Rob?'

'Vincent, on the count of three, you'll be back here with me, with Katie. Count with me, Vincent. One, two, *three*.'

Vincent was nowhere near this earth, nowhere near Rob and Katie, nowhere near this age, this universe.

'Heaven help us,' Katie moaned.

Slowly, a smile appeared on Vincent's face. Not a smile of acknowledgment or lucidity, but the smile of the feeble, a smile of oblivion.

'Rob, what's happening?' Katie asked.

'I don't know. I can't snap him out of it.'

Rob syncopated his breathing with Vincent's, hoping to reestablish whatever connection that had joined them before.

'Let's go, Vincent. Come on, buddy. For me, for Katie. Breathe deep. On the count of three, snap out of it and return to us. We're waiting here, your friends. Come back. One, two, *three*.'

Vincent swayed in the wind, sailing through his dreams, his nightmares, nowhere, everywhere but here.

'Oh, my God. Rob, do something.'

Rob slapped Vincent across the face. Vincent didn't blink. But his smile remained constant.

'He's in some sort of post-traumatic psychotic state,' Rob explained.

Katie felt sick. What had she done? What had they done? She held Vincent's hands, caressed his cheek.

'Vincent. It's Katie. Your sister. Please come back to me. I love you.'

The smile only.

'I beg of you, Vincent.' Katie wrapped her arms around his shoulders. 'Vincent, come home,' she prayed.

'Vincent?' Rob tried again.

'What have we done?' Katie asked.

'I don't know.'

'Oh, my God.'

'But we can't leave him here. Not like this.'

'What do we do?'

'We'll have to take him with us.'

'Take him? How?'

'Maybe he'll walk. Let's see if we can get him to stand.'

Katie released Vincent's fingers from their hold in the earth. 'Come on, brother,' she whispered. 'Let's stand up. Let's go.'

Rob helped Vincent stand. He swayed like a vine in the breeze.

'Come with me, Vincent.' Katie wrapped her arm in his. Vincent followed, one foot, then the other, not looking where he stepped, not caring.

Against the final rays of sun, they walked from the cabin, step by step, along the path that twisted through the forest and down the cliff to the thin beach and Rob's waiting skiff.

Katie lifted Vincent's feet into the boat. She sat him down in front. Rob pushed off and joined Katie facing the wide expanse of ocean and Vincent's saintly smile, unchanged, unfathomable.

She hoped the ocean spray would wake Vincent. She reached into the ocean to wet her hand and wipe his face, praying for salvation with each touch.

The sun sank into the west and the sky cycled through its colors until it reached a deep purple.

'Is he going to be all right?' she asked.

'I don't know.'

'Rob, it wasn't you who killed Lily. We know that now. At least we have that.'

All of a sudden a crow swooped down from the heavens, a big black bird. It spread its giant wings and dived for Vincent's head.

And Vincent came alive.

He shielded his face and eyes from the attack. Fought back with his arms, cried out with the crucible of the truly insane.

Rob swept the bird away. It flew off back to shore, north, toward the cabin and Madame Charay's.

Katie turned to Vincent, but he again wore the smile of oblivion.

'Vincent?' she called with a glimmer of hope.

Not a twitch.

She sighed. 'What was that all about?' she asked.

'Hungry bird,' said Rob.

'Crows don't come out to sea, do they?'

'No, they don't.'

'He responded. Isn't that good?' asked Katie.

'Encouraging,' said Rob.

'I think he's going to be okay.'

'We'll see.'

With her right hand Katie took Rob's hand, and with her left she held Vincent's. She remained that way the rest of the way, holding their hands, a conduit between them, feeling Rob's emotions rise and fall, and Vincent's steady nothingness, a flat line, like the cold hospital machine that had announced the death of Katie's mother a few days ago. Or was it a lifetime ago? Katie didn't know; she didn't care. Only Vincent mattered now. Vincent and Rob.

CHAPTER SIXTEEN

Rob carried Vincent in from the Jeep and laid his limp body on the couch. He cloistered himself in the study, pulled down an armful of books, and with Buster at his feet began the search for the key to unlock the secret of Vincent, if, he prayed, one existed. He studied books he hadn't touched since college and others he had once felt spurious or unworthy of his time. Now he pored through them all, groping for any clue to help him mend Vincent's shattered mind.

Katie grabbed a blanket from the living-room floor and tucked it around her shivering brother, his face the pale white of a candle. Katie tried to get him to sip some water, but the liquid ran down his chin untasted. She swabbed his face with a cloth dipped in warm water and peppermint oil, and stroked the hair from his eyes. She caressed his cheeks, like Lily would have done, she thought. Poor Lily.

Animal mauling. Katie couldn't wait to run to the police to tell them everything, to watch as they led Madame Charay away in handcuffs to the hell of prison where she belonged. And the same for Peter Grow, the savage. Castrate him, that's what Katie would tell the judge.

But vindication would have to wait. Katie closed Vincent's eyelids, hoping it would help him sleep if he wasn't already sleeping. It comforted her to see his eyes remain shut. Only the smile lingered, that beautiful terrifying smile. Katie rubbed his arms and legs to keep the circulation going, to warm him. She didn't know if it helped or if he noticed, but the shivering stopped and she thought she felt his body relax and his breathing deepen. Communication didn't need words, not always. She hummed a lullaby. He was going to be all right, Katie was sure.

She made room for herself on the couch and squished in next to Vincent. She wrapped his arm around her shoulder just like she had dreamed of when she first learned of his existence. She thought about her grandmother, who would be worrying now, sitting by the phone, a suspense novel in her lap, glancing occasionally at the phone, hoping for Katie's call. Katie considered calling, but how could she explain what had happened today? Or yesterday, or the day before? And then there was tomorrow, whatever surprises it would bring. Better wait until all this was resolved before trying to explain it to someone or even understand it herself.

At least she was safe in Vincent's arms, safe in Rob's house. It was the first time she felt like she had a family, a family of men. She closed her eyes and savored the moment, realizing it might pass, like all good things in life.

She didn't want to fall asleep, didn't plan on it, but she was so tired she couldn't help but drift away. Her dreams took her to her childhood, to her only memories of her father. She was two years old, three perhaps, and she was twirling in her father's arms high above his head. Flying and laughing, her arms spread like an eagle, dizzy with delight. It felt so good. All the world was good in her father's strong arms, looking into his handsome face that smiled always. He threw her up into the air, caught her, and twirled her some more. He laughed freely. So beautiful, this God in slacks, smelling of cigars and cologne and the alluring aroma only men can generate.

Like dreams often do, Katie's shifted in time and place. She was flying now, high above the Brenner place, looking down at a solitary figure standing where the house used to be. She turned her wings and swooped down, delighted to see it was Vincent waving his arms. She quickly realized he wasn't waving in friendly recognition but to shoo her away. What's the matter, Vincent? He's waving her away, furiously warning her to move on, to avert the danger. What danger? It's just you, Vincent. There's no danger. But the closer she flew the more emphatic his warning, and as she was ready to land she saw the pained expression on his face and it frightened her. She flew up, up, up, until only the blue of the sky greeted her, and peace again. When she looked down Vincent was gone. But the Brenner farmhouse was intact, and Tippi Hedren was motoring in Rob's boat to the house with two lovebirds in a cage beside her. Only it wasn't Tippi anymore, it was Katie. Katie in that boat with a mischievous look on her face, aiming for the Brenner dock where Rod Taylor stood on the shore smiling and waving his hands, waiting to greet her. Suddenly a bird, a sea gull, swooped down and grazed Katie's forehead, releasing a trickle of blood. Frightened, Katie looked to Rod Taylor for help. But he was gone. And Katie was all alone in the boat, no longer in the serene bay, but in the open ocean, riding tall swells topped with white caps, miles from the nearest shore.

She awoke with a gasp and a thud, and found herself on the floor next to the couch. Dazed, she looked up and saw Vincent, still sleeping, still smiling, his arm dangling off the edge of the couch for Katie to cuddle beside him again.

Rob ran in from the study. 'Are you okay?'

Katie shook herself awake. 'I had a dream, but it was so confusing. I was flying, a little girl with my father, and then I was at the Brenner place, and Vincent was there, but he was warning me of something terrible. Oh, I don't know. I can't remember.'

Rob drew her close and stroked her hair. She closed her eyes and let the solace envelope her.

'Shhh,' Rob whispered. 'Let it go. It's just a dream. It's late, almost dawn. Why don't you go into my bed and get some rest.'

Katie saw the fatigue in Rob's eyes. 'You haven't been resting.'

'No.'

'Vincent? What did you find out?'

Rob closed his eyes for a moment to digest all the information he had covered in the past few hours.

'There's so much I don't know. The hypnosis was too much for him. He saw something during the regression, something that he couldn't bear, and his mind shut itself off. It's a protective measure against a memory too frightful to recall.'

'In that room. The black room.'

'Yes. Something happened in there. Something terrible that persuaded him into believing he killed Lily.'

'What could it possibly be?'

'I don't know. I've read hundreds of cases of war prisoners and captives brainwashed into believing the most bizarre impossibilities.'

'How?'

'Any number of ways. Exposure to their worst fears, continuous indoctrination, even lack of sleep. It doesn't take much to alter the memory of the mind, insert new scenes, change endings. Something happened to Vincent the day of the murder, and when he tried to remember it last night he couldn't handle the ordeal. It was too much to tolerate, even under hypnosis.'

'Can he come out of it? Tell me the truth.'

Rob sighed. 'The human mind is capable of miraculous things. Maybe he will. That's all I can say.'

She gets a brother for five days and puts him into a psychotic trance for the rest of his life.

'And if he doesn't?' Katie cringed at the thought.

'There are places. Homes that are good, that can take care of him. He'll be well fed and clothed. He'll never go in need.'

'No,' Katie said. 'I'll never let that happen. He'll stay with me. I'll care for him, no matter what the sacrifices.'

'Let's not rush to judgment. I found some techniques that may work. We'll try tomorrow; he's sleeping now. He's tired, you're tired. Let him get some rest. We'll all feel better in the morning.'

Katie touched Rob's cheek as she had Vincent's moments ago. 'And you? How about some rest?'

'Not yet. I'm almost done in there. A few more books and I'll get some sleep. Tomorrow we'll take care of everything.'

Rob paused.

Katie saw he wanted to speak. 'What is it?'

'I have to tell you something. About what happened up there tonight.'

'You remembered too, didn't you?'

'Yes, I did.'

Rob told her about his father and Madame Charay and all the images that had returned to him in that moment, and the simple theory that tied so much together.

'My first sexual yearning ended with murder. And the transference was absolute in the impressionable mind of a twelve-year-old boy. It's so basic, a first-year psychology student could have told you that.'

'Unless it had happened to them,' said Katie. It all made so much sense. She hugged him for his tribulation, his courage, his sharing, for so many things.

'We suffer most for the crimes of others, don't we?' she said.

'Yes, I guess we do.'

Suddenly the face of Peter Grow flashed before Katie's eyes and she buried her face in her hands.

'I should have known. He was cashing Vincent's checks. Our encounter at the gas station. When he attacked Lois thinking she was me—'

'How could you have known there was someone else? Two suspects in a murder is more than enough.'

'Let's call the police right now,' said Katie.

'Soon, tomorrow. Let's see what we can do first for Vincent. One step at a time. You get some sleep.'

Maybe he was right. The truth was out now. What had the inscription said on Lily's grave? *Truth, crushed to earth, shall rise again.* There was time.

'I'll fix you some breakfast,' said Katie. 'It's time for me to wake up.'

The first pink of the morning surprised Katie through the kitchen window, a light as sublime as her dreams. She rubbed her eyes and felt her body tingle with awakeness. Outside, two bluebirds searched the ground for seeds. They fluttered around, never straying far from each other.

Katie saw his reflection in the window, hesitating at the door behind her. She urged him on silently, turning her head ever so slightly for a sign. When she saw him moving closer, she closed her eyes, anticipated his touch. Her desire swelled with every sound of his approaching footsteps. He stepped up behind, waited a moment, then lovingly wrapped his strong arms around her. He kissed her hair, drew in her scent, pressed his body against hers.

'Oh, Rob.'

He kissed the nape of her neck, and she felt his warm breath, his tender kisses. She turned to face him, feeling his strength, his desire.

The kiss was open and wet, and everything Katie dreamed it would be. He kissed her eyes, her cheeks. He traced her lips with his fingers, found the small of her back with his hand. He breathed deeply, slowly, an energy of supreme confidence.

He scooped her up, carried her into the bedroom, laid her on the bed like a princess. His hand traced her outline, her shoulders, her stomach, her breasts. His every touch an act of reverence.

Katie felt the divinity within her soul, calling him, wanting him, needing him. Rob felt his hesitancy, borne during years of shame, confusion. Could he do it after all these years? All these failures?

Their bodies fell together, no fears, no concessions, no regrets. They unleashed their passions, rose together like a pair of loons. Ascended gracefully to heights of glory, sailed on the currents of unity, dived into each other with the gravity of their desire. And when Rob entered her, fully and potently, Katie understood the flower, the orchid on Lily's grave. An eternity of pure bliss. For this was hers, as encompassing as birth and death in a place where time is inconsequential, life pure energy, and matter as insignificant as their bodies wrapped together in the dawn light of their union.

They fulfilled themselves until the shadows in the valleys disappeared, the morning fog vanished, and the sunlight radiated upon them, strong and clean.

And in the white light of morning they returned to earth exhausted and fell into a deep sleep in the tangle of each other's arms.

It was Lois's voice that woke them.

'Rob. Rob!'

Katie thought it was her dream taking a sinister turn, but the voice was insistent and tangible. Katie opened an eye on Lois's petite outline framed in the bedroom door and spotlighted by the mid-morning sun.

'Rob!' Lois yapped. 'What is the meaning of this?'

Rob woke leisurely, still in dreamland. And then he realized. 'Lois, what are you doing here?'

Lois's jaw dropped. 'What am *I* doing here? What is *she* doing here?'

Rob quickly drew a sheet around his and Katie's naked bodies. 'Please, let me explain,' he said.

'Explain? How can you explain this? We're engaged to be married, remember?'

Rob hemmed and hawed. 'I'm sorry,' he said finally.

'Sorry for what? For sleeping with her or marrying me?'

'Lois, I—'

'And we were supposed to look at rings today,' said Lois. 'How ironic.'

'Lois, everything has happened so fast. So unexpectedly. I can't marry you, Lois.'

Lois bit her lip. 'Nice way to break it to me.'

'I'm sorry.'

'Sorry?' Lois said, holding back tears.

Katie knew the pain of rejection and wished it upon no one, not even Lois.

'How could you do this to me, Rob?'

Rob grappled for the right words. 'It's not you. It's me. Me.'

'Or maybe it's *her*,' Lois interjected.

'No, Lois. Not Katie. Me. I had so much wrong with me. So many secrets, so much to work through. And whatever dirty bargain you and I made, whatever bound me to you, it was wrong, sinful.'

'So that's it? All these years of waiting for you, wasted.'

'No, not wasted. Ours would have been a life of misery, a misery built upon a lie. A mountain of lies. But now I'm free. And you are too, Lois. I'm sorry.'

'Sorry,' said Lois, fighting back tears. 'That's all I get is sorry. Okay, I'll be sorry. I play that part well, though you'd never know it. Sorry. I guess one more sorry won't hurt.'

'I'm the one who's sorry, sorry for hurting you,' said Rob.

'Cut it, Rob. Let me escape with some dignity. And Katie, congratulations. I can't say I didn't see it coming.'

Now it was Katie's turn to scramble for words. 'It's not like that.'

But before Katie could explain, Lois rushed from the room and out of the house.

Rob fumbled on a pair of shorts and chased after her, but Katie knew that when a woman doesn't want to be caught she isn't. Katie closed her eyes and heard Lois's car start up and race away, Rob's voice calling after her.

Katie rolled over, feeling terrible for Lois. But she was unable to resist the bliss of the early morning, which returned to her in waves of contentment. She smelled the pillow to make sure it was real and listened to Rob's footsteps returning.

'He's gone,' Rob said.

'Who's gone?'

'Vincent.'

Katie leaped out of bed and threw on her clothes, suddenly aware of her nakedness. 'Gone? What do you mean?'

'Gone, not in the house anywhere. Look.'

Katie dashed into the living room. The blankets were strewn on a path to the front door, as if Vincent had shed them with the slow return of his consciousness.

Couldn't they have waited another night to make love? Like foolish children they had rushed in. And now Vincent was gone. Retribution truly is swift and hard.

'Where could he be?' Katie asked.

'Back to Madame Charay's. That's the only place he knows.'

'But he's in danger there. Who knows what she'll do?'

Rob's mind raced with possibilities. 'You wait here, just in case he comes back. I'll drive down there myself.'

'Okay. And Rob?' she whispered.

'Yes?'

Katie wanted to say so many things, to express fear for Vincent, her sorrow for Lois, her elation over this morning, her devotion toward Rob, even if he chose to sail away right now and never return. But she denied herself all these things, and the kiss she wanted so badly, until Vincent was safe in her arms again.

CHAPTER SEVENTEEN

Katie remained on the porch long after Rob's Jeep vanished around the bend. Only after she no longer heard the whir of the engine and the dust had settled did she turn back inside to clean the house, the only outlet she could find for her energy. She scrubbed the dishes, threw the blankets in the washing machine, vacuumed under the bed, dusted the tabletops. Then she started all over again.

Several times as she zoomed by with the vacuum cleaner, she picked up the telephone and punched the number for the police. She slammed down the receiver before connecting each time, fearful of putting Rob and Vincent in danger, fearful of what Madame Charay might do if she knew the police had been alerted.

It was Vincent who worried Katie most. There was no telling what state he was in. Was he still a walking, smiling ghoul, weaving his way absentmindedly through the coast-road traffic, protected only by the hand of fate? Had he awakened replaying in his mind the terrible ordeal of the murder? If so, he might be driven by any number of emotions – revenge, sorrow, suicide, despair. Perhaps he had completely transformed into a homicidal maniac looking to slaughter the first victim he could find. Maybe he was waiting in the bushes right now, planning for Katie a more brutal death than Lily's. Katie searched around for Buster, but the dog had vanished, off to search for his new master or to return to his familiar hell.

And what if Vincent were to run into Peter Grow? Or take it into his own hands to seek revenge? Vincent was no match for anyone; he couldn't hurt a bird, let alone his stepbrother.

Katie glanced nervously out the window every few minutes, hoping to see Vincent returning from a stroll in the woods with a bouquet of handpicked flowers, unaware that he had been gone for so long, sorry for the distress he had caused.

She dusted a vase and peered out the window once again. She saw a car she hadn't seen before, hiding behind the cypress trees. When she recognized it, the vase dropped from her hands and shattered into a thousand pieces across the floor.

It was the devilish Cadillac of Peter Grow.

Katie dashed to the phone. No dial tone – the bastard had cut the wires. *Dial M for Murder.* Oh, God.

The kitchen door clicked open, letting in a slight breeze that fluttered the pages of the magazines on the coffee table. The first leaden footsteps creaked the wooden floor.

Katie caught his odor even before she saw him, the foul stench of a sister killer.

Katie took two steps back and snatched the iron poker from the fireplace. Run, she told herself. Sprint to the car and start it quickly. Run him over if need be. No mercy.

His long shadow turned the corner first, then his seething, livid flesh. Only the blue of his eyes colored the sickness of his smile.

Rob flew down the back roads, banking on his traction to compensate for his recklessness. Though he hadn't driven these roads in years, he knew what lay around each corner. The scenes were etched in his mind from countless trips as a glum and reluctant passenger in his father's wide Chrysler.

Under other circumstances this would be a big occasion, this return to such an important locale in the history of an individual. Rob's practice was to counsel his clients for weeks before advising them to travel back to the house in which they had been abused, neglected, or had witnessed a hideous crime. He had no time now for the luxury of reflection. Only finding

Vincent mattered. Or was it strangling Madame Charay? Rob wasn't sure.

The door knocker was missing so Rob clobbered the door with his fist, knocking incessantly until he heard footsteps approaching, those same wretched footsteps he now remembered so well.

She greeted him in a flowing black evening gown and with a gracious smile, as if expecting him. Her face was caked with rouge, blue eye shadow, and ruby-red lipstick. She had changed little, that same mix of detachment and severity, the same false facade of nobility.

'Good afternoon, Dr Du Maurier. My, how we've grown.'

Rob swept her aside and stepped in. 'Where is Vincent?'

'Good question. I was wondering the same thing myself.'

Rob glanced around, revolted by the decor that had made no sense to him as a child.

Madame Charay wrapped her arm in Rob's to lead him to the sitting room. He pulled away, sickened at her touch.

'What have you done to him?'

Madame Charay threw back her head and laughed, the false laugh of a bad actress. 'Housed him and fed him for the past thirty-some-odd years.'

'Fed him a pack of lies. Kept him trapped and tortured.'

'My, aren't we feisty today. The same trait I admired in your father.'

'You can write his eulogy, then. I'm going to take a look around.'

Madame Charay didn't stop Rob. On the contrary, she delighted in following him from room to room, proud to share her treasures with such an esteemed guest.

Each room brought back a flood of memories for Rob. He remembered peering through the windows as a little boy, watching with a mix of wonderment and disgust as his father clumsily humped Madame Charay on the bed in the *Psycho* room, his bare buttocks rising and falling in the perverse rhythm of adults. In the *Rear Window* room he remembered his father swigging a martini, a fake cast on his leg, and Madame Charay dressed like a grotesque Grace Kelly, rubbing his shoulders and then moving into his pants with her hands. And in the *Rope* room he remembered the worst of it all, Madame Charay tying up his father and stuffing him in that trunk in the middle of the room, only to release him moments later to copulate like animals on the floor.

He remembered it all now, and he fought the urge to belt Madame Charay, to mangle her like Peter had Lily, to take revenge for grievances against him, for all the children.

He ran upstairs and found rooms he had never seen before, surely the sets of more sordid scenes acted out by the sick twosome, and who knows how many more. The memories he had blocked for so long. Rob only imagined the memories Vincent held, memories enough to drive anyone to insanity.

'We know about Lily's murder. We know you convinced my father to falsify the autopsy.'

'Without much persuasion, I assure you. On the other hand, $75,000 a year isn't chicken feed, is it, Dr Du Maurier?'

Rob came to a room that was locked. He pushed against it with his shoulder, but it wouldn't budge. 'What's in there?'

'Nothing. Some memorabilia I haven't catalogued quite yet. Not ready for showing.'

'Open it.'

'I don't have the key. My son does.'

'Peter Grow. We know all about him too.'

'You have the wrong man, good doctor.'

'Give it a break. It's over.'

'Under the veneer of virtue, Vincent is very cunning, you know. I wouldn't believe everything he tells you, even under hypnosis. I've always been very concerned about that boy. Indeed, I thought of bringing him to you several times.'

'Why didn't you? Afraid of what I'd find out?'

'Quite the contrary – afraid he might mislead you, fill you with dangerous notions, as he apparently has.'

'You won't get away with this.'

'I wouldn't be so sure. In fact, I'm surprised you are here. Surprised you left your little girlfriend alone.'

'What are you talking about?'

'Look at you. You're chasing memories like a schoolboy and you leave her undefended at your house. Hitch would never tolerate such a foolish lead character, such an improbable turn of events.'

Rob suddenly realized his mistake. 'You wouldn't,' he said.

'Not I.' Madame Charay smiled.

Katie pulled the car keys from her pocket and flew out the front door, giddy with her impending escape. But one look at her car froze her with dread. The hood had been propped open and the distributor cap was perched atop her antenna, its wires dangling like an abominable sea creature.

Peter reached the screen door and paused there to enjoy Katie's surprise. 'Gotcha now.'

Katie waved the poker like a wand and squinted her eyes as she delivered her demand. 'You get away from me, you scum.'

'Keep talkin' dirty,' Peter winked. 'You're really turning me on.' He batted open the screen door and stepped closer.

'Step back! I'm warning you. The police are on the way. Rob knows. We all know.'

Peter skirted around Katie with his hands lodged in his trench coat like a flasher.

'You think you're going to hurt me with that little poker? I've had transmissions dropped on my face – and liked it.'

With her back to the house, Katie suddenly felt weak, terribly weak. Her fingers trembled, her knees buckled. She turned to run, but like in her dreams her feet would not take her. She stood, paralyzed, cursing herself as he staggered forward, gnashing his tobacco-slimed teeth.

'No!' Katie screamed.

She hurled the poker at his face and hit him all right, hit him good. Right between his filthy eyes. He shrieked in pain. Transmissions, my ass.

Katie raced inside and up the stairs, three steps at a time. She slammed the bathroom door and locked it tight.

His footsteps shook the house as he raced up the stairs.

'Open up!' he said, pounding on the door.

'Not on your life.'

Katie tried the window, but it wouldn't budge. She realized her mistake. She was trapped. Trapped in a tiny bathroom with no way out.

She climbed onto the toilet seat and used her elbow to shatter the window glass and clear the remaining shards from the frame. She peeked out. The drop was long, break-a-leg long.

The sound of his hammering fist stopped, replaced by another sound, a curious heavy scraping.

Then she saw them, the golden claws of the brass door knocker ripping the thin wood of the door and launching sharp splinters into the small room.

Small chunks of wood dropped to her feet with every hit. In no time Peter clawed a hole large enough to take a look inside, his twisted smile seething with anticipation.

Katie grabbed a towel and picked up a shard of glass. When Peter stuck his hand in to unlock the door, Katie slashed him across his wrist.

'You whore!' he cried.

Katie looked around for a weapon, protection. All she could think to do was rip down the plastic shower curtain.

Peter busted through with his shoulder, mumbling a string of profanities as he waved the claw in his hand. 'Now I got you.'

'No, you don't!'

Katie flung the shower curtain over his head, and with a mighty heave shoved him into the bathtub. He hit the back wall with a thud and slid into the tub, his legs kicking in the air like a live chicken in a pot.

'You fuck!' he yelled.

Katie leaped past him and raced down the stairs. She bolted from the house and jumped the stream.

Run forever, she told herself. Run fast, like you did when you were a little girl. Run for your life.

She glanced over her shoulder on Peter galloping behind in his thick boots.

She reached the edge of the clearing, not sure which way to turn, losing precious seconds. She dashed into the woods, but tripped on a root and tumbled into a thicket of blackberry bushes. The thorns snagged her hair and held her captive. She ripped and tugged but for every freed strand of hair another got entangled in the thorns.

Peter's heavy breathing grew louder. His boots crushed brittle grass and twigs as he drew nearer. Katie ripped herself free and dashed off into the forest. Peter nipped at her heels.

When he got close he lunged at Katie but missed by inches and tumbled to the ground. She ran on, but every glance back lost her a step.

He caught up and lunged again, this time grabbing hold of her ankle and tripping her to the ground. She fell face-first, her cheek slamming into the ground.

'Let me go!' she hollered.

'Not on your life.'

Peter planted his thick boot on Katie's back and yanked her arms up behind her, rendering her helpless other than to shriek in pain.

'Now I got you,' he crowed.

He pulled off his belt and wrapped it tightly around her wrists. A second belt came out of nowhere, and he twisted it around her ankles. Then he pulled out a thick section of rope and snapped it taut between his fists.

Katie fought hard against the restraints; she choked on dust, panted for air. When she finally caught her breath she asked: 'What are you going to do to me?'

Peter grinned. 'Lights, camera, action.'

From the upstairs hall window, Madame Charay watched Rob

run to his Jeep, looking as earnest as James Stewart. That boy couldn't hold a candle to his father, Madame Charay thought. Now *there* was a man. A bona fide man unafraid to enter the chamber of illusion for the pleasure it brought. That was what was wrong with movies today, actors today. No illusion. Everything in graphic detail, over the top, on the nose. They would do well to study the master, to see suspense built with negative space, to watch subtext drive a story, to leave the mystery *in*.

But nobody cared to make art anymore. Money drove them now, the whole lot of thieves in Hollywood. Money wrote the scripts, money chose the actors, money directed. At least his legacy was preserved. They could never change his art, thank God. And if they didn't give him the recognition he deserved, they were fools, all of them. He was recognized here, in this house, and they could never take that away.

Madame Charay returned to the door of the black room, as Vincent liked to call it. She pressed her ear against the door, as Rob should have done had he been astute. How easily foiled he was, a pup.

She didn't dare open the door. Not now, not after days of hunger. She listened closely though.

Birds are usually so quick to flutter about, to craw and bark, especially in such closed quarters where petty fights for territory consume them. Not now. Now they were conserving energy, shutting down, praying.

She peeked through the keyhole. She saw one bird falter with weakness then drop to the floor. Her siblings pounced on her and tore the flesh from her bones, even before she had a chance to die. A meal provided by a sister – how fitting.

Madame Charay had waited so long for this moment. Patiently feeding the birds, destroying the sick and timid before they had the chance to reproduce. Breeding the rest for boldness, aggression, fortitude. All for this moment. All for the triumphant reenactment of the scene they said could never be duplicated. And they were right, on film anyway. But in real life, that was a different beast altogether. And to have Gloria's daughter in the starring role – how ironic. How ingenious. How *Al*.

He would have been so proud.

CHAPTER EIGHTEEN

Maybe she couldn't see through the soiled bandanna tied across her eyes. Maybe her screams had been reduced to moans by the sock stuffed in her throat and the duct tape strapped across her mouth. But she could feel. She could feel the air cooling and the sunlight reduced to ripples as the Cadillac turned under the big trees. And she could feel the gravel hitting the floorboards inches from her cheek as they swerved onto the unpaved driveway.

So when Peter came to a stop, when he opened the back door and ripped the bandanna away, when Katie got her first glance upside down and through the frame of Peter's legs, it was no surprise to see the round stones of the mansion and Madame Charay herself approaching, her black dress billowing like smoke. They could bind Katie, gag her, but they couldn't stop her from feeling.

Peter grabbed Katie by the scruff of her neck and slammed her face-first on the drive.

'Don't hurt her!' Madame Charay called out. 'I want her fit.'

He pulled Katie to her feet and dusted her off.

'And unleash her from those ungodly restraints,' said Madame Charay. 'This isn't a slasher film.'

Peter moved quickly. 'Yes, Mama.'

'And what happened to your wrist?'

'She cut me with glass,' he reported incredulously. 'And threw a poker at me.'

'The nerve. Can you imagine?'

Madame Charay turned to Katie. 'But I like an actress with spunk.'

Peter ripped the duct tape from Katie's mouth and unbuckled the belt. He bent to untie the rope at her feet.

'Stay away from me, you jerk.'

Peter looked to Madame Charay for advisement.

'Let her do it herself. And go quickly. Take care of your chores. I'll entertain Katie, here.'

Peter moved sheepishly toward his mother. She extended her cheek for the obligatory kiss, and he obliged with a devout peck.

'Bye, Ma.'

'Good-bye, son. Now go.'

Peter hustled to his car and roared away, leaving a trail of dust in his wake.

Katie rubbed her wrists. Her lips smarted and her neck throbbed, but she wasn't beaten. 'What do you want from me? Where's Vincent?' she demanded.

'Vincent? He's safe asleep upstairs. Safe, as long as you don't try to flee.'

'You'll never get away with this,' said Katie.

Madame Charay sighed with exasperation. 'Another tired cliché. Your boyfriend used the same line. No more inferior movies for you, missy, that's an order. And don't disappoint me like your mother.'

'What's my mother have to do with this?'

Madame Charay raised an eyebrow. 'You mean you don't know?'

'I know you took Vincent away from her.'

'Oh, my. You are an innocent.'

'I know that she was a great actress and she tried to be a good mother.' Katie wasn't going to have anyone disparage her mother, especially Madame Charay.

Madame Charay laughed. 'You'll have to work on your fibbing skills if you plan to make it in life, deary. Your mother was a high-cheekboned blond who couldn't deliver a line to save her life.'

'My mother was a star. A star waiting for a break.'

'My, you are misinformed. Shall I recount a little history for you over a spot of tea?'

'Another time, maybe.'

'You said you wanted to see Vincent again. I think you have time. Shall we?'

Katie peered down the driveway, the dust settling. She could run easily. It was just half a mile to the main road, where she could flag down a car or find a house with a phone. She sized up Madame Charay, so thin and small, no match should it become physical.

'If you insist.' Katie flashed a smile. She would stay and play the game. Whatever Madame Charay had to say about her mother, Katie would simply ignore. The more time she wasted sipping tea, the more time Rob had to get back or call the sheriff for help.

The tea was waiting, piping hot and served on a tray with shortbread biscuits and a shallow china bowl of lemon wedges. Madame Charay poured Katie a cup.

'Do you always have hot tea ready?' Katie blew away the steam.

'Only when I'm expecting guests.'

Katie leaned forward for a sip. It burned her tongue.

'Enjoying Bodega Bay?' asked Madame Charay.

'Let's cut to the chase, shall we? What is it you want with me? With Vincent? Why do you hate my mother so? Why this sick fascination with Hitchcock?'

'My, my. Filled with questions. Let me tell you a story. A story about a girl from Kansas.'

'I don't want to hear any stories,' said Katie.

'Oh, this story, I think you will. Drink your tea. It'll relax you; you look tense.'

'*Notorious*,' said Katie.

'Pardon?'

'In *Notorious* the Nazi's mother poisoned Ingrid Bergman with tea.'

'No, silly girl, it was milk. And the movie was *Spellbound.* And it was Gregory Peck that was poisoned, well, not poisoned but rendered unconscious. Would you like to switch cups with me? I'm in no mood to poison anyone, I assure you.'

'No, this one will be fine,' said Katie. She just wouldn't drink. And it was *Notorious*, she was sure. 'Let's get this story over with.'

'Ah, yes, a girl from Kansas. Doesn't that sound funny? Like Dorothy in *The Wizard of Oz.* The same initial problem, too, for this strange little girl who loved the movies so. How could she possibly stay in Kansas, where the conversation was of hog feed and the next thunder shower? Where the kisses came from repugnant farm boys who looked like immature versions of their fathers and who tried to lure you into the filthy beds of their pickup trucks. No, this girl had her calling, to be a director, the first great female director. And she traveled to Hollywood. Heard of it? It's south of here a tad; they make products that come in tin cans and enamor the world. Hollywood is the Emerald City, beckoning lights, magic wands and ruby slippers, savants and witches. The perfect place for a girl from Kansas who cared never to go home again. And like Oz, Hollywood had only one wizard.'

'Alfred Hitchcock.' Katie rolled her eyes.

'My, you are perceptive. Imagine her surprise when he offered her a job as a script assistant, a lowly position to be sure, but a start, an opportunity to learn from the master, the man behind the curtain.'

Katie shifted with impatience. 'So you were that girl from Kansas. It doesn't take an art-house crowd to figure that out.'

Madame Charay smiled wistfully.

'You've never been under the spell of a master, have you? You've loved men before, or thought you loved them, but they were boys, really. Of course, you have so little opportunity today. There are no masters anymore. Scorsese, Stone, *Ron*

Howard? Please, don't make me laugh. A vanished breed. It's a shame, really, because a master knows things about you that even you don't know. And you can feel it in his subtle gestures, in his casual glance as he infiltrates every fiber of your substance. Let me tell you, mademoiselle, there is no greater stimulation a girl can feel.'

'So what's this have to do with my mother?'

'I remember the very day she stepped into the office, one of a herd of anorexic blonds swarming to the cattle call. The part was Melanie Daniels. Your mother read for it, a thoroughly wooden performance, sorry enough to choke a high-school stage. But Alfred didn't think so. No, he kept her in the mix. She followed one dismal reading with another but was called back, nonetheless. Five girls left, then two, then one. Your mother.

'When word came down that Gloria Jacobs had gotten the nod we were all in shock. The assistants, the writers, the production crew. She was a drudge, a pill, terribly and utterly wrong for the part – any part, if you ask me. She was stunning, yes, alluring and sensual in a sophisticated way, but completely inept. How could he have misjudged so? We could only guess. Only he knew what he was looking for in these creatures of beauty. Grace, Kim, Eva Marie, Tippi, never two at the same time, mind you. Each one in succession, as carefully chosen as a wife. Necessary evils, that's what I called them. Each chosen with exacting care. And now he had chosen your mother, this *monstrosity*.

'Alfred, you know, was a virtuous man. Loyal to the hilt, loyal to his family, to his staff. And each relationship was governed by the established rules of etiquette and station. A true Englishman. Writers understood their position, cinematographers theirs, art directors, leading men, extras, we all understood what was expected of us and what we should expect in return. All of us abided by these precise rules of conduct.

'All except the blonds. They didn't follow the same formalities, they weren't *expected* to. No, their relationship with

Alfred was different, privileged, for no other reason than their beauty. Once chosen, they were not beholden to the common rules of behavior required of the rest of us. These goddesses answered to Alfred, and Alfred alone. That's not to say Alfred employed secrecy to develop the relationship. On the contrary. His sense of decency would never allow him to be alone with these women. Then again, he didn't require secrecy. He was the master. He did it all in front of us, through us even, by his subtle suggestions concerning their makeup, eyes, nylons, waistline, delivery, pout. Oh, I so loathed them for the privilege. Yes, they were beautiful. But shallow. None had the emotional or intellectual depth that I possessed, that any of us possessed on the set. And deceptive. Fluttering their eyes, doting over him, pretending to be virtuous, when off the set they scurried around like schoolgirl tramps. *Yes, Mr Hitchcock. Certainly, Mr Hitchcock,* enough to make one sick. It was painfully obvious to us that these women didn't deserve his attention. But Alfred was generous to a fault. Time and again he forgave their failings, ignored their behavior, pardoned their sins. Thankfully, after one or two pictures, Alfred came to see their inadequacies, and he let them go. Quickly, with a snap of his fingers, delighting us to no end. Nevertheless, you'll understand that the selection of the blond was no trivial matter in the compound. And you'll understand our horror when he chose your mother for the lead role in *The Birds* to be filmed in this wretched birdland.

'I prided myself on my unquestioned devotion to Mr Hitchcock. After all, he had proven time and again his vision with the novel angle of the lens, the pulse of the edit, the manipulation of tension. None of us questioned him. Oh, we prodded him, yes, developed along with him, but he synthesized the disparate minor talents of us all.

'All except your mother. She had no talent to speak of, and she tried to make it up with her so-called intelligence. The relationship with the new blond started quite normally, a polite friendliness. But she was different. Unlike the others, she didn't feign compliance, or attempt to. No, she argued with him about character motivation, suggested dialogue changes, insisted on nuances he hadn't called for. *Her* way; she always wanted to do it *her* way. The rancorous little wretch. Naturally, my work, the work of us all, started to suffer. We were at the critical pre-production stage, four months before shooting was to start. There was much to be done. Hundreds of special-effect shots to be planned, storyboarding, mattes, script meetings, character revisions, casting problems. Alfred was not his usual self. He spent hours brooding, lost his temper, made rash decisions, then changed his mind minutes later. Not Alfred at all, and all thanks to the impertinence of your mother and the pall she cast over the production. You can only imagine our panic.

'What choice did I have? I took it upon myself to speak with him. I found him in his office at an hour we were told never to disturb him. I spoke openly and with dispatch, so as not to squander his time. I voiced my concern clearly, outlining the disastrous effect your mother's presence was having. While speaking solely for myself, I felt it my duty to let him know the staff shared similar views, even though I had not polled them individually.

'Now, I acknowledge being a little light-headed in the presence of the master. I was alone with him for the first time, after all. And in no way was it my intention to approach him so boldly. To get so near him, to touch his hand. It was improper of me, I know. And he rebuffed me resolutely, rightly so. I came to my senses and with a profusion of apologies took my leave. I was lucky I wasn't fired promptly, and I fully accepted the rejection of my fellow workers following the incident.

'But imagine my sense of vindication when I saw the first serious casting conversation between Alfred and producers. One didn't need friends to listen to this grapevine. Luckily, not a frame had been shot. I'm not even sure the ink had dried on your mother's contract. It was all decided very rapidly, and the day Tippi was chosen to replace her, your mother didn't even suspect, the buffoon. The word came by memo during the only morning I can recall Mr Hitchcock's absence. Two sentences, incomplete. *Gloria Jacobs out. Tippi Hedren in.*

'Tippi Hedren. Do you know where she came from? Alfred saw her on a television commercial. A model hawking a diet drink, with no lines to speak. Just an elegant blond passing across the screen and turning amiably in response to a little boy's whistle of approval. That's how desperate things had become. For the most celebrated movie of our age, your mother was being replaced by a female prop. But imagine my delight. I celebrated alone perhaps, but reveled with the crew nonetheless.'

Madame Charay chose a cigarette from a table box. She puckered her lips and sucked away without lighting. 'I'm sure your mother never told you that story.'

Katie sipped her tea, lukewarm now. 'No, she didn't. My guess is if she had, her version might sound a little different. But let's for a moment pretend it is the way you tell it. Is that just cause for the suffering you've imposed on Vincent?'

'Did I say I was finished? I've only just begun. But here, let me warm your tea, dear, and then let me finish.'

Rob's heart sunk the moment he saw the stunt with the distributor cap. He rushed inside and found the pieces of the shattered vase, the vacuum cleaner cord snaking along the floor, and the trail of blood on the stairs leading to the bathroom door ripped apart by a wild animal, the bloody shower curtain, the shattered window.

He followed the blood outside to the clearing where he found fibers of rope, a torn piece of duct tape, and more blood. Lots of it.

How could he have left her alone? How could he have been so foolish? Rob jumped into the Jeep and tore down the road.

But he didn't get far.

He slammed on his brakes to avoid colliding with a black Cadillac blocking the driveway.

Peter Grow stood on the car's roof, one eye closed, and

the other ogling down the length of a double-barreled shotgun aimed right at Rob's head.

The first blast shattered Rob's windshield and sent glass spraying across Rob's face. His ears rang with pain as he dropped to the floorboards.

The second shot followed quickly and ripped through the engine, sending a spray of radiator water gushing into the air.

One shot. Two.

Reloading time. Rob rolled out of the car and dashed for Peter.

In one fluid motion he leaped onto the hood and tackled Peter at the knees, sending the shotgun flying into the brush. The men fell off the car with a grunt, and by a stroke of luck Rob landed on top. He made a tight fist and smacked Peter in the jaw, the first time in his life he had hit someone. It felt good. Damn good.

'Wait, wait,' Peter pleaded. 'I give up.'

Rob's fist froze in midair. He wanted to hit him again, pound him into unconsciousness, but he couldn't hit a man surrendering, and the fury left his fists, just like that.

'You're giving up that easily? You're a coward.'

'I got a thing about pain,' Peter explained.

'Tell it to your prison therapist. We're going to the police.'

'Okay. Just don't hit me.'

Rob wished he didn't hate guns so, or he'd have one right now. 'I'll let you up, but you better do what I say.'

'Anything.' Peter shivered.

'All right, no funny business.'

Rob released Peter, feeling kind of proud for bringing down a criminal so easily.

His pride didn't last long. From the small of his back Peter pulled a Derringer and pointed it at Rob.

'You amateur. You didn't think I'd have a backup gun?'

Rob felt the shot graze his shoulder, a pain as instant as it was disarming. The force sent him stumbling to the ground.

Peter stepped up and hovered over Rob.

'Looky here, this little baby's got two bullets, not one. My lucky day.'

'They'll find you,' said Rob.

'We'll see about that,' Peter said, taking aim. 'Sorry to kill you so fast, but I got to run. I can't wait to poke your little girlfriend. What's her name? Katie? Did you see her pretty titties?'

'You bastard.'

Peter tugged on the trigger. 'See ya, buddy.'

'Hold it right there!' a voice rang out.

Deputy Berwick stood twenty yards up the driveway, half hidden behind a redwood, his service revolver trained on Peter.

'Put the weapon down and step back,' Berwick ordered.

'What the fuck?' Peter muttered.

'Put the weapon down,' Berwick repeated.

'Do it,' said Rob.

Peter sneaked a peek into the woods, then retrained the handgun on Rob. 'I'll shoot him, I swear!'

'Put the weapon down and your hands in the air.'

Peter looked at the deputy, Rob, the woods. He spun around and fired a shot at Berwick. It pinged off a tree and ricocheted into the forest. But it was enough to give Peter a break for the woods.

Berwick moved up and took cover behind the Cadillac.

'Halt!' he called after Peter.

Peter galloped away, a wild horse without a rider.

'Halt or I'll shoot.'

Berwick lifted his revolver, took aim, fired.

Rob heard the shriek of pain and the body tumble to the weeds, followed by Peter's frantic plea. 'Help me, I'm bleeding. Bleeding! Help me, God damn it!'

'Got him in the leg,' said Berwick. 'He'll be okay. Let me look at you.'

Berwick inspected Rob's wound.

'Looks like it grazed the bone and blew clear through.'

'I'm lucky I stopped in town to call you,' said Rob.

'You got that right.'

Peter's howling continued.

'I'll radio for an ambulance,' said Berwick.

'For him, maybe. We've got to get up to Madame Charay's fast.'

'Sorry, buddy, you're in no shape to go anywhere but the hospital.'

'You get me to Madame Charay's or you'll have to shoot me too.'

CHAPTER NINETEEN

Madame Charay pierced a lemon wedge with a small fork and squeezed the juice into her cup. 'Biscuit?'

Katie nodded no. 'Get on with it.'

'Patience, patience, dear child. There are pleasures in life other than instant gratification. The cinema has made children of all of you. As I was saying, that wasn't the last we saw of your mother. Oh, no, we saw her again, four months later during our first week of shooting in this unspoiled little corner of purgatory. With the ambition of our goal finally facing us, tensions were high; a sense of failure permeated the set. The last distraction we needed was the sight of an unwelcome guest. There was no security in those days, but if Alfred wanted someone off the set, it was done. Yet your mother lingered. Oh, how she lingered, like a cat around his feet all day, prancing and preening, strutting and purring. Why he didn't order her off, I don't know. But just as the shooting wrapped, I saw her whisper in Alfred's ear. I'm the only one who did. And then they went away together, two hours in his limousine. The rest of the crew thought nothing of it and shrugged when I pointed it out to them. But I understood the significance, I alone. Upon their return, I offered the driver a small bribe. He confided in me that he had dropped them off at a private residence with instructions to return in fifteen minutes and *no less*.'

'So?'

'So, Alfred was a family man. The only director in Hollywood with virtue outside his craft. That is, until that temptress came along.'

'Stop right there. I've heard enough.'

Katie stood to leave, as she should have long ago. She'd meet Rob or the police on the road. They would be coming soon, any moment; they must be on their way. Enough of this fable.

'How about a little proof, Ms Jacobs?'

'Believe me, there's nothing you can show me that will make me believe this garbage.'

'Such a tough customer. How about Vincent, then? You wanted to see him, didn't you? Let me introduce you to the proof upstairs, and then I'll take you to your brother. I promise.'

'What have you done to him? I don't even think he's here.' Katie could only imagine.

'Indulge me, please.'

Katie knew it was foolish, but if Vincent was upstairs by chance, she would be that much closer to him, she could call to him. He might hear. Que sera, sera. 'One minute, then I want to see Vincent.'

'I'd like nothing more than to see Vincent too. Shall we?'

Katie followed Madame Charay past the movie posters for *I Confess* and *The Lady Vanishes*.

Madame Charay climbed the stairs slowly, past posters for *Family Plot* and *Shadow of a Doubt*. She turned back as she spoke: 'I hope you'll forgive me. I don't clean as adequately upstairs as I should. The air is a little . . . musty.'

Katie got a whiff of the odor, stronger with every step up.

'Where was I?' asked Madame Charay. 'Ah, yes. Melanie Daniels. Tippi played the part well, even brilliantly considering the wooden performance I understand Hitch insisted upon from her. Tippi's critics never understood the encumbrance. But, oh, the terrible tragedy of how Tippi got all cut up and frightened during the week it took to film that final scene. You know, the one in the upstairs bedroom? Tippi versus a room full of birds. The birds win. It took five days to film. Five days of Tippi standing against a door while gloved crew members flung live birds at her under the artful gaze of Alfred. So unnatural. She almost lost an eye, poor thing. But pain is the price of art, and Tippi was a good little soldier. At least, that's what I hear.

'Regrettably, I wasn't around to watch the filming. Indeed, I wasn't around to see any shooting. The day after your mother showed up on the set, I was summarily fired. *Let go*, as they say. No cause given, no need. But I knew who put the bug in his ear. Given the disgrace of my discharge, I was sure never to find employment in Hollywood again, nor was I about to shame myself by attempting to do so. So I was consigned here to this miserable little town. At least I married rich.'

'And what happened to your husband?'

'Oh, dear, no time for that story.'

'It's all very logical, but there's a big hole in your story.'

'And what's that?'

'Why did you adopt Vincent? If my mother got you fired, surely you wouldn't want her child, nor, I imagine, would she care to have you as Vincent's adoptive mother. And why would he keep our last name, Jacobs?'

'You see how little you know about your mother's true nature? That was her only request, that Vincent remain a Jacobs. How utterly selfish.'

They reached the top of the stairs – *Torn Curtain*, *Frenzy* – and made a right turn and stopped two doors down on the left – *Stage Fright*. Madame Charay twirled around proudly. 'Here we are.'

'I suppose this is another one of your sick shrines to Alfred?'

'You could say that. I prefer to call it a living memento.'

Madame Charay glanced around quizzically. 'Hmm, now what did I do with the key? Oh, that's right. I keep it in my pocket. How silly of me.'

The stench was unbearable. Only Katie's desire to find Vincent was stronger than her urge to flee.

Madame Charay slipped the key into the lock. She clutched Katie tightly by the arm. 'You wanted proof, didn't you?'

'There is no proof.'

'Stubborn, just like your mother. You see, it didn't take much to convince your mother to give up Vincent, not much at all. A little threat goes a long way, or haven't you learned that in life yet? Nine months after the limo ride, your mother paid me a visit. She wasn't interested in having anyone reveal the identity of Vincent's father to the world. The scandal would have put a swift and certain end to her dismal career. As it turned out, she needed no assistance to fail miserably, least of all from me. Nevertheless, I promised my complicity for a small price. Isn't it comforting to know your mother traded her firstborn for a slim chance of stardom? What do they say, *vanity, vanity, all is vanity*.'

'You're insane.'

'We all are.'

Suddenly Madame Charay spun behind Katie and twisted her arm behind her back. A shot of pain rifled through Katie's shoulder blades.

'Let me go!' Katie struggled.

'Toodle-loo, dear girl.'

Madame Charay opened the door and thrust Katie inside. The door slammed behind Katie with a sickening surge of hot air.

The room was pitch black, save for one spindle of light projecting through a pinhole in a boarded window on the far wall.

Katie groped for a light switch, found none, and returned her hand to cover her nose and mouth. She choked down heaves of revulsion from the stench.

Through her fingers she called. 'Vincent?'

Katie waited for her words to echo off the walls, but the sound didn't return.

A flutter answered.

She extended a hand into the putrid air.

A cackle.

Oh, God. She felt the force even without seeing it, a million eyes hungering, craving her in this dark theater of the absurd.

A stab at her hand.

Another cackle.

Katie spun around, pounded on the door. She ripped away splinters with her fingernails.

'Let me out. God, please,' she cried.

She pressed her ear to the door and heard Madame Charay's footsteps traveling down the stairs. 'Let me out!'

She turned back to face them. Her eyes adjusted slowly to the thin light, and she detected quick motions of restless wings. The gleam of shiny beaks. Black heads tilting oddly for better views. Crows, ravens, blackbirds. The black room.

A bird nipped her shoelace. She kicked at it, but hit only air. She glanced down and saw scores of birds shuffling away on the floor. And then she heard the *click, click, click* of their claws as they sauntered back.

A swoop of black broke the spindle of light. She followed the line of flight with half-closed eyes until the sharp razor of a spur raked her forehead.

She slapped the air, but it was too late. The bird retreated to devour the tiny morsel of Katie's flesh, his anonymity protected by hundreds of birds just like him, just as hungry.

A stream of blood trickled into Katie's eye.

Her tongue fattened with fear. Her panic was palpable, and she knew the birds tasted it too. Prey and predator heeding the same signal.

They took wing simultaneously, a raucous cacophony of wings: banking, stroking, veering, stalling, halting. A confusion of outstretched claws, angry eyes, sharpened beaks.

They came, tearing her clothes, scratching her face, clawing her feet, nipping her neck, twisting her ears, tugging her hair.

She ripped them away, squeezed her legs, bit the air. She threw them to the ground, pinned them against the wall, crushed bone in her fists, kicked wildly.

A hundred birds followed a hundred more. She swung her arms, they stabbed her face. She kicked, they nabbed her crotch. For every one repelled, three attacked; for every victory a dozen defeats.

The attackers lingered, clawed deeper, faster, nastier, stole her air until her senses deafened. Her body numbed. She slapped and kicked, but her arms grew heavy, her head light.

She sunk to the ground and covered her face. Shock turned the pain into an abstraction, the attack into a nightmare.

Sunlight flooded the room. Katie flashed open an eye to see a single board come down from the far window.

Another board and the top rungs of a ladder.

'Rob?'

Katie pulled herself to her knees, spied through the creases of her fingers.

Through flickering intervals, she saw another board come down, an arm reach into the window, and a figure climbing in.

'Rob?' Katie cried.

He jumped into the room, silhouetted by the sun behind him.

With increased fury beaks plunged into her skin, tormenting her for hoping.

The birds swarmed him, smothered him, weighed him down until he fell to one knee.

Katie shut her eyes, weak, mindless. The light, too, was brilliant, the images fading.

'Please, Lord.'

He rose, stumbled, fell again. Then he stood, sheer will powering him, throwing birds to their deaths.

He tumbled again. Birds covered him like an island, ten deep, thick with ferocity.

'Please get up.'

'Oh, God.' His end too. One last glance.

Then he moved, crept toward her while birds landed and departed, tore and ripped.

Closer, closer.

His hand shot out and groped for her clothing. He clutched her jeans.

The form stood, a hint of human being behind a moving mass of black.

He dragged her by the leg toward the window, toward light and air. Katie slid on her back across the feathers on the floor.

He scooped her up in his arms.

She pressed her face against his chest, wrapped her arms around his neck. And she smelled him through her tears.

'Vincent.'

He struggled toward the bright light. Katie felt the sun's warmth. The first whiff of fresh air filtered through his shirt. The birds wrapped their beaks in strands of her hair and tugged her back. Vincent lumbered toward the window, toward the light.

He leaned Katie against the wall, batted birds away. He thrust her up until her hand grabbed the windowsill, a feeble hold. The birds struck harder, pecking, clawing at her hands, her wrists.

Her muscles wouldn't listen, and she slipped. Her fingernails traced scars on the wall as she fell.

She tumbled onto Vincent, covered him with her body, sure it was the end.

'I love you,' Katie whispered.

But Vincent lifted her up, higher this time, until her waist straddled the windowsill, and her face and shoulders stood free in the open sky.

She climbed through the window and she righted herself on the ladder. She filled her lungs with air, and mind re-awakened.

Suddenly, her foot slipped from the rung, and she tumbled down, two rungs, three.

She caught herself and climbed up, up to save Vincent.

She reached her hand inside. The birds jabbed her arm and hand, but she felt his arm against the wall and grasped it tightly.

'Come on, Vincent.' With every fiber she pulled, but Vincent's arm slipped away, almost willingly.

'Help me, Vincent.'

Her hold slipped to his wrist.

'Vincent. Hold on.'

Three fingers.

'No!'

One finger.

Vincent dropped to the floor, a mad whoosh of the crows and ravens swooped down on top of him, a clash of feather and wing.

She tried to climb back in, to save him, but a wall of angry beaks and claws prevented her.

'Come on, Vincent.'

She groped for Vincent.

'Vincent, please.'

The birds feasted on her dangling arm.

Oh, Vincent.

She withdrew slowly, fumbled down the ladder, her heart racing, body shivering.

She reached the earth and curled into a ball. In her mind the birds attacked her still, clawing, ripping, tearing. Her eyes rolled back, consciousness drifted away.

The image of her mother replaced the birds, her mother draped in a white robe, lit from behind like an angel, a smile of peace on her face. Her mother calling to her, not with words or gestures but with an invisible string attached to her heart. Katie moved toward her, to embrace her, to bask in the shower of maternal grace and light.

Then the vision began to fade, the reception weaken, and the image washed away in a blaze of light as consciousness returned. Katie opened her eyes. She looked up to the window, hoping to see Vincent soar out. Instead she saw hundreds of crows and ravens take wing, away from Katie, away from Vincent, away from Madame Charay's.

She tried to stay alert, to order her body up to help him. But she couldn't. She searched again for the image of her mother, so lovely. Katie smiled weakly, at rest. Redeemed, joyful to have lived. Happy to be going home, to mother at last.

CHAPTER TWENTY

When Katie awoke she heard the screech of a million birds, but as her senses returned she realized it was not birds but the wail of an approaching siren. Through a blur she saw a jumble of concerned faces hovering over her, Rob's among them.

'Vincent,' she heard herself whisper. Her voice sounded muffled and odd, constricted, she realized, by the oxygen mask strapped across her nose and mouth. She thought of her mother, the light.

'Katie. Thank God,' said Rob.

Katie looked up on Rob's face, kind and compassionate. She felt his hand stroking her hair. Her eyes unblurred, then blurred again. Her body was numb with pain.

'I knew you'd come out of it,' said Rob.

'What happened?' asked Katie. Then she remembered, and winced at a fleeting image of attacking birds.

'It's okay,' whispered Rob. 'Everything is going to be all right.'

A paramedic dabbed her forehead wounds, another worked on her arms and legs. Everywhere stung badly. She saw the ambulance nearby and the flashing lights of the sheriff's cars, their doors hanging open and radios thundering messages.

'Vincent?' she asked feebly.

Rob shook his head.

'He saved me.'

'We saw the ladder.'

'But you don't understand.'

The room, his fear; she needed to explain so much. She pulled the mask from her face and tried to rise, but Rob gently pressed her down on the gurney.

'Shhh,' Rob said.

'Please, go help him.'

'Katie, we can't.'

'Maybe he's alive.'

Rob's expression left little doubt. 'Look.'

Katie's eyes painfully followed Rob's finger to the mansion, ablaze in flames with black smoke rising to the heavens.

'She torched it,' said Rob.

Katie watched the flames flutter from every window like the orange wings of a hideous beast. She returned her gaze to Rob and saw his arm in a sling.

'What happened to you?' she asked.

'Brief encounter with a bullet. No harm done.'

'And her?' Katie asked.

'We haven't found her yet.'

'You know what she told me?'

'What?' asked Rob.

'She said my mother . . . that Vincent . . .'

But Katie couldn't remember what Madame Charay had said, though she knew it had been an awful thing. 'I don't remember.'

'Don't think now.'

She tried so hard to recall, but it was like a dream, a childhood smell, someone else's memory, as if the knowledge was stored not in her brain but below the surface of her skin, there but unreachable.

Her thoughts were interrupted by a buzz over the radio. A deputy walked over to Rob and whispered in his ear.

Rob returned and held Katie's hand.

'They found Madame Charay. She's at Vincent's,' said Rob.

Katie saw Rob's hesitation. 'What?' she asked.

'She wants to speak to you.'

'No way.'

'She's threatening to jump if you don't.'

Katie strained to sit up. She looked down at her shredded clothing and the patchwork of gashes and cuts on her skin.

'She's pretty bad,' said the paramedic. 'I wouldn't advise it.'

Katie winced with pain. 'I can do it.'

She jumped off the gurney, wobbled but didn't fall, surprising even herself.

'Are you sure?'

'Let's go.'

Every step hurt like hell. Branches attacked her, scratched her like the claws of the birds, reopened wounds. But Katie kept on, welcoming the pain, a tribute to her slain brother.

Katie stopped midway down the path and plucked the green thread from Tippi's sweater.

'What is it?' asked Rob.

'A little memento,' she said, tucking it in her pocket.

Suddenly she remembered what Madame Charay had said about her mother and Vincent, the awful truth, or half-truth, or outright lie.

They reached the cabin in mid-scene. A small platoon of officers, rifles drawn, surrounded Madame Charay on all sides except the ocean.

She stood alone, ten paces from the cliff, lipstick thick around her lips, applied hastily. She wore a pearl-laced wedding dress that once was white but had yellowed with age, and long white gloves reaching above her elbows. A large ostrich plume accented her veil, and her shoulders were wrapped in a shawl of embroidered silk.

When she saw Katie, Madame Charay waved theatrically with a curl of the fingers.

'I see you survived, dear girl. What a pity. I always preferred his movies in which the pretty girl dies in the end. That's why *Vertigo* was such a treat.'

'Vincent rewrote this script,' said Katie.

'My grand finale ruined by my simple son.'

Katie thought of a thousand things to say, but she stopped herself. All she wished for was to see Madame Charay caged behind prison bars for the rest of her life.

Only then did Katie notice the strange bouquet in Madame Charay's hands. The wild orchids of Borneo, the immortals.

Deputy Berwick, the only unarmed officer of the group, took a step toward Madame Charay and held out a hand of conciliation. 'Please, ma'am, let's step back.'

'Get back!' she ordered, as if Berwick were a servant. 'I wish to be left alone now.'

Rob stepped up. 'Madame Charay, there's no place to go. Why don't you step away from the cliff. Let's talk about this, before someone gets hurt.'

'Dr Du Maurier, maybe your father was wrong about you. You don't seem half bad.'

'Please step away,' Rob pleaded. 'I beg of you.'

'In Greek tragedies there is but one fitting end for a hero. Did you know that? I suppose not. We're so fond of trite little endings to our modern fables, everlasting love, enduring happiness, or some such drivel far more mythical than anything the Greeks would care to invent. Alfred understood that. He knew.'

The orchids began their transformation, from white to flaming purple. Madame Charay paused to admire them, and so did Katie.

Deputy Berwick crept a few feet forward. 'Ma'am? Let's make it easy for everybody. Let's step away from the cliff.'

Madame Charay wasn't listening; she heard only the mad sirens that drove her.

'Our passion was too great for this hellish earth filled with people with no reason to their lives. Ah, but we *created*, Alfred and I. We created in the image of the gods themselves, on screen for all to behold. We created, and that's what separates us from the likes of you, Katie, with your fine cheekbones and languid eyes. They'll hide behind puffy lids and wrinkles one day, and then what will you have?'

'Love.'

'Ha!' Madame Charay chortled. 'Love is a fleeting emotion fueled by lust. It doesn't exist, my dear girl. Not for the masses, not for the likes of you. Do you know what love is? A fabrication designed to hustle movie tickets and convince women to bear children for men they come to despise.'

Deputy Berwick inched closer.

Katie couldn't bear to listen any longer. 'Vincent was love, pure love, and you drove him to insanity.'

'Alfred would have fired you on the spot for such insipid writing.'

'I'll keep on believing until the day I die.'

Deputy Berwick drew closer.

'Enjoy the burden, Katie. I'll join Alfred in our celestial theater and leave wretched reality to you.'

Madame Charay turned to face the crashing waves. 'Adieu,' she said, heaving the orchids into the sea.

'Don't!' Rob implored.

Madame Charay spread her arms wide and formed a pair of graceful wings with her shawl.

'Stop,' called out Berwick. He lunged toward her, but missed her ankle by inches.

Madame Charay rushed toward the sea, her arms undulating gracefully, a ballerina, a swan preparing for flight.

Rifles slapped against shoulders, eyes squinted.

Madame Charay hit full stride with her arms fluttering, ready for flight.

'No!' Rob called out.

At the cliff she threw herself skyward, arching her back, waving her arms in a mockery of flight.

But she didn't fall.

She defied gravity, sailed in thin air, glided higher still. Driven by supernatural powers, she had found an escape where none seemed possible, had fooled them all.

Then gravity reasserted its dominance, and she dropped, slowly at first, then swiftly over the cliff, a flash of white against a sea of blue, a vanishing vision. Only her shawl was left to ride the current of air. And then it, too, drifted down to the crashing surf below.

Katie couldn't see beyond the cliff, but she covered her eyes. Enough death for one day.

Rob ran to join Berwick at the edge just in time to watch the shawl land gently beside Madame Charay, her body strewn on the craggy rocks below.

A crashing wave covered her with foamy surf, a sea gull flew leisurely by.

Berwick called on his hand-held radio for the search and rescue squad. The *chop, chop, chop* of an approaching helicopter filled the air.

'Let's go,' Berwick said, tugging at Rob's arm.

But Rob lingered to make sure she would not rise like a phoenix.

Another wave.

Just to make sure she was truly dead.

Another bird.

So he could put it all to rest.

Katie arranged for Vincent's funeral in San Francisco. There was no reason to hold it in Bodega Bay; no one knew him there, not like he really was. She couldn't bear the thought of him laying next to Madame Charay, even though he would also be near his beloved Lily.

If it were up to Katie, she would have been happy to bury him in the graceful hills of Sonoma County, unbound by fences, with a grand view of the great clear sky above. She would put him there to rest just as if he had fallen asleep, to have the sea breeze sing about him and the deer forage for wild flowers on his grave, while birds circled above in homage.

But such things were not permissible. Death had its restrictions like everything else. Katie ordered a simple wooden casket, guessing Vincent would not be fond of anything ornate. She gave him her plot, the one next to their mother, which had been bought and paid for with Grandma's Social Security checks. *Got to have a place to die*, Grandma had said.

Katie invited the same collection of aging actors that had come to Gloria's funeral. They didn't know Vincent, but Katie wanted a proper farewell, with people who at least knew their mother. They came, surprisingly, perhaps reflexively, to play the part of mourners once again. Katie thanked each one with a handshake or a kiss.

The day was fog gray, fitting, Katie thought. Mama would have approved. A slight aroma of the sea wafted through the air, and a few gulls circled overhead. Rob stood by Katie during the service, which was led by the same young priest who had eulogized Gloria.

'What is the nature of greatness? Is it great works? Benevolence? Artistic genius? Inventiveness? These are all measures of greatness, yes. But what of the simple man? The tortured man? The shackled man? What opportunity does he have for greatness? The answer is every opportunity. And herein lies the great paradox of life. For greatness is not measured by comparing our achievements to others, but by comparing our achievements to our own capabilities. And therefore greatness lies in all of us. Waiting to be tapped, waiting for our will to set it free. Look around, look at your neighbor, look at me. Not one of us is without the potential for greatness. Each a potential hero. So next time you find you're berating yourself for lacking this particular quality or that personality trait, think of Vincent Jacobs. Think of what Vincent did to save his sister. Think of the slim window of opportunity he had for greatness, and think of how he measured up. Now think of your problems again. And reevaluate your opportunities for greatness, and then count your blessings. And be great in whatever way you can.'

'Amen,' said the crowd.

'Amen,' said Katie.

Katie made sure everyone found a ride to the wake, held at

the apartment where Katie had cared for her mother all these years. It felt odd being back, like returning to a museum. Everything seemed familiar yet foreign, as if Katie herself had been disassembled in the past few days and put back together a little differently, a little better. Where once this place seemed corrosive, now Katie looked on it with fondness. Even the ashtrays.

Grandma had insisted on preparing a meal. 'Just a little something,' she said. It was more than that, a pot roast with potatoes and onions, creamed broccoli and steaming sourdough rolls, cranberries and sour cream, strudels and cookies.

The place filled quickly. Perhaps this is why they had come to the funeral, for the free meal afterward. No matter. Vincent would have liked that.

Katie dished out broccoli to hungry guests, some with two plates in hand. Grandma worked beside her, slicing the pot roast and giving the men extra helpings.

As they worked together, Katie gave Grandma a peck on the cheek. 'Thank you, Grandma.'

'Hey, he's my grandson too.'

Grandma gestured toward Rob at the far end of the room, deep in conversation with a crusty actor whose name Katie had once known. 'Handsome guy,' said Grandma.

Katie looked at Rob intently. 'Yes, he is.'

Grandma waited for more details, but none came. 'Wedding bells?'

'I don't know. So much has happened so fast.'

'Adventure. That's what makes for a good marriage.'

Grandma basted the pot roast with gravy from the bottom of the dish. 'You know, your mother would have been proud of you for what you did for Vincent.'

'If only she had told me about him before.' Katie smiled at an aging starlet, mascara running down her tired face.

'Ah, but that's the rub, isn't it?' said Grandma. 'The secrets we keep.'

Secrets. The word struck Katie like a knife.

'Grandma,' began Katie, 'remember at the hospital when you told me about Vincent?'

'Yes.'

'You told me you didn't know who his father was.'

'That's what I said.'

'But you do know, don't you?'

Grandma tidied a stack of napkins, like she did when she didn't want to talk. 'Now, child, don't get me started.'

'I *knew* it,' said Katie. 'Why didn't you tell me?'

'I told you enough that day. I didn't want to overload you. It didn't seem relevant.'

'Not relevant?'

Grandma sighed with confession. 'I didn't think you'd find Vincent up there. I thought he was dead. Why complicate matters with details?'

Katie lowered her voice to a whisper. 'Details? Alfred Hitchcock is no detail.'

Grandma turned to Katie with a quizzical look. 'Alfred Hitchcock?' she asked with a scrunched-up face.

'Yes,' said Katie. 'Isn't that his father?'

Grandma let out a chuckle. 'Dear God, no. Where did you hear that nonsense?'

'From . . . never mind. You mean it wasn't Alfred Hitchcock?'

A starving actor waited patiently for his broccoli, but it hung on the end of Katie's serving spoon.

'Don't make me laugh,' said Grandma.

'May I have some broccoli, extra cheese, please?' asked the actor.

'Here, help yourself.' Katie gave him the spoon.

She wheeled Grandma out to the thin balcony overlooking Lombard Street and the Golden Gate Bridge beyond.

'Well, if it wasn't him, who was Vincent's father?'

Grandma looked around to make sure no one was watching. 'You really want to know?'

'Of course I do,' said Katie.

'But you can't tell anyone. Promise?'

'I can't promise that.'

'Well, then, I can't tell you.'

'Grandma, please.'

Grandma sighed. 'If I tell you, I won't have any secrets left.'

'*Grandma*.'

'Okay, okay. Move closer so I can whisper. Actors have satellites for ears.'

There was no threat of anyone hearing, but Katie moved closer anyway. Grandma cupped her hands tightly and whispered a name in Katie's ear.

The name of an actor.

The name of a very famous actor. Perhaps the most famous actor of his generation.

'You're kidding, right?' said Katie.

'On my honor.' Grandma crossed her heart.

'You mean Vincent's father was—'

'Shhh!' said Grandma with a finger pressed firmly against her lips. 'No one must ever know.'

'Holy smokes,' said Katie. 'Why did Mom keep it a secret?'

'An illegitimate child. It would have ruined his career.'

'But he was fabulously wealthy, and all those years we lived in poverty.'

Grandma sighed. 'The things we do for love.'

'She loved him?'

'More than anything.'

Rob saw the puzzlement on Katie's face. He walked onto to the balcony. 'Katie, is everything okay?'

'Yes, yes.' Katie tried to hide her astonishment.

Grandma gave Rob the once-over. 'You're a nice young man,' said Grandma. 'I hope you stick around.'

Rob smiled. 'Thank you. And Katie says wonderful things about you too.'

'She's just babbling,' said Grandma. 'Anyway, I'd better go inside. Leave you two lovebirds alone.'

Grandma smiled and gave a wink to Katie before rolling her chair inside.

Rob peered into Katie's eyes. 'Are you okay? Because you look kind of pale.'

'Must be the healing process,' Katie said. The vestiges of the cuts and scratches certainly remained, plenty of them, but the pain was subsiding, from her heart to her skin.

'Can I get you anything?' asked Rob.

'Yes.'

'What?'

'A kiss.'

'With pleasure,' he said.

Rob kissed Katie on the mouth, a wet kiss, far too succulent for a gathering like this. But Katie let him. They were on the balcony, and, anyway, who cared?

'Rob?'

'Yes?'

'Can you keep a secret?'

'Yes, what is it?'

Katie looked beyond the bridge to the hills turning green from the rain.

'I love you forever,' she whispered in his ear.

'I love you forever too. But do we have to keep it a secret or can we tell the world?'

'Can we decide in about fifty years, when we're old and gray?' she asked.

'You bet.' Rob kissed her once again, hard. Katie's back pressed against the railing dangerously. A few heads turned inside.

'When we have lots of grandchildren?' she continued.

'A tribe of them.'

Katie wrapped her arms around Rob's neck. 'And a big house in Bodega Bay?'

'Right there on the cliff, if you'd like,' Rob said.

'So we can watch the birds dive at sunset?'

'You betcha.'

Rob kissed her again, a lusty kiss that swept her off her feet.

'Sounds good to me,' Katie giggled.
'Just wait till the cameras start rolling.'
'A real crowd-pleaser, eh?' asked Katie.
'Masterpiece.'